The
Europeans

The
Europeans

A Saga of Settlement Down Under

Gerry Burke

THE EUROPEANS
A SAGA OF SETTLEMENT DOWN UNDER

Editing: Kylie Moreland
Illustration Back Cover: Ben Sullivan

iUniverse books may be ordered through booksellers or by contacting:

iUniverse
1663 Liberty Drive
Bloomington, IN 47403
www.iuniverse.com
1-800-Authors (1-800-288-4677)

ISBN: 978-1-5320-7778-4 (sc)
ISBN: 978-1-5320-7780-7 (hc)
ISBN: 978-1-5320-7779-1 (e)

Library of Congress Control Number: 2019908504

Print information available on the last page.

iUniverse rev. date: 06/28/2019

AUTHOR'S PREVIOUS WORKS

BOOK EXCELLENCE AWARDS — FINALIST

The Snoodle Contract
— a provocative power play of political perfidy

The Replicants
— they come in peace or so they say

Be Dead and Be Damned
— murder with malice in Melbourne

U.S.A. BEST BOOK AWARDS — FINALIST

Pest Takes a Chance
— and other humorous stories from the *Paddy Pest Chronicles*

Pest on the Run
— more humorous short stories from the *Paddy Pest Chronicles*

The Hero of Hucklebuck Drive
— another Paddy Pest mystery

INDEPENDENT PUBLISHER BOOK AWARD

Paddy's People
    — tales of life, love, laughter and smelly horses

COMMUTERS' COMPANION

The Lady on the Train
    — more humorous Paddy Pest yarns for children over thirty

SHORT STORIES & OPINION PIECES

From Beer to Paternity
    — one man's journey through life as we know it

Down-Under Shorts
    — stories to read while they're fumigating your pants

He droned-on incessantly about Lord Rugby and his hookers, and Earl Grey and his Portuguese tarts, and never let-up on how the Duke of Edinburgh could be a Greek.

The dissolute lifestyle of the aristocracy in Europe was a bone of contention for many who searched elsewhere for a more egalitarian way of life.

Some of these people travelled to Australia. It was a land of hope and glorious possibility.

Victoria — 1951 to 1983

MAJOR CHARACTERS

THE SCOT

ABERDEEN HOMESTEAD
Bing McKeon
Helen McKeon (nee Scanlan)
Joe McKeon, Edwin McKeon
Ron Stokes (Horse Trainer)
Clementine, the Rabbit
Omo, the Silver Stallion

MT. BEAUTY
John Mills (Handyman)
Marvin Mills (Handyman)
Chris Dow (Bookkeeper)
Margaret Dow (nee Ryan)
Richard Papworth (Businessman)
Tony Mayor (Shopkeeper)
Johnny Laing (Shopkeeper)

BIDHAWAI PEOPLE
Bunji Waku
Mrs. Waku

THE GREEK

BALLARAT
Peter Papadopoulos
Henrietta Papadopoulos
(nee Hornblower)
Lydia Papadopoulos
Norm Jones (Horse Trainer)
Jack Glover (Car Salesman)

NORTH BY NORTHWEST
Sam Tromans (The Fixer)
Tony McCurry (The Law)

THE PADDY

ALL OVER
Matthew O'Gorman
Pat O'Gorman (nee Malone)
Angela Pride (The Law)
David Walkden (Businessman)

Any similarity between these characters and real individuals is a figment of your imagination. However, certain historical events have been revisited in the hope of obtaining a better outcome. Unfortunately, there are dead people involved in this tale. If this is distressing for you, turn the publication sideways and, with two fingers, shake the book. They should fall out. No animals were harmed in the writing of this story. Thank you for your support.

GB

CHAPTER 1

The Scot

Bing McKeon felt like the loneliest man on the planet. The high country can do that to you if you arrive without a talking companion. Not that there wasn't any conversation. The inquisitive immigrant was throwing his voice at the fearsome looking chasm in front of him, and chasing the echo as it bounced off a precipice above the abyss, before returning to him some seconds later. Who needed a talking companion?

A dog would have been nice. A mutt with malice is always a good foil should there be a vicious presence lurking in the vegetation, as there surely was. In truth, these hunters mostly come out at night and Bing hadn't failed to notice that the light was fading fast. He heard owls, howls, and the strident vowels of the ever-present kookaburras, perched high in the gum trees, which is their designated home base.

That's exactly what the big fellow was looking for: a home amongst the gum trees. The Bogong High Plains was mostly Crown land, but if you were a canny Scot with something to offer, arrangements could be made; and the further from town, the cheaper the property value.

The newcomer was standing in the middle of the plateau, mentally designing his future residence, when the earth began to tremble beneath his feet. The distant thunder that was fast approaching was not a warning from the weather God. The roos knew that. They stopped their feeding and looked at each other with alarm. The brumbies were in flight and coming their way.

"Listen tae that," said Bing to himself, as he placed his hand behind his ear. The small rumble that had disturbed the eerie silence of the early evening was now a roar, significantly announcing the impending arrival of the herd. There was no longer a kangaroo in sight.

"Bloody hell," gasped the gobsmacked intruder, as he saw the leader of the pack stride magnificently into the clearing and head in his direction. The silver steed, stretched to capacity, darted across the plain like a white flame looking for ignition. His head carriage gave off an arrogant impudence that can only be found among leaders, and his gait seemed effortless as he drove fearlessly into the open ground, almost two lengths ahead of his followers. At least forty horses trailed in his wake.

If Bing McKeon had eaten all his porridge that morning, he might have had the strength to make a run for it, but his legs had turned to jelly. If he had been wearing a kilt, he might have been able to shock the mob into a different direction, but probably not. These animals were going wherever their leader was heading and it was straight at the stranger, who may have been wondering what Hopalong Cassidy would do in a similar situation.

Of course, Hoppy would have had a lasso and that does make things easier. Big Mac just braced himself and walked straight at the oncoming herd, flaying his arms in all directions. They parted and let him through. It was a pivotal moment that would help establish his credentials as a genuine mountain man. He was very proud of himself.

The silence and solitude of the high country is satisfying yet intimidating and a challenge for both man and beast. Even the birds prefer to patrol lower regions where the accessibility of food morsels makes life less challenging. "Do you want chips and salad with that, Mr. Seagull?"

The underground residents are not so adventurous and never travel far from their lair. Where would they find the time? There is so much to do before winter sets-in— especially gathering all that tucker to store-up for provisions. One also needs to be alert for predators. They are forever foraging in the undergrowth and don't take kindly to cheeky small pests who antagonise them. It is best to avoid these monsters.

The wild horses are no problem to the resident creatures. You can hear them coming and you know they're showing off. It's in their nature. Being herd animals, they run in packs and run they do. The Bogong High Plains is their territory and has been since White Nose won The Cup—that's the Melbourne Cup—in 1931.

Some twenty years after this momentous victory, Bing McKeon, completely unaware of the home-grown devotion attached to Australia's greatest horse race, moved into the area. He would soon learn that, in this part of the world, the horse was man's best friend.

The fellow's ethnic credentials were there for all to hear, and nobody recognised any city mannerisms. His speech was slow and measured, and he wore a wide-brimmed hat, which immediately identified him as a country yokel. Generous money was on offer with the construction work associated with the Kiewa Hydroelectric Scheme and many recently-arrived Europeans flocked to the region. This newcomer from Britain impressed many with his relaxed and easy-going nature, established and authenticated over a number of years travelling to various godforsaken outposts of this diverse world of ours.

One could only guess at what the Scotsman thought of his new home because he didn't say much. He just went about his business and put away his money diligently. He didn't smoke tobacco or drink at the ale house (both expensive habits) and, although he did hanker for wild women, there didn't appear to be any about.

A carpenter by trade, the six-foot-four chippy arrived with his tool box in tow. To most men, such heavy baggage would present logistical problems, but the man mountain carried his implements with ease. His impressive muscular development was on show and, although the temperature often hovered around zero, the top of his shirt was always unbuttoned—his hairy chest inviting spontaneous appraisal from the opposite sex, should any wild women materialise.

At this time, the project boasted a male-dominated workforce and for good reason. The lads provided the skill and expertise required by the contractor, not that a few of the ladies didn't perform with distinction in the canteen and medical facility.

Two dams were being constructed in concert with several aqueducts, built to process flows into the catchment area. The ugly earthworks saw Caterpillars crawling all over the terrain, but these mechanical marvels would not have been sanctioned by their namesakes, at that time experiencing the trauma associated with the devastation of their flora. The fauna also observed their natural habitat disintegrate before their eyes, and the traditional custodians of the land, the Bidhawai people, looked-on with undisguised horror at this catastrophic turn of events.

Any forthcoming protest would be considered after much discussion and deliberation around a camp fire. All eyes would then turn to the female elders. After all, who else would you expect to make the right decision?

Australia, the continent, is a big country. Divided into six states and two territories, it is a land of sweeping plains and ragged mountain ranges, as described by iconic poet Dorothea Mackellar. The early settlers descended on the eastern seaboard and pushed deep into areas of New South Wales, Victoria and Tasmania; as did Helen Scanlan, many years later. At least, she saw a fair bit of Victoria.

Helen was a novice teacher employed by the Education Department and, as such, qualified for a country posting; the bane of every cadet on the payroll, and the sadistic revenge of education administrators who probably never got to chalk the boards in their own right. Miss Scanlan's first two postings involved towns with unpronounceable names and almost perishable populations. Every death decimated the demographics and only the multiple births of some immigrant families kept the tiny timber schools going. Needless to say, small towns provided limited opportunity to be socially active and this can affect one's mental state.

Therefore, for the sake of sanity, Helen directed her considerable charm where it would be best appreciated, even though the pickings were slim. The likes of Gavin the grease-monkey, Bulldozer Bob, and Jack the Goose, who owned a poultry farm, were but passing fancies in a world that seemed to be leaving her behind. She was fast becoming disillusioned with her profession and wondered if she had been ill-advised.

The young lady had attended a Catholic school and absorbed the traditions of her faith, supplemented by invaluable worldly advice from her mentors, the Sisters of Charity. When it came time to consider her future, Helen concluded that education was a noble vocation, worthy of her life's work, and no doubt the nuns provided solid support and encouragement in helping her make this career choice. Basically, it was just what they were doing, with extra benefits. The possibility of love, sex and marriage had to be the icing on the cake, so where was the downside?

Some people will remember the times when young ladies were only expected to profess carnal knowledge if married. In some country communities, the town's most eligible bachelor might be at least forty years of age with limited education, and if he still possessed half of his teeth, ring the bell and shout hallelujah.

Helen's eventual transfer to Bright in northern Victoria proved to be a blessing and was possibly the result of those nightly entreaties to the Virgin Mary, which the young lady had formulated after obtaining intercession suggestions from the nuns. One doesn't want to belittle the elevated status and veneration afforded the Mother of Christ, but virginity isn't for everybody. This was the message that the country teacher hoped to get across without fear or favour and surely it worked? She received end-of-term notice and instructions to present at her new school in the new year.

The township of Bright is and always has been a mecca for campers. They flock to this part of the world to appreciate the superb spectacle of autumn hues, as the poplar trees drop their leaves in keeping with tourist expectations. Add the ancillary delights of oaks, chestnuts, elms and Japanese maples and you end up with a picture postcard hamlet that is both charming and welcoming. The welcome mat had been dusted and debugged for the new broom and the locals gave the school's old wooden structure a once-over with some surplus paint from Johnny Laing's hardware and soft furnishing store. A new teacher must be embraced by the community and every effort would be made to make her feel comfortable.

The new girl instantly fell in love with her new home. She now taught a full class, and bonded with agreeably friendly mothers of her own age. The town amenities gave her the opportunity to expand her horizons and she spearheaded a theatre group and book club. The sporting facilities proved to be first-class, and the nearby wineries and snow fields were a magnet for communal outings.

Bright also served as a lifeline for the people who lived on the mountain or just below it, and this is where Bing McKeon acquired his provisions. The town was also the centre-point for thrill-seekers who were easily pleased. The Scottish carpenter always stayed at Mrs. McGennisken's guest house, where Helen Scanlan enjoyed permanent tenure.

Conversation at the dinner table was mostly polite and predictable. He would pass her the condiments and she would fetch his second cup of tea. Sometimes they both offered to help Mrs. McGennisken with the washing-up. On his third visit, the man from the mountains made what seemed to be a knowledgeable remark concerning the current atmospheric conditions, and followed it up with an invitation for a walk in the moonlight.

They would have the town to themselves, as the crisp air would deter the bravest and boldest—not that anyone would consider venturing outside during the six o'clock radio serials. Just as Amos 'n' Andy dominated the airwaves in America, Australian households became mesmerised by these soap operas that bounced into their home every evening. Families clustered around the wireless, and sometimes had to declare standing-room only, should a delegation of neighbours drop-in to listen to *Hop Harrigan* or *The Air Adventures of Biggles*.

Out in the cold night air, Bing discovered a woman at ease with herself. She chatted amiably with no obvious sense of self-consciousness and fielded all his questions with admirable honesty. Red-headed women, from his experience, could be forthright and feisty but, it has to be said, his former paramours were all Scots. This angelic creature defined humility itself, and she didn't even appear to be aware of her obvious physical attributes. He tried not to stare.

Her red hair, cut short, provided her face with a page-boy appearance that defined her ruddy complexion, naturally conditioned to defy the elements. The freckles on show appeared understated but they were there, and the dimple just under her right cheekbone was prominent and might have been a birthmark. He noticed these things before he scrutinised her dark brown eyes and waspish smile, which enveloped a pert little nose that reminded him of the new ski jump being built in the alpine region. Some people might construe such a comparison to be uncomplimentary so he decided to remain silent on the subject. However, he did offer the poor thing his handkerchief when her nose started to dribble.

McKeon was not an accomplished romanticist. The girl's features, seen at meal time, acquired increased significance in the moonlight. Her below-shoulder artillery came into play when she snuggled close to avoid a chill wind that danced through the dell where they dallied. If he had formulated plans to return to the guest house prior to the episodic finale to *Biggles*, he shelved such an idea and suggested a walk on the wild side—the path beyond the bakery that led to Cherry Walk along the Ovens River (an appropriate name for this teenage hot spot for after-school liaisons and other clandestine assignations).

For many, the smell of cherry blossom is an inedible aphrodisiac, to be equated with oysters and strawberries, both renowned for erotic characteristics. However, one would not expect a naive bachelor from the colonies (having spent time in India and Rhodesia) to know that. Perhaps Helen did, as teachers are supposed to know everything.

Their first kiss didn't eventuate until their second moonlight walk and a further five weeks went by before he got anywhere with his perennial probing into parts designated as off-limits by devotees of the Virgin Mary. The skinny dip into the Ovens River was not only momentous but outrageous in the extreme. The prospect of hypothermia loomed large and exemplified the difference between July and December. Nevertheless, Helen, emboldened by her adventurous spirit, recently acquired, was first out of her clothes and laying down the challenge.

"I'll race you to the pontoon and back. The loser buys dinner at the *Dew Drop Inn*."

Bing had never been to the *Dew Drop Inn*, but his Scottish frugality would never see him knock back a free meal under any circumstances. She was already half-way to the pontoon when he dipped his toe in the water.

"Oh shite," he cried. "It's as cold as a mother-in-law's kiss."

Given her start, and allowing for their respective height and weight differences, it proved to be an exciting finish. He closed on her as she scrambled up the river bank, and brought her down with what can only be described as a rugby tackle. Of course, everybody knows what can happen when you play naked rugby. Lying huddled together on the riverbank with nothing between them, they concluded that there was only one thing to do to keep warm. So they did it.

News of the pregnancy was relayed to Bing some weeks later. The letter came in with Jed, the sewerage contractor, which was the reason Helen's perfumed parchment had lost some of its zing. Nevertheless, the brazen bachelor considered his options and eventually set off on the road to Bright, where he purchased a dozen roses and picked up a mail-order catalogue. Should the sweet thing accept his proposal of marriage, she could choose her own ring. He hoped it would arrive before the baby.

The lady said yes and the whole community celebrated, even though it would mean the loss of their schoolteacher. Helen would relocate to Mt. Beauty, a town at the foot of Mt. Bogong, which was beginning to open up on the back of the hydro scheme. By virtue of the construction work being undertaken by the electricity company, management blatantly assumed control of the town and services, but nobody complained, as most of the townsfolk now enjoyed employee status. The busy carpenter was in demand and on good terms with the hydro authorities, who were impressed with his work ethic. He managed to strike a deal for some land in the wilderness to build his dream home—in between assignments, of course.

History tells us that most pioneers are handy with an axe and Bing was no exception. The trees in the immediate vicinity of his new property didn't last long. If you wanted timber from town, Solly Simons would get it for you wholesale, but who needs wholesale when free is available? The deforestation operation instigated by the new landowner was not appreciated by the nomadic residents or the environmentalists but what is the point of complaining after the fact?

This high-altitude area was dotted with treeless shrubbery and elongated grassy patches, so the new clearing around the McKeon home was not out of place and the brumbies loved it. And didn't the new man continually eye-off the hurtling herd of horseflesh as they thundered by. He made a mental note to think about rounding-up a few of them but only after completing his residential structure and ancillary buildings. The idea of horses on tap sounded fine but the little lady wanted self-sufficiency animals first—chickens, goats, cows and rabbits. Not that Clementine would ever see the inside of a crock pot. She would be groomed as a companion for the new baby.

"Darling, I want you to build a hutch for the rabbit. Now that he's one of the family, we have to make him feel right at home."

The finished residence proved to be a credit to the builder. The Americans might call it a ranch house but that kind of talk was unwarranted. The amateur architect, having seen cattle stations in Australia and Africa, knew what he wanted. His homestead was not only individual but also practical and accommodating. His initial projections indicated he would sire three children, two boys and a girl, and he based his bedroom designs around this premise. He increased the size of one bedroom on the off-chance that one such delivery might be twins.

Helen could not have been happier with her new home. The rooms were spacious and the rough-hewn finish of the timber beams gave-off a feeling of warmth which she accentuated with well-placed carpets and rugs. Her husband picked-up a second-hand AGA stove from Johnny Laing's store and this further enhanced the homely nature of the residence. Her kitchen came with all the mod-cons of the time—a refrigerator with ice-maker and automatic defroster, a hand-held mixer, an electric skillet, a toaster, even a milkshake appliance. There was always the possibility that Peggy Sue might drop by.

Although he employed no permanent staff, the house-proud husband considered future requirements and added a bunkhouse, outside toilet, chicken coop, a kennel and a couple of corrals. The brumbies would need accommodating when he decided to go horse-hunting.

Joe, the son and heir, arrived in the autumn, much to the delight of all the folks at the Bright General Hospital. Dr. Richardson declared the child to be hale and hearty and predicted a positive future for the lad. His own child, also named Joseph, was a stand-out student at the provincial primary school, now under the control of another teacher from the city.

Most of the farm animals congregated at the front entrance to welcome the new arrival home, including Daisy, the milker, and Clemmie, the rabbit. A passing flock of parakeets also dropped by to see what all the fuss was about. For young Joseph, the deputation in the driveway proved to be a non-event. Coddled in multiple blankets, he slept peacefully. The animals didn't seem offended.

Over the next few days, a trickle of well-wishers and busy-bodies from town dropped-by to lay eyes on the child and provide their opinion. The little tyke passed muster. In fact, it was agreed that he was a dead ringer for Clark Gable, which seemed quite mystifying because nobody had ever seen the actor without his moustache.

The first-time parent had no intentions of spoiling his youngster, but he did dote on the infant. The junior carpentry set he purchased for the lad's first birthday may have been a somewhat premature gift but one that would surely encourage ambition in terms of future aspirations. Helen gave him a rattle. It has to be said that the father of the child was not only proud of the boy but also his own accomplishment, having nailed a son at his first attempt.

Naturally, one had to supplement the dynasty, and this became a priority as the months went by. On Tuesdays and Fridays, the couple would retire to bed shortly after the conclusion of *Leave it to Beaver*, which seemed an appropriate precursor to what they had in mind. Television, in its infancy, could not beguile the viewer beyond bedtime.

With conception confirmed, Bing breathed a sigh of relief and moved-on from that tick-box. He now felt entitled to pursue one of his delayed commitments: to catch and tame some of those unrestrained speedsters who galloped past their kitchen window every evening. He didn't claim to be a rodeo rider and although those cowboys on television could rope a steer or a headstrong bandit with ease, he figured it to be more difficult than it looked.

Tony Mayor ran the general store in town, although he didn't do a line in lariats and lassos. Being a fellow Brit, his relationship with the carpenter hovered between geniality and friendship. This man delivered opinions on most subjects; however, these opinions needed to be disseminated. Nevertheless, roping wild horses was obviously an American thing and he didn't want to volunteer a point of view that might put his friend in harm's way. He did stock twine of various descriptions, but he was faced with a dilemma. His mark-up was sixty per cent, but the force resistance on his product came in at thirty per cent.

"You'd be daft to try this on your own, my friend. I can sell you some rope, but I reckon you need at least two fellas to help out. What about the Mills brothers? They're pretty fearless, although they've got shit for brains."

Johnny Mills and his brother Marvin, the twenty-something sons of one of the electrical contractors, picked up odd jobs when it suited them. These strapping young lads exhibited a devil-may-care attitude to life, and horse rustling probably sounded like a bit of a rush to them. They may also have wanted to ingratiate themselves with the prominent landowner.

The McKeon dinner invitation was received and accepted and, after completing their meal and paying their respects to the baby, the guests joined the homestead owner down by the large corral. Cigarettes were produced by the non-smoker, and the group gazed out at the kangaroos grazing on the pasture. Sundown provided these meandering marsupials with the chance to frolic in the half-light, and few would forgo the opportunity to pig-out on the rich pickings available.

In recognition of his first experience with the high plains brumbies, Bing had named their entry point into his property Thunder Ridge, and it was to this location that he directed their attention.

"Look yonder, laddies. And listen. The herd from heaven is aboot ta arrive, and I'll wager ye have no seen anything like it."

"Get out of here," screamed John Mills, as the sound crescendo climaxed with the arrival of the white stallion over Thunder Ridge. As usual, he was ahead of the pack, and the deputation of two-legged observers didn't seem to surprise him one bit. In fact, he may have craved the attention. You know what blondes are like.

The dash across the plateau was over in a matter of seconds and only the steamy aftermath of the frenetic gallop lingered in the air, mesmerizing the onlookers, and rendering them speechless. Eventually, Bing made his pitch.

"Gentlemen, it is ma intention to capture and tame the snow-white stallion, along with some of his chums. I want you to help me."

Marvin Mills stared at his brother in disbelief and then took a deep breath. This man asked a lot of them. He wondered if he could dampen his enthusiasm.

"Gee, Bing, the horse is magnificent but how are we going to do it? Did you see the heat coming from his nostrils? He could kill us."

"This is true but he might have a gentle nature, and ma garden full of carrots might be used as an enticement. Are you boys up for it?"

If you want to challenge the masculinity of the Australian male, one only has to infer a small degree of cowardice in the nicest possible way. The challenge will be accepted and, in this case, it was. Johnny even followed-up with a plan.

"Why don't we narrow the gap around the ridge, and divert the majority of them into your lower paddock. The leader will probably be clear of the pack, like today, and give us a chance to separate him from the others."

"Oh yeah," interjected his brother. "Who's going to stand in front of forty horses and shoo them away? Not you I'll bet."

It was unusual that Marvin would delve into the realm of practicality as his pragmatism had often been questioned in the past. Both lads, being avid fans of the cowboy movie, had seen various heroes instigate a similar diversion with marauding buffalo. Of course, neither of these boys would consider themselves to be in that class.

"No bad," said the reflective rancher, looking at his young friend with some surprise. "Aye, we can work on that idea. Give me a few days and I'll be in touch."

After Bing escorted his two friends to their car, he joined his wife and baby in the kitchen. Although focused on washing the dinner plates, Helen found time to remark on the team meeting down by the corral.

"They are lovely boys, Bingham, but I would think twice before committing them to your latest hair-brained scheme. They don't have a lot between the ears."

"My God, Hell," responded the breadwinner. "We're just talkin' aboot a wee bit o' rustling. What could be easier than that?"

As his wife turned from the sink with a raised eyebrow, Bing turned to his new-born son for support.

"What does the bairn say, young Joseph? Can the laddies be trusted?"

The baby, yet to come to terms with grown-up discussion, responded by crying loudly and persistently. His father tried to quell the outburst with the child's rattle but to no avail. Only when he produced the spirit-level from the tot's junior carpentry set did he calm down. "What a well-adjusted child," declared his proud father.

It took the would-be rustler almost a week to formulate a plan and, apart from the Mills brothers, four stalwarts from the town's pool hall joined the hunting party on the boundary of the valley property. Seven of them formed a line across the access clearing beside the bend of the ridge and armed themselves with whips, blankets, drover's hats, whistles and anything else that would communicate the fact that there was a barricade in place.

Half of the plan worked. When the galloping herd approached the bulwark, they automatically detoured past his house and the corral, with fourteen carrots hanging from the highest railing. They repeated this regimen for five days running, with no obvious interest in the vegetarian treats on display. On the sixth day, the despairing team assembled by the bunkhouse and debated the value in continuing with the plan. The brumbies had passed fifteen minutes earlier at their usual fevered pace. Marvin first noticed the approaching visitors. "Hey fellas, get a load of this."

Six pairs of eyes redirected their gaze to the five horses picking their way through the open land pasture, with the magnificent white colt leading the pack and slowly heading in their direction. A lone crow could be heard in the distance, but, otherwise, the stillness of the evening provided the equine delegation with their early warning system. Any loud noise or erratic movement and they would be off.

Aware of this, Bing whispered instructions to his pals.

"Get ya ropes ready. Johnny, Marv...you're on the stallion wi' me. The rest of you should round-up as many as ye can."

The next challenge required the boys to move behind the frisky beasts and try and steer them through the open gate of the corral. Should they need to drag them, so be it.

It is hard to know where carrots rate on the pecking list of horses, but the amateur cowpokes probably hoped the dangling delectables would be of some appeal to the inquisitive beast. The lead brumby seemed interested and wherever he went the others followed.

In retrospect, one might question the animal's lax attitude in terms of vigilant caution. Low-hanging fruit is fair game in the wilderness, but these raw vegetables were on high and attached to a man-made structure. He should have known better.

Mr. Mac was lucky to rope the stallion's neck at the first attempt but Marvin was not so fortunate. His lariat ended up around his brother's head. Nevertheless, the siblings regrouped and eventually the freaked-out animal was being pulled on three sides—hardly the end of it.

He snorted, he buck-jumped, he reared and he roared. They came at him; he came at them. Johnny Mills, pinned against the hardwood fence, could only wince as his brother tripped over his own feet. Through it all the main man hung on to his rope for dear life and proved to be a vigorous adversary for the spirited animal. In the end, the defeated stallion surrendered to the overwhelming odds and slinked away to the corner of the enclosure to brood with two of his companions, while the humans closed ranks and shut the gate of their prison. The escapees, who resisted the overtures from the pool-room lads, rejoiced in their freedom and high-tailed it for the safety of the undergrowth.

The Aussie cowboys would celebrate that night with a few cool drinks and a hot bath. Long after they had left the property, the laird would patrol the corral and contemplate his good fortune. Surely, Bing had asserted his capability and mandated his right of passage. Only a brave or foolish person would challenge his authority, or try to deny him his dreams and expectations. That person was closer than he could ever have imagined.

CHAPTER 2

Ron Stokes trained racehorses for most of his life. He occupied a four-room Edwardian weatherboard at the back of the Benalla track and, at one stage, could accommodate up to a dozen horses in purpose-built boxes. These stables were now in disrepair, due to general wear and tear and lack of maintenance. The last winner from this yard remains a memory but a distant one. The man's wife was long gone and his only son subsequently moved-on from the country home.

The area around Benalla, a mid-sized provincial town, geographically situated two and a half hour's drive from Melbourne, was regarded as good horse country. A few acres of land is not a bad inheritance, but if your own flesh and blood has no interest in maintaining the family tradition, there is little you can do about it. The only son visited every now and then, but it was obvious that his former home no longer stimulated his interest. Ron decided to re-evaluate his situation and consider options—a bold move for a senior citizen, set in his ways. Not that he was that old. Sixty-four years of age only became a terminal indictment because of the Beatles and their infectious ditty. Ron didn't see it that way. Nevertheless, he did feel that he needed to forget old memories and search for new challenges.

The ad for a wrangler with a sound horse pedigree first appeared in the *Wangaratta Chronicle*, whose reach and influence touched most areas in the northeast. The initial response underwhelmed the prospective hirer, but he appreciated the fact that the remoteness of the locality might deter would-be applicants. Little was offered in the way of spousal support, so Ron's status as an unattached male gave him a leg-up and a look-in.

Bing McKeon, the hirer, met the applicant in Bright and produced pictures of his property and outlined his prospective duties and living conditions. The chap, who Ron thought to be most personable, admitted that his primary occupation prevented him from giving enough attention to his burgeoning equine business and he needed help—a good man tried and true.

In those days, a handshake was as acceptable as any legal contract and both parties appeared happy with the arrangements. The new employee put his house on the market and disposed of most of his possessions. He arrived at the McKeon property (now named Aberdeen) and took up residence in the bunkhouse. The sight of the rampaging herd at sundown tickled the new man's fancy and he never tired of it. By now, many of the brumbies had been rounded-up and languished in their corral, but this didn't stop their pals from stopping by for a whinny and a whine. The white leader had been captured but he was still *numero uno*.

In the next few months, Bing learnt more from Ron than he could ever imagine. The bumkin from Benalla proved to be a magician around these untamed steeds and knew when to cajole and when to constrain. He became a valued adviser to the landowner and gave him the benefit of all his experience. Because of the difficult terrain around this area, there was quite a demand for capable workhorses and nobody ever considered buying from anyone but Bing, although he did have a competitor operating from the flatlands.

Only when the trading business had been well and truly established did Ron decide to float an idea past his boss. He produced most of his ideas at dinner time, when discussion and debate often transpired between courses. With lamb's fry on the menu, there was every chance the head of the house would be in a receptive mood.

During this period of consolidation, it is important to reflect on the little women's role in the decision-making process. The times demanded that wives know their place (mostly in the kitchen), but many women could manipulate and manage their husbands through their stomachs. This protocol even related to guests. Helen often put sheep's brains on the menu when Johnny and Marvin shared their table but, alas, their powers of concentration and understanding remained minimal. Nevertheless, their part in the initial herding operation was never forgotten and Bing always kept the boys on stand-by for any odd jobs that might arise. The two roustabouts also got-on quite well with Ron, now officially designated as foreman of the property.

The big idea was the installation of a training track for the horses with the possibility that the educated brumbies might be able to contest some of the events at the race meetings scheduled at many country towns throughout the state. Ron made his point as Bing tried to accommodate an overlarge piece of bacon in his mouth. He still listened with interest, as his wife stared him down and frowned at his masticating efforts.

The foreman would not be stopped. "We've got the natural inclination of the hill and half a bend around Thunder Ridge and at the peak of the rise. That's all we need. I know where we can obtain some barrier stalls for education purposes and we can run the potential stayers up the mountain tracks to develop their stamina."

Helen fiddled with her lamb's fry and took time to fill her wine glass, rather than instigate eye contact with her husband. This was a decision he would have to make on his own, although her veto could always be implemented at a later date. This authority is never stipulated in the wedding vows but it is generally accepted as the way things are going to be—at least by the bride.

Half a smile on Bing's face was enough for Ron and he felt encouraged. The Mills brothers also thought this was a great idea but they thought everything was a great idea, with no conception of the skill necessary to progress a revolutionary plan past the chairwoman of the board. In this instance, that person sat between them and gave no indication of approval or otherwise...at that time.

"Gentlemen, we have sticky date pudding for dessert, with cream and fresh fruit. I'll put the coffee on while you discuss this ridiculous proposal."

So much for the unanimous decision, but isn't impartial dialogue and objective consideration the balm that soothes disagreement and inspires understanding and accord? Bing thought so, and winked at his co-conspirators.

"Dinna worry, ma friends. She'll come 'round. I think it's a braw plan for sure. I reckon we can borrow Ferret Grilla's bulldozer to clear us a galloping track. Ye can drive one of those units, can you no Marvin?"

"Sure I can," confirmed the younger of the two brothers. "But it's not Ferret's dozer. It belongs to the power company."

"So?" replied the enthused ally, aware that the company never knew where their heavy equipment was, and that his mate was always up for a bribe. Being a keen punter, Ferret always needed money.

The departure of their guests signalled the commencement of the impartial dialogue and objective consideration. The initial advantage lay with Helen, as she was handling a number of sharp utensils in the sink. He was only armed with a tea towel. Fortunately, the frostiness of the lady's earlier resistance dissipated in the hot water and she capitulated.

In truth, Bing was surprised his wife had caved-in so quickly but, on reflection, he realised he had traded away a number of non-negotiable indulgences. Perhaps she was not as opposed to the plan as he first thought.

Ferret Grilla arrived with his bulldozer five days later. The power company's work crews knocked-off promptly at 5 p.m. and this was the way it was going to be—as much as could be done by sundown. The long summer evenings gave the small group a bigger window of opportunity and the efficiency of the program became enhanced when Ferret refused to let Marvin anywhere near his 'dozer. He would operate the unit at a reduced rate for his friend, and also provide access to the company compound should any other land-clearing equipment be required.

Trees and shrubs needed to be cut and uprooted and this task fell to Johnny and Marvin. The siblings handled the chainsaws and the landowner chipped in with his considerable physique on display. Any plant with a delicate root system was in trouble. The workers just grabbed it and pulled hard. Nobody thought about damage to the ecology or all those spiders and blue-tailed lizards forced to move on to greener pastures. This would be a problem for later generations

After a number of weeks, the wreckers surveyed their work and were satisfied that progress was being made. One onlooker felt embarrassed as she watched from her kitchen window and saw the amount of discarded waste lying across the length and breadth of the tableland. When the instigator came in for lunch, Helen quizzed him relentlessly.

"Darling, the mess you're making is shocking. I've been deterring people from visiting us because if they see the parlous state of the plateau, they'll go straight to the shire council, and you know they'll shut you down if they get the opportunity. God knows what the electricity company will do when they discover you've been using their equipment. At the very least, they will fire Ferret."

In all their time together, this was the longest speech the winter bride had ever made. Her chastised spouse accepted that he would have to do something about a clean-up but he should have conceded this point immediately, rather than pander to the cravings of his stomach.

"That mince was a feast, lass. Have ye nae more?"

The pot with the meat in it landed with a thud on the table beside his elbow and it was obvious that self-service would be the order of the day. Some of the regional stores had already embraced this contemporary shopping trend, which had been endorsed by the housewife alliance. The mince-muncher wondered if a new wave of spousal independence might be making in-roads into accepted family traditions. He now thought it appropriate to comment on his wife's criticisms.

"You're absolutely right. It was nae our intention to leave such a mess long-term but I can understand the need for a clear-as-we-go policy. Dinna ye worry. The logs will be chopped-up for firewood and the excess soil used for planting small trees along the track. We'll burn the rest. How does that sound?"

A small smile provided the reassurance he was looking for and order was resumed. She even poured his coffee for him. What a gal! Later that afternoon, Bing looked down from the upper paddock and saw his wife gathering rubbish and carrying it to the bonfire. The workforce could no longer be regarded as gender-specific. No wonder he was a proud man.

Although the land-clearing operation didn't have shire approval, some members of the council became aware of it but were happy to look the other way. There were also silent observers, who hovered in the scrub a little north of Bing's property. The elder statesman of the Bidhawai people was known to be a man of few words but most of his tribe rejoiced in his leadership. When Bunji Waku frowned, the whole tribe murmured. When he slammed his walking stick against a tree, a babble of consternation broke out.

The fellow was in an invidious position. He had, on past occasions, locked horns with land developers and his relationship with the electricity company was tenuous at best. On the other hand, his people appreciated the handouts that emanated from the general community and the tribal leader enthusiastically endorsed the overtures from the local schoolmarm to accommodate a few of their youngsters, with books provided free of charge. He could see this very teacher collecting refuse for the fire.

The onlookers had no idea the completed project would involve a training track for racehorses; otherwise they might have approved. The indigenous people, over time, had embraced just about every self-indulgent practice the white fella initiated and there were quite a few. In this case, it appeared as if the designated space for their corroborees was being redeveloped, and they may need to put on their war-paint to convey their statement of disapproval.

Helen first saw the face in the window and screamed. By the time Bing arrived in the kitchen, there were three painted warriors staring at them from the eerie half-light that always heralds the oncoming darkness of night. Anybody can be a cool customer when they stand six foot plenty, so the homeowner was not agitated, in contrast to his wife. He gently prised her hand off the handle of the frying pan and explained to her that he would talk to the delegation on the verandah.

The lads were frocked-up for war, not that these warriors were wearing much in the way of clothes. Clothing can interfere with the white paint that is essentially daubed onto most parts of one's body—a mix of clay compound, water and Dulux Weathershield. Some of the young studs didn't have the patience of their elders and sometimes tradition and custom are lost in the flurry of innovation. Tony Mayor reckoned ten cans of paint went missing from his retail outlet every month.

McKeon and Bunji Waku were not strangers to each other. Earlier in the year they considered joining forces to promote regular corroboree evenings for the tourists, and had picked out a spot near the perimeter of the property.

"Hey, big fella Gubba man! What this bulldozer shit on blackfella land? Momma Waku very upset—sacred burial site cannot be disturbed."

It is always prudent when dealing with Australian natives that you acquaint yourself with their history and be prepared to recognise their territorial claims, even if you are sceptical. One should also be aware that the female members of the tribe call the shots, just as they do in western society. Land is a central part of their identity and the indigenous people regard themselves as custodians of this piece of dirt by sea named

Australia. Unfortunately, the geographical position of their sacred burial sites is only identified when the dirt appears to be of some value to the white man. Over time, the various tribes have become superb negotiators and a fragile relationship usually develops between the negotiating parties.

Nevertheless, one cannot argue with the degree of cultural exchange that has now existed for many years. We, the invaders, introduced the indigenous people to our many idiosyncratic pastimes, such as alcohol consumption, gambling, shameless fornication and bingo. With this knowledge locked-away in his portfolio of promises, the canny Scot reckoned he had a fifty-fifty chance of appeasing his greased-up associate.

"Bunji, my friend! What we have here is a fabulous opportunity for us both—a training track for racehorses. We can condition our animals here in secret and present them when we know they can salute. You and I will be well placed to win much money. Momma Waku is sure to be pleased."

The wiry old warrior might well have been secretly enthused, but one doesn't give-in to the white man this readily.

"What about sacred burial site? Blackfella ancestors cannot go to races. Blackfella ancestors must be respected."

"And so they shall be," replied the negotiator. "We'll gie oor first few horses aboriginal names. This is a tremendous honour and they will be recognised everywhere throughout the land. We might name one of them after you."

Way to go, Bing. This chap really knew how to clinch a deal and with a little bit of flattery and devious rhetoric, he had the tribe eating out of his hand, literally. They all gathered around as he handed out chewing tobacco. What a schmoozer!

Helen gazed apprehensively out of the kitchen window as the would-be warriors trudged back to their home among the gum trees. Her husband slipped his arm around her waist and assured her that there would be no trouble. In fact, the next two months were indeed trouble-free and the project was finalised in time for the grand opening and horse auction, publicised for the last Sunday in summer.

Country people always know how to put on a show and Mt. Beauty had never seen the likes of this one before. Those who had never been invited to Aberdeen saw an opportunity to snoop and swap scuttlebutt with their fellow critics. Helen expected the colour of her curtains would be under scrutiny, as well as her garden, vegetable patch and dining-room settings. Her husband only fretted about the degree of interest in his horseflesh. He needn't have worried.

There were two dozen brumbies for sale and he must have counted that many horse floats in the parking area—a credit to Bing's marketing campaign, which embraced all of the surrounding areas to a radius of ninety miles. Of course, in many of these communities, there isn't much to do on Sundays, so an exciting trip to the high plains is a given.

Helen organised the family entertainment and put on pony rides, fairy floss, a lemonade stall and a Punch and Judy show. Clemmie the rabbit patrolled the animal farmyard and made herself available for petting from the young people. The Country Women's Association was not invited but they came anyway and set up their tent for refreshments. A nice Devonshire Tea with scones and fresh cream would set you back a few shillings, and good luck to anyone contemplating a competing franchise.

The strip of track, which started by Thunder Ridge, plateaued near the homestead, then inclined upwards towards the distant tree-line, where it curved on a right-handed camber. It was here that Bing hand-painted his friendship sign—Bidhawai Bend. Bunji and his people set up a firepit and barbecued kangaroos, wombats and other traditional fare for the visitors. Momma Waku, seated at the cash counter, looked smug and full of herself.

Bing's pledge to establish some sort of green edge was not a false promise. Instead of the conventional white railing at the side of the track, he planted a line of Lombardy poplar trees, which would also provide a windbreak to protect the residence. Ferret Grilla and his bulldozer were entitled to be congratulated for the excellent galloping surface, not that anyone bragged about the fact. All the executives from the power company were in attendance but not one of them queried where the landscapers acquired their equipment. They did comment, however, on the quality of his wine.

For a Scot, mine host proved to be a generous soul and those with a bidding ticket were able to access free beer or vino. Naturally, the auction would start late in the day, after the prospective bidders had imbibed sufficiently. The canny fellow figured their purse strings would have been loosened by then.

The livestock expert came from Bright and his reputation revolved around pigs and sheep. He had no idea what use these people would have for the horses they bought but it didn't matter to a gifted communicator. The procedure was simple. The horse galloped a few furlongs up the track and then paraded in front of the assembled throng. The auctioneer would comment on the pony's bright eyes, his rein, and strength behind the saddle (he had a big bum). Further observations related to the animal's sexual orientation and political convictions. By the end of his dissertation, Bing wondered whether he should buy the nag back. He hadn't reckoned on the brute being such a fine specimen.

By that evening, the master of Aberdeen was rolling in cash, as were Bunji Waku and the Country Women's Association. All the horses sold, as had the scones and barbecued delights. By the time the last vehicle departed the property, the residents craved a hot bath and a warm bed. Notwithstanding their weariness, they were overjoyed with the success of the day and relieved they had found a new income stream. The only disappointed soul was the silver stallion who lost all his companions to commercial interests.

He wasn't alone for long. Much to the delight of the Aberdeen onlookers, the gangly gang of gallopers recommenced their twilight rumble along the plateau and embraced the new track with relish. They came out of the mist behind a new leader and attacked the rise with gusto. Some of them often returned for a reunion with their captive friend, securely imprisoned in his corral. If you don't have a chinwag, how do you know what's going on?

The boss man would have to instigate another rustling operation to replenish his stock but he would do it away from the house and surrounds. He didn't want the animals to feel threatened as he sized them up for future consideration. The homesteader, now a discerning stockman, could isolate and choose between work horses and possible racehorses. Ron Stokes taught him well.

CHAPTER 3

Winter in the high country can be very cold. The mist lingers, the air is clammy and the rain seems never-ending. However, the aftermath of a seasonal storm can be exhilarating as the verdant countryside comes alive with the sounds of survival. You'll hear a concert of bush melodies featuring birdsong, the babble of a brook or the raging river flow, making its way down from alpine regions. Sadly, the wet leaves shiver in their seclusion, knowing they'll not be caressed and warmed by the sun god any time soon.

Ron Stokes had known bleak winters in Benalla but not like this. His boss, having been brought-up in the foothills of Ben Nevis, considered himself to be an expert on arctic conditions and never complained. "It's a state of mind," he often claimed, and continued to wear his kilt throughout winter. Most highlanders only trotted out their clan garments to titillate the tourists.

Down on the farm, residents of Aberdeen kept the home fires burning brightly and coped with winter in the traditional manner. The long dark nights kept them indoors and there was no better place to be than around the hearth with a good book. At least for Helen! Her husband preferred listening to the radio, and the huge aerial on top of the roof gave him the opportunity to intercept transmissions from near and far. Bing remembered when country folk needed crystal sets to make contact with the outside world. Of course, he didn't advertise this little known morsel of information because there was no need to divulge the fact that his life experience went back further than most people thought.

The fireside rug was the domain of young Joe and his companion, the incorrigible Clementine. The bunny had put on a few pounds since summer and everybody blamed Mrs. McKeon's comfort food, curtesy of the cookbook she discovered under the Christmas tree. Such was the nature of gift-giving in those times. Exciting presents for the lady of the house included carpet cleaners, dishwashers, steam irons, pots and frying pans etc. On one occasion Helen received a voucher for a year's supply of Omo. Her husband explained that Blue Omo, the best soap powder on Earth, also happened to be the most expensive. She only continued to love him because of the latter fact, as the Scots are universally renowned for their frugality.

Should Clemmie expire, the bereaved would need to invest in a garbage disposal unit, to take over from the present arrangement, currently responsible for Clementine's expanded girth. The extra pounds slowed her down and the journey from house to hutch saw her at her most vulnerable. Undoubtedly, the carnivores in the bush became aware of the fat cottontail in residence at Aberdeen and these critters are nothing if not single minded. They eat and they sleep. If perchance they dreamed, it would involve the desire for fresh rabbit, washed down with an ice cold beverage, sourced from a nearby mountain stream.

The bunny's master had moved on from his rattle and now experimented with his junior carpentry set. His favourite tool, the hammer, had already caused havoc throughout the residence and the lad's mother made a point of relocating much of her Bric-à-brac to higher ground. The current damage report included a porcelain tea set and Helen's lifetime achievement award from the Country Women's Association. The coloured glass depiction of a scone with cream and jam defied description and replacement proved impossible (thank God).

The horses accepted their lot and found shelter from the inclement weather wherever and whenever. Those earmarked for a racing career received special treatment and were entitled to their own blanket. The early morning gallops stimulated their heart beat and these consistent work-outs tightened muscles and improved stamina. Ron was too old to ride the beasts and Bing too big. A young lad named Tommy turned-up every morning for track-work and stayed for two hours. Helen provided the lad with breakfast and then escorted him to class, thus ensuring his participation. Truancy was a major problem in her school and the native kids in particular were unreliable.

For a number of months, the trainer sat on the fence with his stopwatch and his boss supervised the workload from his position aboard the silver stallion. One day, the crusty old codger slipped down from his railing and approached the white horse. Bingham McKeon looked on suspiciously as his foreman ran his hands all over the animal. He looked the steed straight in the eye and then did the same to his employer.

"You know, we've been educating all the others and we haven't even bothered to see what this fella can do. Why don't we try him out? He has the constitution of an ox and the physique of a body builder."

"He's ma horse," replied the boss. "He does nae have to race and I will never sell him."

Ron Stokes smiled weakly, as he often did when taken aback. He hadn't anticipated such a combative response to his suggestion and realised he would have to follow up with tactical logic.

"I'm not saying you have to sell him. I know you are empowered by the success of your auction but I would hope that you would like to retain some horses to race. After all, this is why you put in the training track, isn't it?"

The big man, after due consideration, agreed with his foreman and conceded the point he made. A grunt from the horse indicated that the vote was unanimous. Anything to get that giant off his back!

The next morning Tommy arrived to find the stallion under saddle and ready to go. Ron hoped he wouldn't dump the hoop and head for the hills. Bing, of similar mind, warned the over-confident youngster of what might happen.

"Tom, this horse is different to the others. Be careful he does nae try to unseat you. I dinnae want to see you on your butt, waving goodbye to my prize possession. Is that understood?"

"Sure thing Mr. McKeon! This is his first hit-out so I'll take it easy. Perhaps a couple of furlongs at cruising speed. That should do it."

As the young rider trotted the horse towards Thunder Ridge, the binoculars came out. Usually, the old guy didn't bother and Bing had to search the house to locate his glasses. Two sets of eyes were transfixed on the galloper as he travelled towards them at speed. They could see the lad was having trouble restraining the animal, as the colt passed them like a flash of white lightning and headed up the rise at speed. The trainer screamed with joy and his companion was buoyed by his enthusiasm. Ron hadn't been that animated since he won the meat tray at the Benalla RSL.

"My God, did you see that action? He covers the ground like a gazelle. I've never seen a first trial like that before. He's a natural."

The horse came back to the enclosure covered in sweat and breathing heavily. Ron produced water and the thirsty animal plunged his head into the bucket.

"Gee," said the enthusiastic rider. "He's one hell of a horse. I tried to hold him but he had the better of me. I reckon over time he will realise you can't go hard all the time. When that time comes, you'll have yourself a pretty handy neddy."

Over the next few weeks, trainer and jockey conspired to restrain the animal and, when they achieved that aim, they instigated a scheduled program that would condition the horse in order to properly assess him. Part of this regime involved a walk in the black forest: the virgin territory beyond the homestead and adjoining plateau. The local people had established walking tracks and trails through the undergrowth but the ground could be uneven and unpredictable. However, the colt didn't seem to mind. Perhaps he harboured thoughts of running into his old mates from the pack, but surely those times were over? With two meals a day and regular grooming, life couldn't be better. He also mingled with animals of a different breed. He was not to know that social intercourse with a rabbit didn't amount to much.

Some people might want to commiserate with a creature plucked from his natural environment and forced to indulge in the ways of man... or woman. After a while, one learns to live with a change in the order of things and the alert and even-tempered can adapt quickly. However, there are always instances where acceptance is difficult and confusion reigns. In this case, the white charger's new owner had given him a stable name— Omo. Where did that come from?

The name was the least of his trainer's problems. There was the matter of his heritage, and as soon as Ron Stokes realised he had a potential racehorse on his hands, he recognised the fact that subterfuge would be needed in order to register him. The astute horseman explained the situation to the owner.

"These thoroughbred people are pretty fussy. They demand birth records and protect their lineage to the point of fanaticism. Did you know the racing industry trace all thoroughbreds back to three Arab stallions imported into Britain in the late 17th and early 18th centuries?"

"I did nae know that," exclaimed the surprised Scot. "Did Bonnie Prince Charlie have one?"

"Not to my knowledge. However, I do know the Victorian registrar, Charlie Lenegan. We might be able to arrange something."

The amount of conniving and scheming in the horse-racing industry is best left unsaid but it does happen when money changes hands; not that anyone would infer such skulduggery in relation to the registration of an unnamed colt out of the mare Clementine, sired by an unnamed stallion. Often, parental legitimacy is questioned on the basis that sometimes a horse gets into the wrong paddock. However, in this case, the dopey clerk thought the father's name was Unknown. When Bing received the papers, he couldn't have been more pleased and invited his man up to the house, cracked open an aged bottle of single malt whisky, and congratulated him on his perspicacity. Ahhh, the generosity of the occasional imbiber!

It goes without saying that the contribution of Tommy to the family operation was well and truly above the call of duty. Certainly, he received a stipend (not much) for his equine duties but he also proved to be a great help to Helen. Every day she bundled young Joe up in blankets, put him in a straw basket, and carted the young dynamo off to school with her. Actually, her student did the carrying. Tom would take charge of the rattle and sometimes let the kid play with his slingshot.

Joseph McKeon enjoyed pride of place during maths class, just left of the blackboard with a window view. Although the outlook rarely varied, he didn't bore easily and kept quiet most of the time. Sometimes he would start to wail for no apparent reason and it was no surprise that these occasions coincided with Helen's interpretation of trigonometry. Tommy had a standing brief to carry the basket of disquiet outside and quell the outburst, which suited him, as he shared the baby's opinion of this mystifying subject.

It is unclear whether the Department of Education provided guidelines as to the number of ancillary attendees allowed in a state schoolroom, but the teacher reckoned they were well away from meddling bureaucracy in Mt. Beauty. Richard Papworth often brought his blue heeler along to classes and Priscilla Bond never went anywhere without her pussy. The feline patrolled the room and crept over all the desks, which proved particularly galling during an exam. Richie maintained that the moggy was a spy on the department's payroll.

These were not the only animals that appreciated the warmth of the schoolhouse. The discovery of a brown snake in the naughty corner had everyone up on their chairs, and when a pig rampaged through the streets, they cornered it in the school grounds. Solly Simons wanted to kill the hog on the spot but Helen intervened. For that she received the eternal gratitude of the owner, who always sent her a few rashers of bacon every Hanukkah. Who says country folks don't have a sense of humour?

CHAPTER 4

The Greek

There was a sense of pride in this one-horse town called Mt. Beauty, even though McKeon, the entrepreneur, tried his best to make the place a multi-horse town. Change can sometimes be an ugly word in small communities, and there is often opposition to the best ideas. Prickly Peter Papadopoulos, the town grocer and resident grump, felt aggrieved about everything. Rumours of a self-service supermarket opening in the main street got him going and understandably so. Such an innovative arrival would impact on his own business, with the strong possibility that his present customers would be delighted to transfer their allegiance to a more agreeable trader. The man vilified Catholics, Jews, parking inspectors and the Girl Guide movement. Street parking, not a problem in Mt. Beauty, always became an issue in Bright during the tourist season. The young girls kept dobbing him in and delighted in doing so.

Bing also had issues with the grump. On Sunday, his day off, the fellow would pan for gold in the creek near Aberdeen homestead, which was his right. However, he lit fires on days of high fire danger and messed-up the environment with his garbage. Furthermore, he often deliberately strayed onto Bing's turf for no other reason than to pry and snoop. Thoroughly sick of it, Helen asked her husband to get a dog, which he did.

Then there was the nasty incident.

Settler's Cemetery, situated adjacent to the waterway where the shopkeeper did his fossicking, was the venue for the Challenge Cup, an annual cricket match between the town youngsters and the children of the power company's executives. Richie Papworth captained the locals;

ten strapping lads and one girl, Mary Dwyer. Being a bit of a tomboy, she was afforded honorary male status for the day. The graveyard picked itself as an obvious location to hold this fixture—Grubber Kelly's headstone was the exact linear measurement of a wicket, and other important prerequisites, as stipulated by the international sporting authority, were invoked. Notwithstanding that, the contest bore no resemblance to a conventional game of cricket.

Being bushwhackers, the language of the participants and their supporters was ripe and personal. They had mastered sledging before it came into vogue and savage taunts accompanied most balls, which mostly didn't comply with the law regarding straight arm delivery. At the time, the cricket world continually debated the controversy over chucking and the authorities would have been aghast at the action of these eager amateurs.

Nevertheless, the contest proved to be an exciting game. The local kids amassed a fair total and their parents, seated on the most comfortable graves, indicated their loyalties in no uncertain manner. Some dads, nicely lubricated, egged-on their offspring with invective that embarrassed their wives.

"Harry, for Christ's sake; it's bloody Sunday."

The run chase was spirited and in the pursuit of quick runs, one of the opposition lashed out at Richie's arm-ball and belted it over the boundary for six.

The ball not only sailed over the graveyard fence but headed straight for the creek where Peter Papadopoulos industriously panned for gold. The fellow had just noticed two tiny yellow specs at the bottom of his sieve when the missile cannoned into his pan and knocked it into the water. His verbal response would have been censored in any family journal. The following transcript has been retrieved.

"What the ####! Who is #### responsible for this ##### ###? I'm going to #### murder some ####."

In retrospect, young Mary, just eleven years of age, should never have been fielding at long-on. She didn't have a strong arm and outfielders need pace, agility and strength. However, the ball flew over her head and one expected her to retrieve it. Having seen exactly where it landed, she headed-off in the direction of the prospector.

31

There was no warm welcome in the offing. The chap seemed to be frothing at the mouth, and may have temporarily lost his mind. He picked up the pan and hit her across the head, drawing blood, which spurted freely over her clothes and his. Her eyes opened wide in shock, her knees buckled and her body trembled. She fell to the ground.

From the edge of the graveyard, some of the boys had assembled in order to relay the ball back to the wicket and, when they saw what had happened, they were aghast. The brute was now kicking the girl and she screamed in agony. Richard Papworth was first on the scene, carrying a cricket bat which he brandished with menace. His first blow landed on the grocer's back, making him stand to attention and open for the teen's second strike, which landed with pinpoint accuracy on his kneecap. The grocer didn't drop. He just screamed in pain.

When the rest of the lads swarmed, he offered no effective resistance. He did go down and they gave him his just desserts, kicking him, spitting on him and wrecking his camp site. When he managed to fend them off, Richie stepped-up and smacked him with his bat again. It was left to the adults to restore order and they tried to work out what had transpired. Young people don't make the best witnesses and reports can be varied. Mary appeared to be in a parlous state and was whisked-off to the medical facility in town for tests. Bing McKeon took it upon himself to escort Papadopoulos to the same place, with the Mills brothers supervising the lynching party.

The victim ended-up sore and sorry but suffered no long-term injuries. The grocer was charged and instructed to appear at Bright Court before a magistrate. His lawyer produced a defence that largely related to his bad luck—his wife had left him, his kids hated him, poor toilet training as a child; that kind of thing.

In the end, Peter Pap got-off lightly with a fine and a good behaviour bond, but life would never be the same for him in Mt. Beauty. The united mothers chose not to shop at his store and implemented a weekly trip to Bright for essential supplies. They also put the hard word on their menfolk to fast-track the supermarket being proposed for the town. Peter Papadopoulos, having being sent to Coventry, should have gone there. He would be long remembered as Despicable Pap, in contrast to Perfect Pap, self-labelled by local hero Richie Papworth.

This transgressor wasn't the only son of Hellas with a retail outlook in the main street. Christoph and Michael Tzanlis, proud owners of the fish and chip shop, did great business, especially on Fridays. Catholics didn't eat meat on Fridays and most folks sent their kids down the road to collect the parcels of hot seafood, snugly wrapped in newspaper. In later years, the gourmet providores served similar food in cardboard boxes and charged twice as much. These people were regarded as poofters and poonces.

Condiments were always provided by the two brothers and this included salt, vinegar and a piece of lemon for female customers. The boys were still young but feeling dispossessed, given their unsuccessful attempts in trying to acquire a mail-order bride. Some catalogues included desperate virgins on the books, but one assumes these ladies saw little appeal in spending their life hovering around a deep fryer.

Replenishing male stocks in Australia after the Second World War involved deft population policies and Victoria became a hot spot for Greek immigration. Melbourne's vibrant city life appealed to most bachelors, although some newcomers related to a country environment. It was the family disagreements that confused matters.

"Gee, Christoph," said Michael, "We grew-up in a fishing village. What are we doing in the mountains?"

"All the fish aren't in the sea, little brother. There are lakes and rivers in the country and, with projects like this new hydro-electric scheme, there's big money to be made in far-away places."

Papadopoulos thought along similar lines when he arrived in the high country, but he didn't need to fret about his social life. He had a wife in tow and a ten year-old. The family unit didn't last long as she soon became dispirited with the continual beatings she received from her spouse, and ran away with a door-to-door salesman, taking her son with her.

Peter Pap's woes only increased after his spat with Mary Dwyer and he was forced to close his grocery business, due to lack of interest. The locals would never support him again, so he decided to aim at the tourist market. The new signage went up late on a Monday when Peter's Gift Shop opened for business. By Tuesday morning the graffiti was there for all to see—"Beware of Greeks bearing gifts."

Co-incidence loomed large when the culprit turned out to be a teenager named Troy. Everybody recognised the artwork because the fellow was a repeat offender, but the rebuke from the schoolmarm didn't have him trembling with remorse.

"Troy, you've got to stop stealing paint from Mr. Mayor's shop. Those cans on the boardwalk are for advertising purposes. They are not free samples."

Apart from the likes of Troy and a few recalcitrant youths, the schoolmarm had everything under control. Life for Helen had become easier as school attendance improved, and she now supervised two female assistants, although the younger one was a trainee teacher. Margaret Ryan, a likeable country girl, beguiled most of the town-folk but there were grumblings from certain quarters. Evidently, she always received bigger portions from the guys at the fish shop.

Now and then, the lass competed on the equestrian circuit, and this information was quickly relayed to Bing, who quickly offered her part time employment as a work rider. With a second jockey at his disposal, the operation was up and running. Margaret's early-morning punctuality left a lot to be desired, but she did have her own car and was keen. Ron Stokes explained to his superior that women had a way with horses and the new girl brought with her a certain degree of calm and patience. She would receive her instructions and then walk the steed to the galloping area, all the while explaining her requirements to the horse. It has yet to be established whether these animals understand human dialogue but it is relevant to point out that they often snorted while under instruction.

CHAPTER 5

Margaret Ryan was chuffed. A few years into her teaching career and she was only a pregnancy away from being vice principal. Sure, there were only three teachers in the school, but people who lived beyond a fifty-mile radius didn't know that. And she wasn't the one who was pregnant. The girl was smart, ebullient, sympathetic and loyal— everybody's idea of a well brought-up young woman. She wrote to her relatives in their small town at least once a week and kept them abreast of all the coming and goings in the high country. Many in the community would have been shocked to learn that a couple of old grannies in central Victoria knew more about the local gossip than they did.

Being an unattached girl with admirers, the teacher sometimes became the subject matter of the tittle-tattle. Marg kept three young fellows on the leash but didn't make it easy for them to fully demonstrate their unfulfilled desires. The three chaps all became demoralised and deflated when they discovered they were romancing another devotee of the Virgin Mary, but hope forever springs eternal when you are dealing with a contemporary woman, open to rational discussion, should the subject of sex arise.

Chris Dow, a purchasing officer from Bogong, the small village en route to the peak, produced the most debateable argument. He maintained that the use-by date on virginity expired when the girl turned seventeen years of age (Margaret was twenty). Not wanting to refute his verbal submission out of hand, she promised to check his facts with the school's *Encyclopaedia Britannica*. Helen had purchased ten volumes from a door-to-door salesman shortly before he ran off with the grocer's wife and child.

Marg's other two suiters came to the dance with diverse backgrounds and varying credentials. One was an excitable Italian with a fine body, as befits a manual labourer. He worked the road gang, currently cutting a path through the jungle to the peak. The other, who kept his nationality a secret, might have been a man on the run, and this surely excited the girl. Being a member of the racquet club with Miss Ryan probably gave him the inside running in the race for her affections.

Margaret impressed as an athlete, which is not uncommon among country girls. Observers readily attested to her riding skills, and she proved more than capable on the tennis court. Her students often experienced her backhand, if they played-up. Another success related to her sterling efforts in helping to establish a permanent library, replacing the mobile unit which called once a fortnight.

On Sunday night, "the pictures" dictated the social scene. The community hall, recently completed under the project management of Bing McKeon, was a multi-purpose venue. Every week after church, members of the congregation met for morning tea and then transformed the premises into a cinema. Folks didn't know the name of the movie unless they telephoned someone on the weekly route. The reels travelled from Wangaratta for Saturday night in Bright, and then up the hill to Mt. Beauty for a Sunday showing. The kids appreciated any afternoon matinee that saw John Wayne or Randolph Scott scouring the Wild West for Apache and Sioux Indians. The Taylors, Robert and Elizabeth (not related), often dominated the evening sessions. *Screenplay*, one of the most popular magazines around, featured Liz on the cover more times than Bugs Bunny, who was the biggest Hollywood star of that time.

Margaret's on-going appearance at these Sunday film showings with different partners continued to be a source of gossip for the women of the town and they regularly debated the merits and otherwise of her companions. After all, having an unmarried female around was considered to be a bit untidy. Similar conjecture was bandied around the dinner table at the Aberdeen homestead but only after other matters had been dealt with. The diners shared an opinion in favour of Chris Dow. Like Margaret, he understood the four-legged beasts and Bing approved of their weekend outings, making sure they teamed-up with the sensible horses. They never left without a word of warning from the boss man.

"Now, I dinna want you kids to get-off the beaten track. It's easy tae get lost in the bush."

Did they get lost? They sure did and set in motion one of the biggest search and rescue operations seen for many a day.

"Where do you think that trails leads, Christopher? Should we give it a go?"

Marg Ryan, the inquisitive one! Everybody said that, and Chris was so full of bravado that he wouldn't dare come down on the side of caution.

"Sure thing, babe. Perhaps I'll go first in case there are wild animals that might jump out at us. I wouldn't want you to get hurt under my care."

It is hard to know whether the damsel thought this action to be chivalrous or just plain audacity. However, she let him coerce his horse in front of her and winced as it stumbled up the rise that seemed to lead nowhere. In fact, the trail disappeared after two hundred yards at the entrance to a small clearing. When the two chaff bandits spied some pasture, they took control of navigation and bent their heads for some sustenance. This is always a good time to initiate a horseback meeting, but you have to be careful not to slip down the shaggy incline.

"Did you bring a compass, Chris? I'm not sure where we are."

Although the purchase of such a device is de rigueur for the inexperienced mountaineer, the lad had not got around to it. However, the potential life-saver was on his list.

"No, but I do have hot coffee and chocolate biscuits. You're not on a diet are you?"

With a wry smile, the girl reined in her steed and gave him a belt in the nether-region. Horse and rider darted along another trail and Chris found himself left behind with a surprised look on his face. It took all his riding skill to catch up with his partner, hell bent on reaching an elevated ridge that might give them a panoramic view of the surroundings and a clue to their whereabouts.

All they got was the panoramic view. The stretch of wooded wilderness seemed endless and the towering cliffs of the overhanging mountains appeared stark and foreboding, made more so by the mist that was starting to form above the treetops. The reality of time then became an issue as darkness crept up on them.

"We may have to stay the night," exclaimed the dominant male, while contemplating all kinds of romantic possibilities, should such an extended sojourn eventuate.

"Are you mad?" responded the voice of reason. "Do you know how cold it gets out here at night?"

So they decided to bed down in the bush, as if there was any alternative. Spying another clearing just down from the ridge, the intrepid adventurers unsaddled the horses and left them to nibble on the available grass. If there is one thing to say about the equine species, it is their predictability. They love to nibble.

Chris and Marg snuggled-up in their blankets against their saddles and the hot coffee went down a treat. The animal noises coming out of the undergrowth were quite spine-chilling, but neither admitted to being nervous. Should the truth be known, Chris was not at ease with those slithering sounds he heard from the jungle. He hated animals that slithered. All in all, the two lost souls experienced a comfortable night—at least until 3 a.m. That's when it rained.

When you are in the outback, a fresh morning will titillate all your senses. This is when bacon and eggs come to life on a griddle, the smell of hot coffee invigorates your very being, and you give thanks to God for your very existence. The wet wanderers had none of that—just chocolate biscuits and cold coffee.

They were also a bit bedraggled. Night rain in the high country can be light but it is always persistent. Waterproof riding jackets, invented by stockmen for stockmen, should have been an obvious accessory for this trip but they appeared on Chris's to-do list just below the compass. So, rather than the romantic interlude first envisaged, he now contemplated life with a wife, complete with runny make-up, sodden hair and saturated clothes. He wondered if he might divorce her before they married.

The second day in the wild proved a challenge as the couple covered substantial territory without being aware of the direction they were travelling. The perplexed steeds remained faithful, but blind Freddy could tell they were losing their enthusiasm for this adventure. You didn't need to be a genius to understand negative horse vibes.

Late in the afternoon, the decision was made to set up camp, and then try and attract anyone who might be looking for them. Chris was a smoker and this fact may have been the reason they didn't die of the cold.

The bookkeeper owned the only Zippo cigarette lighter in Bogong and he flashed it at every opportunity. In their new clearing, the durable duo built a makeshift hut, hunted for berries and other edible fruit, and prepared a fire from the deadwood that littered the surrounding undergrowth, hoping that searchers might see the smoke.

There were searchers out there. Bing had alerted the community and they responded, but they didn't see any smoke. To make a long day shorter, Margaret devised a story-telling routine that would help while away the hours. She decided on some of Dr. Seuss's most popular yarns, which her five-year-olds loved. Chris learnt all about *The Cat in the Hat* and the *Fox in Socks*. For his part, he spoke at length about double-entry accounting, declining balance depreciation and stock control: the kind of commentary that brings on the desire for an afternoon nap.

When his consort slipped-off into Noddyland, her protector decided to investigate their surrounds, in the hope that he might discover a food source. He directed some words of encouragement at the horses, as he passed them, but they only looked at him with distain. Ten minutes later he heard a recognizable sound: water on the run. Yes, a babbling brook—a crystal clean, fast-moving torrent of alpine liberation. Seeing fish in the stream gave the young man every confidence they would be dining on fresh mountain trout that evening.

Margaret was still asleep when he returned to base. He didn't disturb her as he rummaged for his Swiss Army Knife. You're not worth a pinch of salt if you don't carry one of these at all times. They're great for whittling and the corkscrew and toenail cutter are essential items one can't live without. It took Christopher Dow five minutes to sharpen the end of a big stick, before he relocated back to the babbling brook, armed with his weapon. Although the inhabitants of the stream may not have experienced riverside aggression before, they avoided his thrusts with ease, apart from Tristan the trout and his cousin Teresa. They found themselves impaled on a makeshift skewer above the burning embers of a fire that transmitted a temperature which they had never experienced before.

In the realm of the senses, one doesn't rate barbecued fish but the smell was enough to wake Margaret from her slumber. She looked around for her pal but he was not to be seen. Little did she know that Chris was foraging in the forest for a side-dish for their supper! It is amazing how many edible plants grow in the outback, including nutritional food which has sustained the aborigines for years. The wild mushrooms that he found had been growing by the side of a small rising, and he didn't think for a minute that they might be poisonous. They weren't.

"A shame we don't have a cheeky little Barossa Valley Riesling to wash down this superb dinner," exclaimed the chef, now basking in his own glory.

The comment elicited a wry smile from his associate, but she still found it hard to be whimsical about their situation.

"That's all very well, but what if this is our last meal on Earth? We've been lost for two days with no sign of any help whatsoever. How long can we last in this cold? I'm freezing."

Cue the cuddle. Chris put his arms around his girl and squeezed her to him. Even if he was also feeling forsaken and abandoned, he didn't admit it. Time for a man to show his mettle.

Once the young fellow settled Margaret into their sleeping quarters, he went about building up the fire. It would need to glow through the night and remain alight for as long as possible. Chris wondered at the absence of aircraft noises because the Bright Aero Club regarded themselves as the go-to people in these situations.

As it happened, their most reliable Cessna was loaded-up and ready to rumble at dawn. Bing had been on their case since the second day of the search and supplies had been delivered to the airstrip. Dropping a food parcel accurately is often difficult, with flares, blankets and a local newspaper part of this package. Once in the air, it would be critical to establish contact of some sort, so the fly-boys could provide a compass reading for the ground team.

When Chris and Marg awoke next morning, they had company—three rabbits, a brown snake and a fox. There's something about a fire that attracts on-lookers, but this party didn't last long, because once Mr. Fox arrived on the scene, the other animals scampered. Chris noticed the horses had also broken their tether and departed. He shooed the nosy predator off and started to stoke the fire, when his twenty-twenty hearing reacted to the far-off buzz of a light aeroplane.

"Hey, girl, let's get these flames going. I can hear the sounds of salvation."

If you're hoping to see smoke from the air, don't depart too early in the morning. The mist takes a while to dissipate and it is difficult to see fire through the fog. However, pilot Skye Shanahan, renowned for having the sharpest eyes in the business, wheeled her craft around and headed for what she thought was a puff of irregularity. Her sidekick Billy Mackintosh, glued to his binoculars, was excited.

"I think you've got them, Skye baby. That definitely looks like movement down there."

Marg and Chris coordinated jumping hand-flaps as the Cessna passed over them on their reconnaissance run. The second fly-over was more difficult and at a lower level. Billy needed to release the relief package at the right moment but also had to avoid falling out of the plane. Skye, evading the taller treetops, looked out for any sudden downdraft that might dump them into the jungle.

The parcel drop nearly bombed out, only barely making the clearing. It landed on the fox, still greedily patrolling the perimeter. The larger package came with the next run and demolished their sleeping quarters. Having performed their task to perfection, the aviators departed. Silence returned to the area around the campsite but with less foreboding. Bing, still on the ground with the walking group, received the coordinates from Bright, and let-off a flare. The rescue team all cheered when they saw an immediate response from higher ground. Johnny Mills reckoned the couple to be no more than an hour away.

Not everyone at Mt. Beauty was rooting for the safe deliverance of the youngsters. The gift store proprietor, still smarting from his gold-panning experience, had the girl and her possible saviour at the top of his most-hated list, for no other reason than they were friends of Bing McKeon. Because his new venture was closed on Mondays, the fellow sometimes let loose on the Retsina, and liked to conjure-up dastardly deeds in his black moments. With his adversary overnighting in the hills, he thought this a great opportunity to implement one of his mean and vicious ploys. Papadopoulos had arson on his mind.

With her husband away, Helen McKeon was isolated and vulnerable, with limited protection provided by an ageing horse trainer and an Alsatian hound named Hero. However, Hero was already on Peter Pap's case, as someone had acquired a piece of his clothing and made the animal familiar with the scent. When the storekeeper's head appeared from behind a time-worn gum tree just after midnight, there was movement at the station. Hero's nose began to twitch and Omo started prancing about in his corral. Sadly, his agitated uneasiness failed to alert Ron Stokes, snoring profusely in the bunkhouse. Even Cammie sensed something was wrong and made a beeline for her master's cot.

When Agamemnon and Achilles made their assault on the Trojans, they probably thought all was fair in love and war. Sure, that wooden horse was a bit sneaky but they didn't arrive carrying a canister of Shell petroleum, three milk bottles and rags for a wick. The inebriated opportunist was going to firebomb the McKeon residence. What a heel!

The chap only got-off two incendiaries before Hero came at him. In the interests of self-preservation, the arsonist left behind the petrol can and the third bottle and only made his escape because of the hunk of sirloin steak he had left by the bushes. There is always time to delay a chase if there is an appetising morsel by the wayside, and one had to consider that the dog had limited experience in the ways of the world. Let's face it—who would expect such a tasty treat to be laced with rat poison? The canine dropped dead on the spot.

The two bumps on the ceiling were enough to wake Helen, and when the fire took hold, she scooped up young Joe and put him in a basket with the rabbit. The foreman reacted to her screams and the two of them managed a bucket brigade that would eventually quell the blaze. The roofing at the back side of the house had been destroyed but the beam struts only scorched. The damage could have been much worse with loss of life a possibility. Did the drink-sodden arsonist consider that?

When the search party exited the forest, Bing stopped in his tracks. He couldn't believe his eyes. His beautiful house was smouldering and friends and family were standing around contemplating the damage. Leaving the youngsters with the Mills brothers, the landowner rushed over to his property, looking for answers. By this time, his wife had regained her composure and was systematically giving orders to all the volunteers who were there to help.

"My God, lassie. What happened?" asked the concerned parent. "Is the bairn orright?"

"He's fine, but somebody doesn't like us. A couple of fire-bombs onto the roof. Ron found a petrol container in the bush...along with Hero's body."

"Nae way!" screamed the agitated Scotsman. Bing McKeon didn't get agitated very often but when he did, the usual suspects copped the brunt of his ire. In this case, it was a wealthy English settler who had been trying to buy him out.

"The bloody aristocracy," he fumed. "An irresponsible, immoral lot with nae clue aboot the struggle of hard workin' men and wimmen."

Helen had heard all this before. Was it Mary Queen of Scots, Bonnie Prince Charlie or William Wallace who had planted distrust of the English into the hearts of every laddie who wore a kilt? Bing was still trying to come to terms with the fact that Australia was an egalitarian society with no ruling classes. Nevertheless, he still droned-on incessantly about Lord Rugby and his hookers and Earl Grey and his Portuguese tarts, and never let up on how the Duke of Edinburgh could be a Greek. Perhaps this is why he wasn't pleasantly disposed towards Peter Papadopoulos.

Strangely, the latter gentleman didn't come to mind as a suspect, because the owner of the property wanted to look elsewhere—the pompous British git who owned a big spread near Bright. This fellow ran sheep, cattle and thoroughbreds and rated as Bing's biggest competitor in the horse trading business. He was the closest thing to aristocracy in this country, as one of his forebears had been the only member of the royal family to be sent Down Under as a convict.

When the dust settled and the investigation completed, the royal convict was exonerated. He claimed he wouldn't be seen dead with Shell Petroleum, being a Caltex man. The local constable accepted him at his word. After all, he was a law-abiding citizen and a gentleman.

This limited inquiry would take place in the future. For the time being, Helen needed to forget about the house and provide comfort for her fellow teacher. As the two women embraced in a delayed reunion, Bing decided to curtail his indignation and went off to investigate the damage to his house. His wife looked at her friend at arm's length and pitied the very scraggy under-nourished young girl, who would be all the better for a good square meal.

"Come inside, pet. We'll clean you up and give you some warm clothes. I guess a nice bowl of chicken broth wouldn't go astray, either. The kitchen hasn't been damaged by the fire."

Chris Dow, also bedraggled and unkempt, was left standing alone and unfussed. The bookkeeper from Bogong just followed the two ladies, hoping for a bacon sandwich. He didn't like chicken much.

The ensuing few months proved difficult for the McKeon family. A temporary tarpaulin had been put in place while the Mills boys, working under instructions from Bing, replaced the slate tiles and returned the structure to its former glory. Although the strong arm of the law proved ineffective in tracking down the culprit, the laird was not ready to let this atrocity go unpunished. He instigated his own investigation. The fuel can gave off no clue, nor the milk bottle, as most folks possessed these glass containers, delivered to their doorstep on a daily basis. It was probably surprising that no-one noticed that the cloth wick was part of a torn-up pair of pyjamas with a Hellenic brand name. Bing decided to hone-in on the rat poison that was used to dope the Alsatian dog. He traced the last known purchase of such an item to Laing's hardware store in Bright.

"Ahhh, yes, the rat poison," mused John Laing, trying to recall when he had last noticed this item as a movement on his regular stocktake configuration. "Not a big seller, especially in your region. The rodents don't like the cold, although storekeepers who sell food like to have some on hand."

His last prognostication may have given Bing time to ruminate on the fact that Peter Pap operated a general store before the gold panning incident, but the proprietor was not stopping his diatribe for anyone.

"Of course, the big run on the stuff was last November when tricky Dicky Morabito won the council election, after stiffing his popular competitor with those outrageous morals accusations. Then, of-course, there was the garbage strike of 1963. We actually ran out of stock."

"There's really nae need to gae back any further, Mr. Laing. I think I get the picture. By the way, is that the same Richard Morabito who's patron of the Girl Guide's Association?"

"That's the one, my Scottish friend. It was one of the girls from F troop who purchased the rat poison."

CHAPTER 6

The years following Bing McKeon's expansion and consolidation were prosperous for the productive pioneer. Whenever a property came on the market, he acquired same and often refurbished the building with the help of his trusty friend John Mills.

"You've furnished into a handy carpenter, ma friend. I think it's time to put you on the permanent payroll...Mr. Foreman."

Together, they erected many of the essential buildings in the town and created goodwill in doing so. These were people who could be trusted, and it was relevant that Bing was now considered an honorary Australian. They even asked him to be mayor, an offer he declined gracefully.

Mt. Beauty was thriving and rentals for properties on the main street proved to be a lucrative return on Bing's investment. The only business not to take off was the one owned by Peter the pariah, so he sold his shop to Chris Dow and headed for the southern goldfields.

The forthcoming wedding of Margaret Ryan and Christopher stifled all other conversation in the butcher shop. The lady's other suitors threw-in the towel not long after they learnt that the young tearaway spent three nights in the wild, alone with the maiden. The new businessman's sustained charm offensive outlasted Margaret's devotion to the Virgin Mary, and she finally caved-in and accepted his proposal of marriage.

With the gradual reduction of the workforce attached to the power company, the purchasing officer anticipated he would soon be made redundant, and began to seriously think about his future and how he would provide for the woman he loved. The ambitious clerk, almost through his part-time accountancy course, thought it time to give private enterprise a chance.

"Hey babe, this town needs someone with accounting and book-keeping skills, and nobody else appeared interested in the child-beater's store. I got it for a song."

"That's because nobody would touch anything connected to that creep. But you've done well. With my salary raise, we can now afford it."

"You have to be kidding. Has Helen become generous in her old age? I can't believe it."

"No, lame-brain. She's retired in her old age. I'm the new school principal, which means you'll have to stop calling me babe."

In the aftermath of this announcement, the accommodating accountant made a beeline for the liquor outlet and came back with a bottle of Champagne. It would be a night to remember, as it would over at the McKeon household, but for different reasons. Young Joe, now almost eight years old and ever-loyal to his trusted friend, was devastated when informed of Clementine's passing.

In recent years, the bunny had put on the pounds, thus reducing her mobility, which meant those forays to the edge of the wilderness continued to be fraught with danger. It was not surprising that the fox got her and didn't leave much for the mourners. Nevertheless, they buried the head in a moving service performed by the laird in the finest traditions of the Scottish church. The animal may have been Catholic for all anyone knew, but the important thing was that everyone shared an ecumenical feeling of loss for the boy's devoted friend. Even Omo and a few of the brumbies came out of their corral to witness the last rites. It is pertinent to make comment that the distraught son was not completely left in the lurch with the demise of the rabbit. His brother Edwin, born some years earlier, demonstrated acceptable personality traits but couldn't be compared to Big Ears. Easter would be forever tinged with sadness.

The following Christmas, there would be another death: the royal convict from the flatlands. Bing attended the funeral and then negotiated with the widow to purchase the manor house and adjoining acreage. On completion of the deal, he would become the largest landowner in the district.

The land extended from the back access road to Bright, to the Ovens River, a natural waterway which would supply irrigation where and when required. This showpiece estate could be improved and converted into a stud farm, if this was Bing's wish. It was.

The builders came in, followed by the painters, the landscape gardeners, and the agronomists. Stables were built, as was a covering barn for the stallions, plus ancillary buildings for office staff and hospitality functions. The laird hedge-fenced some of the paddocks and landscaped the surrounds of the house with gardens and small waterways. The new barns were state-of-the-art constructions and the bunkhouses would accommodate half-a-dozen lads in comfort.

Once the business was up and running, regular stallion parades would be organised and that required first class catering support and an area to entertain. The refurbished main house included guest quarters, which is where the owner would stay when visiting. The yet-to-be appointed overseer and his family would live in grand style in the three bedroom homestead. Only the architect of this rebuild could see the end result, and he did it on the back of ridicule and scorn, which didn't faze him one bit. In fact, he enjoyed the challenge.

What the Scottish fireball had done to this acreage soon became the talk of the valley towns, and how lucky to be able to appoint a manager with a minimum of fuss? An English itinerant, recently arrived in the region, claimed to have equine management skills. His credentials stood the test of limited scrutiny and Luke Andrews was hired within days of his application. He immediately impressed with his enthusiasm and work ethic.

Stocking the place with horseflesh became the responsibility of the owner, trying to run a training establishment at Aberdeen and a breeding enterprise at Gretna Green. His desire to name the branding shed Robbie Burns was knocked on the head by Ron Stokes. Bushfires in this country could not to be taken lightly and might break out at any time. Such a warning would be well-remembered. The green state of the pasture often changed in the blink of an eye under the rays of a summer sun.

A busy schedule saw the man travelling the state, looking for prospects, and he did this knowing the animals would be properly looked after when they arrived at their new home. In the meantime, Bing reckoned his new manager needed a wife and cajoled him into convivial experiments involving eligible ladies in the district. The poor man often tagged along when the popular couple attended civic celebrations, tea parties, curry nights and fondue dinners. On such an occasion, Luke met his bride-to-be: blonde, buxom and beautifully preserved. One doesn't like to guess a woman's age or wonder if there had ever been a wedding ring on her finger, but these questions often surface. Should the truth be known, the girdle of grief currently held together a small water pipe in her bathroom.

Many women will be smitten by a refined accent, mistaking it as an indicator of wealth and social standing. It is history that five serial killers and two axe murderers boasted a cultured British affectation, but who's counting? Cheryl marked Luke's book early in the piece but played hard to get. She didn't sleep with him until their second date and pondered a move to the manor house for all of two minutes. They married in the autumn. Although the new groom could provide no friends or relatives, nobody seemed perturbed or mystified by this lack of support. Helen, the secondary matchmaker, beamed incessantly during the ceremony and her husband seemed relieved. The marital padlock provided initial contentment for his key employee with security of tenure a bonus. He could now move on to other projects, knowing that Gretna Green would be in good hands.

The patriarch's long-term plan might have been optimistic but he could see it all come to fruition within the next decade, when Joseph would be old enough to take over the Aberdeen property. Edwin the younger, presently a mummy's boy, would surely step up and also progress the McKeon dynasty. One day they would own the mountain and most of the surrounds. He was sure of it.

"Bing, would you please take the rubbish out to the bin and, for God's sake, get that foal out of our carrot patch."

Perhaps world domination might still be a way off. Helen had become aware that her husband's expansion plans had diverted his attention away from mundane matters and frequently reminded him of his responsibilities at home. Joe was seven and Ed five and their father's lack of interest in Lego and the Sundance Kid seemed irresponsible. The babysitter filled the parental gap and bonded well with the children but, in time, the boys might look on two women as their parents. Only in a later era would such a thing be regarded as acceptable.

The compromise proved tolerable and McKeon's office in Bright was transferred to Mt. Beauty, where he put Johnny Mills in the big chair. The foreman had been married for just over twelve months, with a rug rat at home. His new title of associate director gave him the security he needed, and both men went home for lunch on alternate days, duly placating their respective wives.

Without a project on the go, it could be a slow day for the associate director, who just looked out the window while his boss rabbited-on all day on the phone. During the winter months there was plenty of traffic going up the hill and JM could only guess how much money Richie Papworth collected from his ski-hire business. Then there was the trickle-down effect, as Chris Dow maintained his books and prepared tax returns for everybody who was making a buck.

With the opening-up of the snowfields, the top town at the bottom of the mountain flourished and those dwellings left behind in the wake of the power company departures were snapped-up and converted into accommodation for the weekenders. It was much cheaper to stay away from the peak and commute to the ski-runs. For the locals, sporting associations, book clubs, and women's groups operated on rain-free days and attendances remained strong throughout the year. Mrs. Mac, now a lady of leisure, found time to attend and provide her opinion on matters important to a small community. The school fair always loomed large as one of her pet projects and everybody chipped-in to help because children were the future. Some smarty ripped-off that little gem from the television. Philosophers are a dime a dozen when they can purloin and plagiarise.

Bingham Alastair McKeon was still the most influential guy in town and, since the ghastly Greek left the area, no one wanted to question his authority. His generosity knew no bounds, and he supported many of the initiatives promoted by his fellow residents. These initiatives didn't get off the ground unless he or Richie Papworth provided at least partial funding.

Setting-up his new enterprise would involve a great deal of frustration and the days and weeks would see him as a frequent traveller to and from the renovated property. Sourcing broodmares and racing stock could be initiated by phone, but the would-be breeder would have to attend horse sales in the city and pursue other opportunities in well-known thoroughbred regions. Omo, his much loved homebred, would be retired as a racehorse and shuttled to the new farm as its first resident stallion.

"Well, Hell, say goodbye to auld faithful. He's been a bonnie friend to us all and fully deserves his new life w' the fillies. If only we had a few more like him."

Helen would not have said as much in so many words but she did agree with the general sentiment. Edwin hovered around her skirt and her other son skipped beside the silver flash as Bing loaded him onto the float and then waved the driver on his journey. Certainly, visiting rights rested with the family and his new paddock was only forty minutes away, but Mt. Bogong and the brumby were synonymous with each other. Twenty odd miles seemed like the other end of the world.

The years would roll by and the canny Scot would get richer and Joe would get taller: *big enough and tall enough to start riding,* thought the laird. He asked Margaret Dow to teach him the basics and she did.

"Gee, Bing, he's not bad. I'll have him doing tricks in no time at all."

Margaret Dow: The Queen of the Contest

CHAPTER 7

Nothing gets the heart pounding more than hope and anticipation and great expectations were rampant during the Victorian gold rush of 1850. The area around Ballarat and Clunes featured in early discoveries, as did Bendigo and Bright, which is where Peter Papadopoulos obtained his fossicking equipment prior to his arrival in Mt. Beauty.

To this day, mining activity flourishes in the aforementioned area and, although the infamous gold rush had run its course, there was always room for some lucky sod. Enter Panhandle Pete, the optimist who managed to leave the highlands without suffering retribution for his act of arson. He resettled near deserted diggings.

Perhaps it was his destiny to relocate to a region redolent of reward, or was it reminiscent of Rhodes, the place of his birth? After he fled from northern parts, the degenerate took-up residence in a historic hotel at Amphitheatre, a small village in the shadow of the Pyrenees Mountains. This hamlet was noted for its lack of roads, with only one sealed street accessible for passing traffic, but few vehicles ever bothered to stop.

Not far from the celebrated diggings, this town had seen its own share of prosperity, but not for a long time. The remaining residents struggled with the lack of service facilities and the commercial trade was almost non-existent, giving the blow-in the opportunity to strike an affordable weekly rate with the publican. He could pan for precious metals at his leisure and not be worried by the pressure and pain of mounting debt.

Amphitheatre and excitement are two words you never find in the same sentence, but one enticement sparked the new arrival's interest. Her name was Nellie Hammerstein, the thirty-something daughter of the postmaster, presently unmarried and available. Being close at hand

and clean-shaven gave panting Pete an advantage, and he often escorted the butterball to the cinema in Ararat and the picnic races at Avoca, the racetrack being a short distance from the hotel.

Then Terry Parry appeared on the scene. Terry had philandered his way through two marriages, but now the liquor salesman was footloose and fancy free. Recognising this hostelry as a cheap place to call home, he signed the register and became the second permanent guest. The two lodgers held divergent views on many subjects, but they existed harmoniously—until the town's resident virgin asked to be introduced to the new arrival.

When Parry met Nellie, the planets aligned for the first time since 561 BC, and sparks began to fly. This didn't sit well with yesterday's man, who felt discarded and forsaken. The innkeeper couldn't help but remark that he thought they were the perfect couple, a comment which he expected would fire-up the jealous prospector. He would never know and understand how this insensitive observation of his would change the course of history; at least for one individual. That individual headed for the creek bed in a foul mood.

He directed most of his profane comments at the clay banks that provided the watercourse with its direction and flow-rate, not that there was much water flow that morning. He walked along the dry section of the almost empty creek, kicking stones and pebbles unceasingly and maliciously. He even lashed-out at a very large rock, which retaliated in kind. He needed to sit down to nurse the pain in his foot.

The largest nugget in the world was found in Victoria during that state's pre-eminent mining boom and weighed 210 lbs. The senior sedimentary surveyor had to break it in three to weigh the bugger, thereafter called the Welcome Stranger.

Pap's discovery didn't quite reach those proportions, but, at 160 lbs, it rated the biggest single find this century. The gold price was high so he became an instant millionaire and owed it all to his lost love, the bitch.

Peter christened the precious nugget Broken Toe, because of what happened when he kicked that glimmering gift from the gods. At first, he sought vengeance and reached for his pick-axe. That's when he saw the yellow flecks glistening in the sunshine, and all negative thoughts disappeared as he looked to the heavens, just as the sun slipped silently behind a cloud. An unlucky man may have missed it by that much.

The priority for this lucky man was to upgrade his living accommodation, so good-bye smelly room in termite territory and hello Ballarat Lodge, a temporary arrangement that would satisfy him until more salubrious digs became available. The real estate guys and gals were there two days before he was, and the landlady presented him with a swag of business cards. Nobody wants to see you without a roof over your head, do they?

The two hundred acres he eventually purchased consisted of many fenced fields and a lovely stately home. His personal specifications required the property to be superior to the one owned by the giant Scot. There's always a child in us waiting to get out, isn't there?

Dowling Forest, fifteen minutes from Ballarat, boasted a racetrack situated not far from the recently-acquired residence. Familiarity with the Avoca course had given Peter Pap an interest in the sport, just like his nemesis at Mt. Beauty, who also dabbled. He wanted to dabble better. A friend from the Pyrenees region was horse whisperer Norm Jones, and the landowner convinced him to move into the foreman's cottage on his property and populate the paddocks with thoroughbreds. They both attended the sales in Sydney and soon built-up an impressive array of stock, consisting of juveniles and broodmares. Of course, the very nature of thoroughbred breeding demands time and patience: a long-term project. More immediate tasks on the fellow's agenda included investment diversification, and it was probably time to think about remarrying, not that the likes of Nellie Hammerstein would get a look-in this time around. He treasured a voodoo doll of her in his office, and people marvelled at the fact that she still smiled with so many needles sticking into her fragile torso.

Sometimes it takes a little time for a lucky chap to be accepted by the local community. There is a bit of snobbery regarding old money and new money, but one is still granted access to the delights of social hobnobbing. Fraternising with a confirmed moneybags is always acceptable behaviour and should that person also be a bachelor, may the best girl win.

Henrietta Hornblower was no girl. Well, she had been once. Time and a couple of husbands had robbed her of her youthful countenance but not her exuberance. The lady remained attractive for her age and, with a little help from the cosmetic industry, she managed to retain that age for six years running. She still possessed the verve and energy to throw the best parties, with no holding back on the French Champagne. Should the horny hostess manage to get one of her sugar daddies to bankroll the event, the shindig would be particularly extravagant.

The socialite had done rather well for someone with limited credentials. Not being well-born and not being from one of the recognised first families, she should have been shunned, but folks were prepared to believe she was the grand-daughter of a famous naval hero. It is true that many people knew this person to be a literary figure but few of her contemporaries possessed enough nerve to challenge her. One doesn't wish to be black-balled from a major social event and she really did have that power.

By the time the cashed-up prospector came to town, Ms. Hornblower had already thrown her lot in with another mining magnate, the irrepressible "Diamond Joe" Nairobi. Rumours persisted that Joe struck it rich in the Pilbara but another train of thought identified him as a jewel thief. There was no hiding the fact that he wanted to avoid marriage at all costs, having survived two leap years and countless hints and entreaties from the professional spinster. People jump ship for less and one wonders what Horatio Hornblower would have thought of that.

The multi-millionaire from Ballarat appeared at the charity shindig knowing little about the patron or his companion, who welcomed everyone at the front door with a kiss and an invoice. This particular private foundation supported homeless kids, whose passion for urban mischief knew no boundaries. Their benefactor cashed-in a few of his diamonds and started a holiday camp for the lads, which put pressure on the other movers and shakers to unzip their wallets. Nobody likes to underbid while in the public eye, but they needn't have worried. The gushing Greek took out his pocket book and not only wrote a six-figure sum but signed the cheque. Saint Peter found himself surrounded by women for the rest of the evening, and repeatedly fended-off question about his background and marital status.

The kind and generous donor would spend time with the hostess and was delighted to learn that she loved moussaka, taramasalata, spanakopita and Nana Mouskouri. Aristotle Onassis had recently been snapped-up by that Kennedy woman, and bachelor billionaires were now in short supply. This snippet of gratuitous society gossip is of no relevance to this story but might give an insight into the thinking of one of the key players.

An attentive host should always look after the stranger in town so introductions seemed appropriate and, although disappointed to be separated from his female fans, Peter appreciated the networking opportunities in the room. Henrietta possessed the ability and charm to bring together people of opposing political and financial persuasions, and a number of influential businessmen readily accepted her invitation, including the chairman of the Reserve Bank.

"Mr. Papadopoulos, I'd like you to meet Mr. Moneybags. Sir Douglas does deals with dollars. I'm sure you two will find something to talk about."

And talk they did—for over forty minutes. The morning after the party, Peter consumed a light breakfast and then summoned his financial adviser around to his quarters at the Kelvin Club. Yes, the investment expert was aware that one of the stateside breweries was in strife and looking to sell at a grossly undervalued price. Their products couldn't match those of the dominant market leader, whose brands remained firmly entrenched in the hearts and minds of most Victorians.

You needed courage to compete against such a conglomerate, or a lot of capital. The new guy in town had both and, for some reason, people who come into money quickly always seem happy to dispose of it quickly. Penelope Wise, the adviser, wondered where he had acquired his information, but supported the proposed takeover. However, she was quick to point out the pitfalls.

"As it is, today, the company is going nowhere because it doesn't have the budget for substantial marketing expenditure. If you succeed with your takeover, you will need to spend up big on advertising and this can be a bottomless pit."

"In that case, we'll outlay what we have to. Let's do it." said the wannabe brewery owner. "Let's see if we can't make the mouse roar. People in this city drink beer like I've never seen before, so there has to be room for an alternative choice."

Penny Wise smiled ruefully at her new client, the chancer, but it was his money to lose. Nevertheless, she encouraged him to consider even the most basic due diligence.

"Don't you want to try the brew before you commit? After all, there may be a flaw in the basic ingredient."

"Nope, I don't like ale of any sort," said the investor to his surprised associate. "We'll retain the current staff and if our man can't replicate

United's product, we'll hijack a brewer from their workforce. Make him an offer he can't refuse.

In the meantime, get me an ad agent who can set-up a campaign that will make inroads into the opposition's market share."

It was hard to believe that a man who had lost all his self-belief and confidence now called the shots at the sharp end of town. Little did his confreres know that twelve months earlier he presented as a country shopkeeper with no prospects. Money often provides the self-assurance you didn't know you had. Needless to say, when the new beer baron returned to Dowling Forest, he was feeling very contented, and diarised the need to include Bright and Mt. Beauty on his company's distribution schedule.

Three high-profile advertising agencies appeared to have the capability and understanding to provide him with the visibility he required. In turn, they made submissions in Penny's office, after which Peter analysed the relative merits of each presentation, including the recommendations for the product names.

"Pap's Blue Ribbon is quite clever," said Penny. "You mentioned a hijack in our last discussion. This is what they've done with an American favourite, Pabst Blue Ribbon. Whether there would be any symmetry here is problematic."

"I like "Pap's Premium Lager," offered the new owner, weighing-up the merits of the two submitted visuals. You could tell that Peter's Pilsener was also favoured by the man who didn't mind corporate nepotism, as long as it rolled-off the tongue easily.

"You do realise Peter's Ice Cream is the brand leader in their field. It might be confusing."

Penelope's comment went by without a response. The client, now looking at artwork from the third agency, was absorbed, continually repeating the proposed slogan with differing inflections.

"Kangaroo Beer—made from the finest hops."

Two of the best-selling beers from interstate, Swan and Emu, were named after feathered friends, but did animal names give them any kind of marketing advantage? Nobody thought so.

Corporate nepotism won the day and the successful agency retired to their ideas factory to produce the marketing blitz. The light pale product was renamed Pete's Pilsener to avoid confusion with the ice cream people and everyone seemed happy. Well, not quite. The board members at Carlton & United Breweries were still smarting from the loss of their chief brewer, who decamped to the competition.

Within nine months, the new lager was the beer on everybody's lips, and the same chief brewer sat behind the wheel of a Porsche Targa. Peter Pap was first in line on every invitation list and as often as not arrived with Ms. Hornblower on his arm. Her relationship with "Diamond Joe" had waned on the back of an unfortunate downturn in his fortunes, having appeared in court on charges relating to a betting swindle. Diamonds aren't always a girl's best friend.

The marriage that everyone expected took place at the Royal Brighton Yacht Club and, in the absence of any naval relatives, Hen was given away by Commodore Paul Davies. He was not family but had certainly been involved in a navel relationship with the lady. They now regarded themselves as platonic friends, and Paul became a frequent invitee at Henrietta's parties and soirées.

The speeches, mercifully short but eloquent, gave no cause for embarrassment and the mirth level may have surprised many, because those in the bridal party were not usually a bundle of laughs. The commodore winged it with references to noble seafarers such as Jason and Ulysses. Henrietta had known many sailors in her time, but most of them swept her off her feet on dry land.

The honeymoon was a first class journey back to the country of Peter's birth and then a grand tour that incorporated Paris, London and Aberdeen, Scotland. The callow fellow just had to acquire some knowledge of the place where Bing McKeon called home, in case he could use it against him one day. Old wounds still ran deep and there would always be considerable rancour between the sensible Scot and the grisly Greek, should they ever meet again.

Mr. and Mrs. Papadopoulos Sr. had both gone to God, but an ageing grandmother rose to greet them in Rhodes, and Peter's siblings came over from other areas of Greece. The ancient one uncorked the ouzo and they all broke a few plates, which is customary for any happy occasion. The brothers danced with each other, as Greeks do, and the sun shone down unmercifully on the married couple. Then it was on to Paris.

"Look, darling; they're having a Jackson Pollack retrospective at the Galerie Perrotin. We must go."

Although not artistically inclined, Peter thought seriously about art as an investment and this particular artist had received a lot of publicity in Australia. The government splashed out $1.3 million dollars for one of his abstract paintings called Blue Poles, which would hang in the National Gallery. If community outrage could be any guide, heads would surely roll on the back of such extravagant use of the public purse. All this money for a picture of some squiggly sticks! It is history that this significant work of abstract expressionism still adorns a wall in said gallery, and one of the current estimates values the painting at more than three hundred million dollars.

"Sure thing, sweet lips, if it doesn't clash with the *Poule d'Essai des Poulains* at Longchamp. This is one of the classic Group 1 events on the international calendar."

As luck would have it, they did both and the amateur art lover managed to pick up a small Jackson Pollock, which he envisaged hanging above the cistern in their toilet. They continued on to London, consumed strawberries at Wimbledon, and made it to Ascot Racecourse in time to see Queen Elizabeth in her landau carriage with her consort, Prince Phillip of Greece. The only disappointment was Scotland. The light rain turned torrential, and the people were mean in Aberdeen. Then again, perhaps they weren't. Neither of the travellers understood a word said.

The day after their return home, the journeyman stood before his bathroom mirror, reflected on the size of his girth, and promised to do something about it. His wife put together a health and fitness regime that, by coincidence, kept him out of the house for long periods. The morning walk around the perimeter of his spread also suited the landowner as he could wheel-by the foreman's cottage and discuss thoroughbred matters. Norm Jones always had plenty to say.

"We've got six youngsters ready to go, boss. Two of them are first-up propositions, not produced at the city trials, so we will get fancy odds. I expect you'll want to bet-up on them."

A knowing grin confirmed that this assumption was correct, but the equine conditioner would be embarrassed if the nag didn't salute. The first animal, Zorba the Geek, beat all-comers at 60/1 when he stepped out at

Seymour, a provincial track not far from Melbourne. The second starter, a filly, collected the cookies at 33/1—another coup for the dynamic duo. After that, bookies became suspicious of this new player in the training ranks and the informed punters from out of town would not see these odds for a long time to come.

Because many Australians have an inherent gambling problem, the local bookmaker is accepted as a respected member of society and a trusted friend. Every Saturday, you will see the bagmen lined-up in a row at Flemington or Caulfield, trying to seduce the poor punters into entering a contest they rarely win. Most of these gentlemen will be wearing a felt hat and a bad suit, in recognition of the fact that a satchel full of money draped over one's shoulders will never be a fashion accessory. The process is simple: they take your cash and don't like to give it back. It's a living. The chaps in the main ring all drive a late-model car, which is garaged in a leafy suburb. They're well-fed and many of them smoke cigars. This is the kind of entitlement and self-confidence that permeated throughout this profession for many years…and then along came Jones.

Norm Jones was the type of individual who would set a horse for a particular race and delight in seeing it salute. With his boss's money behind him, he quickly cut a swathe through bookmaking circles and even sent a few of them to the wall. One poor bloke had to sell-up his elegant home and move to the western suburbs, which wasn't such a thrill for the people in his new locality. Residents who live in these parts enjoy the experience because they don't expect to rub shoulders with anyone from the east.

Zorba the Geek proved a money-spinner for connections and a crowd favourite to boot, especially adored by computer nerds and technocrats. The colt won four races in his first preparation and the filly racked-up five on end. Punting Pete was in seventh heaven and ready to reach for the stars, with the Melbourne Cup his number one priority.

As good as these two thoroughbreds were, they didn't have the pedigree or long-distance ability to contest Australia's richest race. His dream could be put on hold, but he already favoured a name if one of his neddies displayed exceptional staying potential. He wanted to call his contender Colossus of Rhodes. Home is where the heart is.

CHAPTER 8

Peter put it down to that romantic dinner at the Le Cinq restaurant in Paris or the allure of the flower-filled bedroom at the Hotel George V. Whatever the motivation or reason, the fact remained that Henrietta discovered she was pregnant, and subsequently announced to one and all that the family dynasty would continue into the next century, all things being equal.

All things are never equal but this didn't stop the prospective father from making plans, starting with an expansion of his empire. His investment in alcoholic beverages had been a real winner, but he figured that, should his first-born be a girl, she wouldn't be interested in a brewery. However, a winery would be a nice fit for a lady from his loins with a bubbling personality. He just needed to find a takeover target.

Because of post-war tension, Helmut and Ingrid Poppledof's boutique business in the Pyrenees didn't cut the mustard in this country. They planted vines not long after being released from detention, and if you liked a good hock or Riesling, this is where you went for your tipple. Unfortunately, not many people sampled this selection, possibly because of the bottling notes relating to the various vintages. The original grapes came from Worms, which sounded a bit off-putting. Most tipplers didn't know Worms as a city in the Rhineland.

The wine industry is often structured along family lines but the immediate Poppledof lineage was no more. Their only son, killed during an allied raid over Dresden in 1944, might have been their next winemaker, but those slimy limeys from Engelterre put an end to that. Helmut would certainly have baulked at selling his property to an Englishman, but there were no such reservations with this European magnate. The deal was done over a glass of Spätburgunder Blanc de Noir and Frau Poppledof produced a nice low-calorie cheese from her larder.

The immediate task for the new owner involved planting more vines and expanding the acreage under cultivation. Papadopoulos would appoint a farm manager and also a new winemaker, a woman. This type of gender equality, unheard of at the time, raised a few eyebrows, but the lady was a true professional and would make a go of it. Her achievements at a number of notable vineyards around Rutherglen and Wahgunyah had flagged her as the newcomer most likely. It is pertinent to mention that these properties were adjacent to Bing McKeon's holdings. Yes, Peter Pap's nemesis was also growing vines and doing very well.

As luck would have it, the little bundle of female joy arrived conveniently mid-morning at the Ballarat Base Hospital and was named Lydia Iris Zoe; the nursing staff just called her Liz. The sweet thing charmed everyone with her penetrating dark eyes and whimsical smile, and exasperated the night staff with her lung capacity. She could almost shatter ear-drums. The delighted father was so excited he immediately contacted his financial advisor, giving her instructions to acquire another winery.

Now he was really serious—one thousand acres near the town of Great Western in the foothills of the Grampians, an impressive mountain range etched into Victoria's historical footprint like no other. The auction didn't take long and the best bid came via a telephone link from the maternity ward at the regional hospital in Ballarat. Peter Pap's financial adviser Penelope Wise accepted his instructions in her usual stoic manner and prepared to make arrangements.

"I want you to tie up the paperwork quickly, Penny. As soon as Lydia is fit to travel, I want to take her up-country to view her inheritance."

Because the baby's ticket to ride needed to be endorsed by her mother, the trip didn't take place for four weeks, and the planning was reminiscent of a royal visit. The tyke was dressed immaculately in a blue and white wool jumpsuit with matching bonnet, and the staff at the winery stood to attention as she was carried through to the tasting room in a wicker basket. Henrietta refused to let her husband pour white wine down her throat, but agreed to a quick baby walk around the vat of recently picked grapes. Her jumpsuit was now very much blue, white and purple.

Lydia was back in the same tasting room to celebrate her first birthday and, from then on, it was a bit of a procession. As the Greek goddess progressed through her early years, her father celebrated each birthday with a gift of some sort. His appropriations and annexations no longer equated to the major conquest which marked the celebration of her birth, but he did like to invest in catering and related products. He successfully formulated acquisition bids for a small olive producer, two restaurant chains, a bakery, a deli and even a company that primarily sold duck pâté, readily available at his *Duck Inn* franchises. He had more or less plagiarised the name from the *Dew Drop Inn* in Bright.

The long-range plan was to put Lydia through school and university, give her some retail experience, and then place her where she belonged, as chair of Papadopoulos Products. It seemed a good plan at the time but how often do things go according to plan?

Peter Pap was out of town when Lydia got busted for cocaine possession, otherwise he might have had a coronary. It was all a misunderstanding according to the witnesses at the house party that attracted thirty guests and over four hundred gatecrashers. The girl was only thirteen years of age, naïve to the ways of the world, and certainly not promiscuous, as suggested by those law officers who responded to the call-out.

There was a court appearance, but strings were pulled and a large donation made to the victims of social injustice. It was only when the parents brought the girl back to Ballarat that the excrement hit the cooling device. Mrs. P walked into her daughter's bedroom unannounced and discovered a lewd tattoo on her bottom. When this fact was relayed to the master of the house, all hell broke loose. What else could they do but send the girl to a convent in the country? The nuns would sort her out.

Throughout history, the brides of Christ have enjoyed a fearsome reputation for discipline and puritanical chastisement, the likes of which we rarely see these days. If anyone could beat the lewdness off Lydia's bottom, it would be the nuns and Peter Pap knew it. He bid her farewell with some trepidation.

"They may appear a little uncaring but they have your best interests at heart, angel. I want to see you back here at term end, happy and healthy."

"Sure thing, Pa" replied the girl circumspectly. "The school has a great reputation. What could go wrong?"

Fire, flood, famine and failure to make the second round of the World Cup were the obvious answers to that question, but the manipulating mogul could probably overcome any of those setbacks. What would he do if his girl was lost to him forever? Already, there was a hovering presence on a motorbike and he needed to cut the snake off at the head. In the end, this was done for him and he became forever grateful to the Sisters of Charity and their country prison, for that's what it was.

Over time, Lydia succumbed to the rigours and authoritarian rule of the convent and was a better person for it. Her inappropriate associates quickly forgot about her, with the exception of the tattooed knight rider, who often fronted the chapel entrance on his motorbike, seeking a passenger for the pillion seat. It took one shot across his bow from Sister Mary Joseph's twelve-gauge shotgun to deter the amorous fortune hunter.

Of course, this vestal virgin wasn't as fearsome as one might think. Rabbit stew or venison always appeared on the Sunday lunch menu, and Sister Mary was the designated poacher.

Sometimes, Peter and Henrietta made the visitation trip and were always offered Sunday lunch with their daughter in the dining room annexe. It was a time to reflect on the past and plan for the future. On this occasion, there had already been a pre-luncheon agreement between Mother Superior and the student's father, who knew his daughter would be pleased with what he had to say.

"Sweetheart, we have good news. Because you've shown outstanding equestrian ability in your Outward-Bound course, the nuns have agreed to let you team up with your own horse. Geoffrey is on his way."

The screech of joy was all a father could hope for and there was no mistaking the genuine gratitude that Lydia felt as she wrapped her arms around him. Henrietta smiled benignly and pondered the loss of Geoffrey from the back paddock. He was a fine-looking animal but could display temperamental fits of displeasure if he didn't like you. For some reason he didn't approve of black hats and had taken a chunk out of most of hers. She wondered what he would make of the habits worn by the nuns.

Peter and Henrietta drove home from the convent relieved and satisfied that their only child was back on track, which gave them the opportunity to concentrate on other matters, foremost among these being the upcoming extravaganza at Flemington: Cup Week. Both were committed in different ways, but the four-day carnival of horse racing and associated events would tax them physically and mentally. For a start, Peter had a runner in the Victoria Derby, one of the most prestigious events listed for renewal. The winner would be sashed and saluted as the pre-eminent three-year-old colt of the season, thus earmarking him as a future stallion prospect with the potential to earn the lucky owners untold riches. The participation of fillies was a rarity as these girls preferred to race their own kind in the Oaks.

Peter Pap silently salivated as the bookmakers crowned his champion Brewery Boy the 3/1 favourite. On the morning after final acceptances, the confident brewer scanned the sports section of the morning newspaper and noted that his hated rival Bing McKeon had accepted with two entries, Dry Wine and Gurner's Lane. Both animals would go around at 50/1, a fair assessment of their ability according to Peter and the pundits.

Henrietta, still a revered fashion plate, embraced the carnival for different reasons. Her table on Oaks Day attracted the cream of Melbourne society and the millinery on display provided for every possibility except rain. Light years before the introduction of fascinators, these sculptured head-dresses were extremely creative and some defied the laws of aerodynamics. Needless to say, the Members Dining Room would be resplendent with colour and coordination, unlike on Derby Day, when tradition demanded black and white, conservatism and a token effort to notice the equine participants. Possibly, memories of 1965 still lingered, when a slip of a girl arrived with no hat, no stockings and no idea. "Ya got trouble, folks. Right here in River City."

The committee of this fabulous racetrack by the Maribyrnong River shelled-out big money to lure the world's top model, Jean Shrimpton, to judge the Fashions on the Field, a nice little competition for the ladies, while their husbands and lovers gambled away their hard-earned on the main event. Evidently, Miss Shrimpton ran out of material for her dress and it came up short, exactly four inches above her knee. Some women fainted. Certainly, the Lady Mayoress was one of these, a first for the Committee Room. Throughout the racecourse, the female patrons whispered in collective unison while consuming record amounts of Champagne. One of the starters in the mares race refused to enter the mounting enclosure; however, it could not be confirmed that the model's attire contributed to this dysfunctional behaviour.

The mounting yard can be frenetic or solemn, depending on the state of mind of the combatants, human or otherwise. If the neddies don't like the proximity of the crowd, they may become fractious, and nervous owners are often lost for words as they absorb the final instruction given to the hoop by the equally nervous trainer. The connections huddle together in a circle of solidarity, and this is why Peter Pap and Bing McKeon didn't make eye contact. The latter-named gentleman, with two horses to observe, was preoccupied, and Henrietta had distracted her husband with a personal problem. The elastic in her knickers had snapped.

As the jockeys trotted their mounts around to the starting stalls, the course broadcaster announced a betting update, with an outpouring of support for Dry Wine by the members, while Brewery Boy's odds firmed with off-course investors. Nearly every pub in the land was overflowing with excited punters, and SP bookies popped-up in bars and back lanes throughout the city. The police always turned a blind eye to these rogues during the Spring Carnival, with no quarter given at other times, unless the bagman happened to be an off-duty cop.

Gurner's Lane blew the start, but his supporters weren't worried as he didn't possess early speed. Birchwood, one of the fancies, was not favoured by a wide barrier and the rider found himself three out with no cover. Super-jock Harry White, burdened with the unkind sobriquet Handbrake Harry, threw caution to the wind and sooled the horse forward. Back on the rails, smoking his pipe, Wayne Treloar nursed the favourite along, waiting for his chance. It came and so did Brewery Boy. The judges ratified the winning margin of two lengths and Peter Papadopoulos was over the moon. Birchwood held-on for second and the stablemate Venus and Mars finished fourth. The connections of those horses were also over the moon.

The feuding heavyweights never did get to exchange pleasantries, as the delighted owner needed to participate in the presentation ceremony. Unfortunately, his wife could not join him, due to a wardrobe malfunction. The McKeon deputation quietly slipped away from the festivities and yearned for another day. Bing didn't even attend the Melbourne Cup on the following Tuesday, won by Just a Dash. It was a great year for the liquor industry.

The day after the night before, Peter Pap did the rounds of the radio stations, revelling in the spoils of victory. Sunday is always a slow news day so he was able to regale the listeners with stories of his childhood in Rhodes and his affinity with the bluebloods. This fabricated fiction fooled everyone except Bing McKeon, at that time driving back to their home in the high country,

"What a Cretan," exclaimed Bing, who knew something of Greek islands. "The guy is a complete charlatan. They only allow horses with carts on Rhodes. I know. I've been there."

"Now, dear, don't get excited. You know what the doctor said about your blood pressure."

Ahhh, the soothing serenity of the female pacifier—the gift from God that keeps on giving. There's no need for the little woman to raise her voice or pass any kind of judgement. Being the fount of all wisdom, it is her intercession that always placates stormy waters. In this instance, intervention proved timely as the man behind the wheel had a habit of pressing down on the accelerator when he became agitated. Highway Patrol aside, why arrive home an hour early? A pitstop would dilute the adrenalin.

"Oh look, darling. One of those new roadside diners! Let's stop for an espresso coffee."

No response was required. The navigator had spoken. The driver immediately eased the car out of the traffic and along the feeder road to the recently built service station/restaurant facility. The times they were a-changin' and self-service had really taken on. Bing filled his own petrol tank, and Helen ordered the coffee, available to go. What was the world coming to?

At dinner that night, Joe commiserated with his father, having seen the Derby with the other local lads in Bright. Their review of the race continued through two courses but no-one dared desecrate the moment when Helen's apple crumble and cream arrived. Having consumed same in record time, they repaired to the living room for their port, and mapped out a plan for next year.

"Dry Wine will be more mature," said Bing, "and Gurner's Lane will relish the extra distance."

Joseph McKeon knew the necessity of long-term planning with stayers but he hadn't realised his father wanted to go for the big one.

"You're talking about the Melbourne Cup."

"I am," confirmed the patriarch. "It has always been ma dream and I think both of these colts have a chance. Brewery Boy is all froth and bubble and will nae get the trip. Mark my words."

As Helen joined them with her coffee, she couldn't help but shudder at the look of aggression on her husband's face. This feud was getting out of hand and she hoped there wasn't more heartbreak on the horizon.

The Mt. Beauty Pony Club was the inspiration of Margaret Dow. Joseph McKeon, now a young man, supplied the horses, Solly Symons donated timber for the obstacles and the postmistress let them use vacant land behind the post office. Richie Papworth, one of the richest men in town, sponsored the young riders and they elected him president, on the condition that he learnt to ride a horse. Initially, Joe supervised half a dozen young girls and Margaret trained those with advanced skills. It would take some months to prepare a four-person team capable of competing in the various gymkhana and eventing programs regularly scheduled across the northeast, from Mansfield to Myrtleford. Joe and Marg would lead the assault at these one or three-day events in disciplines of dressage, show-jumping and cross-country.

Having a well-heeled sponsor proved to be important because these forays into distant locations could be expensive. Petrol was an on-going overhead, uniforms needed to be dry cleaned and pressed and grooming expenses are never cheap, animal or human. Time also comes at a cost but, when you love doing something, you find the time. Bing was a little disappointed that his son preferred equestrian to thoroughbred, but the lad made a fair fist of combining duty and leisure.

The team's first professional appearance saw them at the Yackandandah Show. Yack was an old mining town with a population problem, and their welcome sign displayed their inferiority complex: "It's cold here, but we've got gold here."

The inexperienced team from the high country would not win gold that day. Even a minor ribbon would have been acceptable, but experience is everything and the contestants and their supporters were thrilled with the outing. Bring on Beechworth, the next contest on the calendar.

The months rolled by and so did the competitions—Wangaratta, Wodonga, Strathbogie and Euroa. During this time, the competitors became familiar with the opposition, because the same people turned-up every week, and the same people usually won. Socialising after the close of competition was encouraged, but no-one ended-up drunk enough to fall off their mount the next day. Could anybody think of a better way to spend a weekend?

"Can I offer you a small glass of something?" Joe asked the pretty lass with the dark eyes. He knew her as a fearsome competitor, talented but unproven. Euroa wasn't far from her patch, which meant she had a home-town advantage, especially in the cross-country event.

"Thank you. Is that wine? It looks rather pale for a red."

"Rosé," replied the helpful host. "My people bottle it at Milawa. I'm Joe. This is Margaret, Millie, and that's Neil, fossicking around for his *Hot August Night* record." "Cracklin' Rosie" seemed appropriate for the occasion and Neil had DJ status.

Lydia nodded at her friendly rivals and introduced herself. "We're fifteen points behind you in dressage but we hope to make ground with the cross-country."

As McKeon Jr. poured the girl an ample sample of the family tipple, Mrs. Dow frowned and attempted to spoil the party.

"Excuse me for saying this, but are you old enough to drink alcohol?"

Lydia's face reddened in embarrassment, and Joe forced himself to intercede.

"Don't mind her. She's a teacher. They hate to see anyone having fun. You look every bit of thirty-five to me."

This comment brought a laugh from the young girl, who admitted to being of age, just. "I'm entitled to imbibe but I know the nuns would not approve. I'm a student at St. Masochist's in Kilmore."

Only Margaret was aware of the cruel nom de plume awarded to Lacryma Christi (tears of Christ) Convent by its students. This institution frequently attained excellent academic results but suffered because of its unholy reputation as the harshest discipline-orientated school in Victoria. Marg Dow found herself in an invidious position. As the senior adult in the group, she carried moral responsibility, but, on the other hand, if she interfered with Joe's pleasure pursuits, there might be repercussions. Surely the nuns would understand that.

"Well, Lydia whatever your name is, let's compromise. One drink, no more. Are we friends?"

Neil ramped up his recording of *You're so Sweet* and they all had a jolly time. The following day the aura of affability disappeared as both teams strived relentlessly for points. Lydia creamed them all with her cross-country display aboard her mount Geoffrey, but Margaret held on for a commendable effort, keeping her foursome in contention for the final day. That night, she lifted her alcohol embargo on the convent girl and plied her with drinks of every description. Such are the demands of competition.

In terms of predictability, the winner of the individual trophy was not expected to challenge. A lass from Violet Town came from the clouds to pip Lydia, when Geoffrey stumbled at the penultimate hurdle. Margaret's mount baulked at the last fence and Joe fell off when his steed decided to bypass the water jump. Nevertheless, it was the first time the team sponsored by Papworth's Ski Hire & Chain Service had figured in a finish of any sort. They came in third, even allowing for the last day's disappointment. The teenager also turned heads and looked to have a bright future, according to those people who knew about these things.

At the conclusion of these meetings, the carpark clears quickly as many of the contestants and their animals have a long trek home. Margaret noticed Joe's gear already packed and loaded in the back of the horse float, and saw him hovering with the Kilmore crew, saying his goodbyes. He and the girl were holding hands.

To say that this relationship blossomed would be an understatement. Yes, the senior member of the Mt. Beauty team did advise, in her role as travelling mother hen, and her view that the girl was too young was noted and ignored. The dark beauty's undoubted charm propelled her into the limelight, and her improved equestrian skills kept her under notice. The schoolgirl was defeated at Dargo and Daylesford but slayed then at Seymour and Shepparton. However, questions were asked. How did she get so much time away from the convent? Had the Sisters of Charity been too charitable?

Joseph McKeon celebrated his twenty-first birthday five days before they put the family's first employee in the ground. The retiree was ready to go and asked that they bury him on flat land near Thunder Ridge, rather than the local cemetery: an appropriate request, readily granted by the landowner.

For Joe's party, a tent had been erected on the plateau near the house, and outside catering was the order of the day; a rarity for country folk who usually provide their own nourishment. Bing had set-up a dozen Roman Candles to brighten-up the entertainment area, and this light source now became a temporary marker for Ron's grave. The flames would burn through the night before flickering and dying—a final salute to a generous soul, beloved by all.

During his time at Aberdeen, Ron Stokes had formed a solid alliance with the Bidhawai people, and often attended their corroborees near Thunder Ridge, after which he advised the local nomads on the sharp end of the horse-racing business.

Joe, having been tutored by the wily horse trainer, assumed his responsibilities. In recent times, the old man provided no more than a guiding presence, due to his on-going attacks of arthritis, sciatica, gout and general weariness. Helen always made him comfortable on the verandah rocker, and he appeared happy enough with his blanket and meerschaum.

As much as she accepted the relationship between Ron and his protégé, the boy's mother wasn't thrilled with her son's career choice, as she hoped he would pursue a vocation in medicine, law or academia. The lad spent his formative years at an all-male boarding school in Kilmore, but his grades didn't warrant continued studies at university, so back home he came. Helen didn't love him any less and, in fact, realised she would see more of him in his new role. He was still the heir apparent.

Another victim of advanced years was the silver flash. His loyal owner had moved Omo to the new property some year's earlier, to become the stud's first resident stallion. The neddy performed well as a racehorse without being sensational, and conjugal opportunities are very much dependent on reputation. Nevertheless, the farm's best mares visited the steed and he kept his end up. Half a dozen of his prodigy were stakes winners. The Bogong brumby had seen twenty-five good years by the time the vet put him down, and the farm manager buried the animal halfway along the driveway that led to the homestead. The three-hundred-foot sweep to the manor-house was lined with magnificent popular trees, well-grown and established. One of them had died and the stump had been removed to accommodate the grave.

The departure of Omo to greener pastures left Bing in a blue mood for quite a while, but, on reflection, he reckoned it was the end of one era and the start of another. There was an itch that needed scratching and it related to his increasing interest in viticulture. Small vineyards came on the market at Milawa, the King Valley and the alpine perimeter around Myrtleford, where cool climate wines were being produced from plantings first introduced by European settlers. There could be no doubt regarding his interest but did he have the smarts to make the right decisions? After all, this man only consumed alcohol moderately on special occasions, and winemaking required considerable expertise and precise decision-making. One cannot fully control the process without being able to scrutinise, analyse and assess the product at various times during production. You can't just wing-it. Exhibiting a knowing and agreeable reaction to the uncorked beverage is what it's all about, and who would want to deprive him of this satisfaction?

"Darling, are you sure you want to go along this path?" queried the woman who knew what strings to pull and when to pull them. "Your heritage is whisky. Name me one Scot who has ever made a world-class wine product."

"I cannae answer that, lass, but I know plenty who know how to drink it."

Of course, the unmentionable would always be Peter Papadopoulos. The burgeoning profits of his brewery interests had been reported in all the financial journals and Bing felt challenged. Pap's Premium Lager, blackballed in Mt. Beauty, sold well in bars all over the northeast. The man from the mountains craved another acquisition and the purchase of a winery would show this upstart a thing or two. He was in the grip of the grape.

Six months after purchasing his first vineyard near Bright, along came blight. Vine disease occurs now and then, being just one of the many tribulations winegrowers have to endure. However, for the man flush with funds, an opportunity arose to profit from other people's misery. The blight actually highlighted his capability, and provided him with a profile in an aggressive and ever-expanding industry. Some of his competitors went to the wall and he purchased their holdings for a figure well below market price. However, some of those folks, forced to sell their properties to Johnny-on-the-spot, retained grudges and regarded the settler from Scotland as a new-wave carpetbagger. When the dust settled, there would be retribution.

CHAPTER 9

A bushfire can take hold quickly. Joseph McKeon was first to see the billowing smoke darken the horizon as it sought a friendly breeze to advance its journey of expediency. This natural warning from the valley preceded the Country Fire Authority's alert by two hours and the young man managed to cobble together a team of resistance, including his mother, the Mills brothers and half of the Bidhawai tribe. Unbeknown to these desperate people, their benefactor, Bing, giant among men, was fighting fires at his other property, where the disaster possibly started.

Joe manned the command post and put into effect what he had learned at the regular fire drills, so much part and parcel of life in rural Victoria. He believed a firebreak, introduced south of the main residence, would deny the flames the oxygen they needed, and turn the path of the inferno away from his family home. The youngster, showing no signs of panic, initiated the supervised back-burn and, in so doing, destroyed the succulent growth that would feed the flames.

He received plenty of support from his indigenous friends, who were there for good reason. Their dwellings would be no match for the approaching wall of fire and so they brought their women to the McKeon spread. These terrified mothers and daughters looked-on in horror from the bunkhouse as their menfolk rushed about, trying to manipulate the burn. Quite often these organised firebreaks can get out of control but not in this case.

By early evening, the worst of it was over. The break had worked a treat and the demigod of destruction bypassed the homestead to cause havoc elsewhere. The town and its occupants remained at risk as did Bogong, just up the road. In Mt. Beauty, Richard Papworth lost his ski-hire business, and there were anxious moments at the schoolhouse. Margaret Dow shepherded the children to relative safety, and then returned to help with the bucket brigade.

Was the blaze the work of an arsonist? Suffice to say it ravaged much of the area around Bright and quickly climbed the mountain. The alpine road became inaccessible and fire-trucks turned back in frustration. Light planes and rescue helicopters water-bombed the terrain in the immediate vicinity of these areas but there would need to be a change in the weather to provide any real resistance. And that damn wind—when would it die down?

Helen supervised a soup kitchen, operating from her back door, while in town all the residents huddled together inside their multi-purpose meeting place. At about 9 p.m., the sound of thunder heralded a change in weather conditions. The rains came shortly after and it poured non-stop for seven hours. The conditions became so cold and miserable that someone started a fire with the remains of Richie Papworth's skis. He didn't seem upset.

The elements can turn on each other in the same aggressive way that humans interact. The brash, impertinent, out-of-control inferno raced up into the high country, causing untold damage and desolation—until the heavens unleashed retaliation in the form of torrential rain, uncompromising and very damp. This was welcome relief for the scorched vegetation, but the trees, with their burnt and scarred trunks, would be blemished for many months to come, if not years.

It is a measure of nature's resilience that the forest never dies, so the depleted undergrowth would green-up over time. This is a natural transition. For the dispossessed who suffered extreme loss, the way back would be more difficult.

The town-folk assembled in the shire hall to shelter from the weather, and count their blessings if their home or business had been spared. The others, with no home to return to, relied on comfort and assistance from their friends and neighbours. Tea and coffee remained in constant demand and, for those women not on kitchen duty, the containment of bored children was responsibility shared. The postmistress suggested they bring forward the Sunday movie for the benefit of the kids. Surely, that would keep them quiet.

"I'm sorry but the film is not appropriate," replied the projectionist, a self-appointed censor.

Hollywood had gone out on a limb with this one, serving-up two major male stars dressed in women's clothes. The youngsters would have loved it, but the title *Some Like it Hot* seemed inappropriate, considering the circumstances of the previous few days.

"Why don't you get Marg to take them down to the school for some calisthenics? That will sap their energy."

In the face of adversity, kids can sometimes be more resilient than their parents and Margaret had an ally in her eldest pupil Catherine, who always exhibited great organisational skills. She managed to marshal all the children together and herd them into the still smouldering school room, where she took them through many of their favourite routines. Given that the girl would not be sleeping in her own bed that night (her family home had been destroyed), her stoic efforts provided a fine example of community spirit.

Unfortunately, community spirit was somewhat dampened in the ensuing days and weeks after the tragic carnage. Restitution was in the hands of the insurance assessors and many of them were displaying scant respect in terms of urgency.

"You can't be serious. The assessor is in Antarctica!" screamed Richie Papworth into the phone.

Although the first snowflake of winter was some time off, Richard was keen to have his business rebuilt and restocked. It was cold comfort to know the person responsible for his policy was prancing with penguins down south.

A few miles away at Aberdeen, young Joe was branded a hero. His firebreak saved the homestead, outhouses and all the animals. Even Helen's hybrid orchids survived the holocaust. Further down the valley at Gretna Green, it was a different story. All that magnificent white fencing, recently erected, could not be saved. The voracious appetite of the firestorm knew no bounds and every post and pillar had been desecrated and devoured in minutes. The manor-house escaped unscathed, but what was left to oversee? The frightened stallions and mares all bolted and headed for who knew where. With minimal visibility, how could man or beast know where they were going?

Bing might have contributed more to the defence of his estate if he had been aware his family at his other property were safe. Eventually, he received the confirmation he was seeking from the senior CFA volunteer, who kept an open line to the air-wing operating over the mountain towns. Sitting on the verandah of John Laing's hardware shop, the dejected landowner silently reflected on his reversal of fortune. Nothing like this had ever happened to him before. The store proprietor, similarly disheartened, sat beside him and commiserated. Having just lost his whole inventory of shovels and buckets to the CFA, he wasn't expecting much compensation.

In normal circumstances, the shrewd storekeeper would wait on the passage of time and then invoice the town council, but, in this instance, Mrs. Laing would be having none of that. The good woman was an inspiration to the disenfranchised and forever generous in the disbursement of her favours or her husband's merchandise. Because Bright was not as badly damaged as other places, some of those water pails and spades would be coming back and marked down as second-hand items. Would it be too gross to call it a fire sale?

"Bing," declared the maudlin merchant. "Some people are saying the fire started on your patch, and was deliberately lit. What do you think of that?"

It would have been hard to comprehend what Mr. McKeon thought because he just stared at his friend and produced a vacant look of amazement. His reply came after long consideration.

"Where is this coming from? I've heard naething of the sort. We respect the environment as much as anyone and I can tell you ma foreman is a stickler for best practice farm management."

"Hey, buddy, this is no reflection on you or your team. The word is that someone has it in for you and might have been seeking revenge for something or other. Did you sell someone a dud racehorse?"

This comment brought a smile to Bing's face. Everyone blamed him if his yearlings didn't perform but buying into a top-quality thoroughbred is harder than winning the lottery. It will happen sometime for someone but often only once in a lifetime.

"All ma clients are satisfied customers, even if they don't become instant millionaires. Tell your friends, the gossip-mongers, they should look elsewhere if they be tryin' to lay the blame on ma doorstep."

Such were his parting words, as the big man extracted himself from his verandah chair and stomped-off into the evening mist, now starting to envelope the town and its surrounds. No, he hadn't sold anyone a dud neddy but, now that he thought about it, he could envisage the possibility of reprisal emanating from another source.

His most recent vineyard purchase had not been conducted in a very friendly manner and the aggrieved seller had definitely been displeased with the price offered. "I'll see you in hell" is not the kind of language you hear in a solicitor's office and, perhaps, Bing should have taken heed at the time. All the same, it was a long bow to think one solitary individual would destroy the forest in a fit of pique. It was usually the people with long bows who lived in the forest.

Did McKeon share his thoughts with the local gendarmes? No, he did not and neither did he confide in his wife or children. Perhaps he didn't want to share his reputation as a hard-ball negotiator with them. After all, they thought he was a soft touch and this was partially true. He always caved-in when the kids broke curfew, and he would never say no to Helen, whatever she wanted.

A practical man doesn't dwell on the past, and there was a lot to be done if the pastures of paradise were to be returned to their former state. The insurance would cover the rebuild costs, but when one has put so much effort into a dream, it is difficult to get over the nightmare. Nevertheless, Bing rolled-up his sleeves and went to work, as did Luke Andrews, who had already covered himself in glory with his heroic efforts at the height of the blaze.

Wood burns first and fastest in a fire and most of the fencing had been made of timber. The insurance assessors wanted to replace all the railing with aluminium, quoting all the advantages of this latter-day product. Bing would have none of it.

"Like for like. That's why I pay ma premiums, ma friend. Don't try and shirk your responsibility."

When you breathe fire and brimstone from a great height, those down below often take fright and this is exactly what transpired. The assessors backtracked from the fire scene and reported to their superiors that complete restitution was in order. Once approval was given, the rebuild commenced, with local tradesman getting the lion's share of the work.

The horses had already been rounded up and were being kept at various farms in the neighbourhood; a typical example of community support for those in need. Sure, Bing's needs were usually less than most people's but country folks don't stop to consider bank balances. If you live in the bush, you're a pal. Ain't that the truth?

The untold loss would be the interruption to service and this would be particularly relevant for those clients and prospective clients who would now send their mares elsewhere to be served. It was a good time to concentrate on other business and Bing's burgeoning wine enterprises awaited the pleasure of his interest. Some of his investments had involved cooperative synergy. He purchased a majority holding and left the previous owners to continue to manage the operation. In that way, his inexperience would not jeopardise the going concern and the minority shareholders could stay involved with cash in hand.

However, he did contribute in other areas like marketing and innovation. His decision to distribute and sell cask wine brought cries of derision from his conservative partners, dyed-in-the-wool traditionalists who couldn't comprehend a bottle without a cork in it. This bag-in-a-box technology was relatively new and brought with it obvious cost savings. The cardboard casks were also easier to store and transport. His son Joe thought it was a great idea.

"Brilliant, Dad, absolutely brilliant! You've got a whole new market out there and they will love it, especially the young people, if they can take Chateau Cardboard to parties and barbecues. And what a great way to get rid of your crap wine."

Perhaps the last comment deflated McKeon's pride a little, as he poured a glass of vino for his wife and both sons. He was no longer even partially teetotal and could now tell the difference between claret and Chardonnay. It was doubtful whether many of Joe's generation were that accomplished.

"Because of these very efficient taps, no air gets into the bag. There is very little oxidation and the wine will remain drinkable for three or four weeks. Can you believe that?"

For all of Bing's bluster and enthusiasm, it would be left to Helen to pass judgement, as she was the epitome of good taste and arbiter of all matters requiring sensible solutions. She sniffed the vino in a professional manner and sipped the dark red fluid.

"It's a bit immature and really needs to be put away for a while," suggested the matriarch, well aware that patience was not one of her husband's best attributes. "But I think it will do for what you want."

"Well said, lass. We're going to package it at our new vineyard near Wangaratta: the acquisition I picked-up for a song. The previous owner did nae have a clue."

CHAPTER 10

The Paddy

As a young boy, Matthew O'Gorman was christened Mog by his contemporaries but some of his bullying class-mates shared a different slant on his moniker. Because of his family's low level of social acceptance, he became "Mog from the Bog."

Schoolyard bullying flourished in Irish schools, especially during the most turbulent period of their history. There is no point in rehashing the tribulations of "The Troubles," and the circumstances that would lead to civil war. It is fact that Erin's men and women committed to their disputes with Mother England and then ended up fighting each other.

Through it all, the O'Gorman family managed to keep food on their table, albeit daily variations of their staple diet, the humble potato. The provider barely passed muster as his responsibilities were sullied somewhat by his dedication to the demon drink. His way home always involved a detour via the ale house and he frequently appeared at the dinner table the worse for wear. The brute could be surly, insulting, crude and daringly demonstrative—not a good example for three children looking for a role model. However, the boy's mother was a saint. Whether the spuds be roasted, basted, boiled, fried, chipped, sautéed, scalloped or mashed, the good woman would supplement the meal with other garden delights, always served with soda bread on the side.

Being an IRA family, it came as no surprise to see Matt displaying ill will and hostility at an early age, having been weaned on bitterness and vengeance. It didn't help that the older students at school treated him like a doormat.

As the years went by, it became apparent the young man would not be heading to Dublin to become a doctor, a lawyer or an engineer. However, he did show some talent as a musician and his mother confided to her neighbours that she had saved enough cash to get him some drums for his birthday. Fearing permanent ear damage, the folks next door responded by donating their old piano and asking her to spend the money on herself.

In terms of a musical career, the likes of Liberace and Peter Nero would not be challenged by this upstart, who took forever to play the Minute Waltz. With no other options available, Matt joined his father in the peat bogs. Hand-cutting fossil fuel while standing knee-deep in a quagmire is nobody's idea of fun, offering little future for the men of tomorrow, locked in a nation's past. The guy with no future prospects was just twenty-two years old when his tearful mother waved him goodbye at the Cork docks. Australia was a brave new world, according to the publicity.

The Australian publicists may well have employed the best spin doctors of the time because the deal sounded too good to be true. Get yourself an assisted passage, co-funded by the British Government, and obtain immediate access to wide open spaces, pristine beaches and glorious sunshine. Because the Aussies were bent on populating their huge country, the promoters considered it imprudent to mention that the heat regularly climbed to well over 100 degrees. Some sixty venomous animals, from snakes to box jellyfish and spiders, also missed out on the publicity. The crocodiles and sharks only became a problem if you wanted to swim in the water, so they were also afforded a low profile.

Starved of this information, the expatriates saw nothing but the silver lining, and so the ships overflowed with enthusiastic Paddywhackers—enthusiastic because their forebears had made the trip as convicts and established a power base. Even after the Irish Free State came into power in 1922, the inhabitants of this small green island remained eligible for a discounted ride to the colonies. Where was the downside?

The voyage would be no walk in the park. In fact, during the six-week journey, there were only two opportunities to stretch one's legs on dry ground: Bombay or Colombo. In either city, the natives were likely to steal your shoes, so many passengers walked around the deck and did their sightseeing with binoculars. On his reconnaissance walk, Matthew would discover many religious people in steerage, heading for Victoria to progress their vocation. In the first twenty-five years of the twentieth century, Irish priests dominated the archdiocese, wisely lauded over by the ubiquitous Daniel Mannix, the Archbishop of Melbourne, formerly from County Cork.

There weren't many from County Kilkenny who weren't religious but Matthew was one of them. He generally avoided these clerics, whose presence put a damper on his potentially licentious behaviour. Interested in social and sexual intercourse with the opposite sex, he scoured the ship for unchaperoned prospects. The decks were awash with convent girls, so there would be mountains to climb, as the Virgin Mary expected her flock to reflect in her own glory. Madonna's own descriptive title gave-off negative vibes, as far as Matt was concerned, and that is why he often called her Molly, a singularly Irish derivative.

He figured his best bet lay with a certain honey blonde, and lying with her was his ambition. Pat Malone, not long removed from Ardglass in County Down, came across as a solitary figure and sought comfort in her books and her dedicated letter-writing regime. Every day she composed a letter to her friends and relatives, describing shipboard life and the people she met. The pragmatic observer couldn't understand how one day differed from the next, and also queried the frequency of the post-box clearance on their floating prison. Notwithstanding this perceived absurdity, he was impressed with her intelligence, noting her knowledgeable understanding of many subjects, obviously gleaned from her library of literature. Actually, the library facility operated for the benefit of the crew, but who can resist the pleas of an attractive woman with a knockout smile?

For her part, he was sure she surreptitiously sized-up his superior physique, naturally acquired while working in the pits. Some of the young male passengers worked-out on the forward deck, and also took part in supervised boxing matches. Matt sometimes arrived at the dinner table battered, bruised, grouchy and short-tempered, but he had good pecs so what else mattered?

"Would you be starting-up a haberdashery business, like your grand-parents?" commented the colleen, as the conversation piece over the mid-day meal reached epic proportions of tedium. This was not the direction the horny voyager wanted their dialogue to go. Still, he remained polite and attentive.

"No, I wouldn't. I hated our shop in our provincial town and I disliked all our customers. I'm going to enrol in a viticulture course and make Guinness for the Aussies. I'm sure they'll love it."

The girl at the end of the table couldn't help but smile at his eagerness but thought the potential brewer may have been in for a shock when they pulled anchor Down Under.

"You do know that viticulture relates to wine and the production of stout is a different process? And I don't believe the Australians care for it. At least, that's what my uncle says, and he has lived in Victoria for some years."

"You have an uncle in Australia?" countered her surprised compatriot.

The lonely traveller understood the ramifications and advantages of having family in this God-forsaken part of the world. She would leave the vessel and fall into welcoming arms, acquire rent-free accommodation, and be fed and clothed by her kinfolk. Matt needed to find a job, his own digs, and feed himself. He contemplated proposing on the spot, thus qualifying as an instant member of the family. It was a thought but one that only lasted until he spied another girl in a short dress.

When the ship berthed, Pat and Matt exchanged contact details, not that he offered much in the way of detail, but she promised to look out for MOG brand beverages, if they should appear in the marketplace. Such was her expectation of ever meeting him again, although she probably wouldn't have minded. After all, he did have good pecs.

The kid travelled light so, after disembarking from the ship, he headed to the unemployment agency as quickly as possible. First there gets the best jobs, right? The young man with few skills hoped his self-awarded degree in Blarney would secure him an appointment in keeping with his expectations. The desk clerk had seen the likes of these Irishmen before.

"I'm afraid, sir, the position of chairman of the stock exchange is no longer available but we can offer you an agricultural post which may be to your liking. It is rare to find such a position in a city environment."

Thirty minutes later, Matthew found himself outside the perimeter of a football oval, right beside a major suburban railway station. The huge billboard towering above him gave-off a blood-chilling message: "The Home of the Tigers — Eat 'em Alive."

The stipend for an assistant curator at this ground was ten pounds ten shillings per week, which covered some costs, but would not leave much for leisure activities. His living quarters, provided free of charge, would never feature in *House & Garden*, but his windowless cubby hole under the grandstand proved to be relatively comfortable. He used the players' bathroom for ablutions.

The chief groundsman, an old soldier named Dave "Digger" Dudley, observed his new apprentice taking short cuts and soon nipped that in the bud. Surprisingly, the old man managed to teach the young tearaway a few things about the earth and its idiosyncrasies, stressing that there was more to groundskeeping than cutting the grass. In a cultural exchange over morning coffee, the Irishman educated his boss in the ways of his ancestors, and announced the existence of a sporting alternative called hurling, a team contest slightly safer than war.

The discussion regarding the healing properties of Guinness grew from this exchange. The banter between the two men was vibrant and sometimes heated, but they agreed that one should keep drinking the black brew until a definitive rejection of the theory surfaced. If the conversation had progressed further, beer may have ended up on the National Health Scheme. They were indeed an odd couple but got on very well, with the elder man admitting his protégé had been well-grounded. After all, spending time in the bogs of Eire gave one an affinity with the earth.

As a spectacle, Australian Rules is quite entertaining and infectious. Although the hurling devotee didn't understand the rules, he soon became an ardent supporter of the Tigers and attended all their football games. In the off-season, the ground was used for cricket and constant supervision was required to protect the wicket and surrounds from the elements. Matt's love of football wasn't replicated with the summer replacement, a sport established by the Brits last century. Old memories die hard.

The immigrant soon learned that he would not be introducing Ireland's favourite refreshment to this country because the first barrels had already come and gone. Patricia's analysis in respect of local appeal proved to be correct but, with so many Irishmen in Melbourne, the black beverage was in constant demand, especially on St. Patrick's Day when the annual march paraded through the city streets. The archbishop would sit erect in the back seat of his open-top limousine, blessing his fellow countrymen, who lurched out from various public houses to receive the passing benediction.

Matt would regularly chew the fat with his compadres in one of these pubs, also exchanging gossip with other labourers, who generally liked to talk about football, girls and money, not necessarily in that order. Money-making schemes quite often dominated the conversation and it was refreshing to hear those from the workers' union providing solutions to the worldwide financial crisis.

"You can't be talkin' about growth without thinking about land," said the orator from the public bar, during one of his pontificating sermons to a poor lad who had drifted into the hostelry for a quiet drink. They only knew each other on a nodding basis, he being the only guy who didn't retreat when the blarney poured forth.

"If you buy a small plot now, a great profit may eventuate down the line and, in the meantime, your investment is productive. You can grow things. Do you see that, brother?"

"I do," replied his acquaintance, "but tell me, Matthew, how do you find the money to purchase this small plot?"

"Begorrah, a needle through the heart," shouted the somewhat inebriated sermoniser, now prepared to change the subject. However, he didn't think ill of the man who denounced and deflated his one and only economic rationale in a simple sentence.

"In light of your wisdom, my friend, can I buy you a jar of God's liniment? Two heads together might solve the meaning of life and liquidity. You don't happen to be a bank robber, do you?"

Hardly a thief but not far from it! During the week, Michael Shine drew wages as a public servant, but on Saturdays he pencilled for one of the influential bookmakers at Flemington and Caulfield racetracks. Mick thought about expanding the parameters of their dialogue by providing details of his second job, but decided to maintain the conversation in the direction his new pal had initiated. In his capacity as general dog's body for the Department of Agriculture, he knew something about land values.

"You know, you're on solid ground with your ideas on agronomy and there are great deals to be made up-country, right now. Farmers are going to the wall in numbers. Have you thought about wine?"

"Wine?" repeated his attentive associate. "Who drinks that shite but the Frogs and Nancy Boys? I was keen on viticulture once but I was deterred by a stronger voice,"

"Ahhh," chuckled his friend. "You do know something about grape production. I didn't take you for a complete knucklehead."

In truth, once you took the obvious out of the equation, the Paddy didn't know much about anything. He thought agronomy was a deviate sexual practice but a Catholic education can't teach you everything. There would be no shame in admitting he harboured thoughts of taking on part-time study in something or other, but he was completely taken-aback when the little bugger offered to fast-track him into a government-funded scheme for would-be wine-growers.

This weekly evening course failed to attract your average red-blooded macho male, not afraid to roll up his sleeves and get dirty. Matthew shared the classroom with Collins Street farmers, French people and homosexuals. Nevertheless, enthused and excited, he planted vines on the hill beside the grandstand where he lived, just to see whether they might grow. Unfortunately, the first game of the new season drew a record crowd at the Punt Road oval, and the grapes were trampled before their time.

Matt would meet Mick every Friday night for drinks and finally learnt of his trackside activities. The curator didn't earn enough money to gamble on horses but he did get involved as a middle man. His new partner would obtain the trackside tip and some of the players would invest. Because the lads played their games on Saturday, they could not attend the meeting but ran onto the field with a form-guide in their sock, ready to view the results on the scoreboard. Should the horse salute, the middle men would take a commission. A nice little earner!

Occasionally, members of the jockey fraternity put on a boat race. This is a situation where all the human participants in the event financially support the same animal. In doing this, they have the full backing and encouragement of certain people who are colloquially known as lowlife. Mr. Shine proudly knew most of these people and obtained valuable information in exchange for his silence.

"Matthew, I shouldn't be telling you this, but I am aware of a great opportunity to make a killing on a sure-fire thing at Caulfield. You've made a pile from all your commissions and so have I. Let's invest it all on the anointed animal and finance our dreams—a one-in-a-million punt to set us up for life.

It was a long speech which ended abruptly. He produced a quick smile, skolled his beer and left the premises with a few chosen words.

"Think about it, my friend. I'll talk to you next week."

What a week! The gallivanting gardener rarely shied away from big decisions but someone was asking him to invest his life savings on a horse. As Wednesday rolled into Friday, he realised he had changed his mind on at least three occasions. In the end, he sought proverbial guidance and he found one—easy come, easy go.

The money went on and the runaway won by three lengths at 50/1. The conspirators were elated. The punters were furious as were the stewards, but they were also a bit slow. The bookmaker's clerk had collected the winnings and given them to his friend, with a railway ticket to Albury, which was in another state. Dave Dudley received Matthew's resignation by mail on the following Tuesday, the same day a certain public servant departed for Queensland on long service leave.

Life in Albury can be a little confusing for a new guy in town. The border town serves booze from New South Wales but most of the thinking is Victorian. Perhaps that's why the place seems a little old fashioned. The O'Gorman presence was valued by his bank manager, who openly drooled when he laid eyes on the size of the chap's first deposit. The zealous real estate agent was also enthused, when he received a brief to find the newcomer some arable land with potential.

The new resident had discreetly transferred Mick's share of the sting to him in the sunshine state, where he now enjoyed a soft life of self-indulgence. The Irishman might have envied this lifestyle, but his complexion didn't suit such an environment. When the realtor identified a possible purchase opportunity, Matthew was relieved to discover that the vineyard nestled at the bottom of a mountain ridge where the sun rarely shined. Memories of Ireland, to be sure.

Although he maintained his advisers in Albury, Matt wanted practical wine-growing experience, and served an apprenticeship of sorts in Rutherglen, a town which would eventually be recognised as the home of the hearty red. He learnt enough to avoid the mistake a recently bankrupted vigneron had made. You needed cold climate grapes to grow in cold climates. You also needed hard currency and a friendly bank manager.

So, the first-time landowner came into possession of a run-down vineyard. He also procured fallow paddocks from some of the neighbours, recently fallen on hard times. In a nearby town, Patricia Malone had just accepted the exalted position of chief librarian for the municipality of Wangaratta. Such was the providence of possibility on a continent where destiny and chance were constant bedfellows.

When the owner moved into to his new house, he surveyed his kingdom and contemplated the job ahead. There was much work to be done before he would see a return on his investment and, if he wanted to expand, his pal, the bank manager, would need to come to the party. He discovered he had also inherited a wayfaring worker, who came and went as he pleased. They touched base in wet ground beside the leaking water tank.

"Well, Mr. O'Gorman," said the handyman. "You can get hardware supplies from the store in Myrtleford. For anything bigger, you go to Wangaratta. This is the largest town in this region and they put on a great rodeo."

"That sounds like a lot of craic, but are there any pubs there? And what about a cinema? I like to go to the movies."

"All of that, and if you need any literature on agriculture, there's a first-class library on Main Street."

"Main Street, eh," mused the man in the mud hole. "That shouldn't be too hard to find."

Pat from Ardglass was up a ladder when her former shipmate walked into the library and spied two long legs trying to escape from a conservative tweed skirt. As he gazed on the lithe figure, he tried to guess her age (Although it doesn't impair their efficiency, some librarians can be on the wrong side of forty). When the sweet thing backed-down the ladder and turned around, the resilient Romeo let out an almighty howl.

"Feckin hell, Jesus, Mary and Joseph! If it's not the star of the County Down. I can't believe it."

Miss Malone couldn't believe it, either. Her mouth dropped open and she stared at the apparition in front of her. It had been two years since they had seen each other but recognition was instant.

"Matthew O'Gorman, as I live and breathe," she gasped. "What on Earth are you doing in my library? In my town! Are you a Guinness salesman?"

Matt laughed, a rare occurrence, and explained his circumstances, which astonished the lady. After all, two years off the ship and he was a landowner. The extent of his holdings would remain a secret for another time. One always likes to save surprises for special occasions.

"I'm lookin' for some books on wine production. Perhaps you can see what you have and we can meet later for a brew."

That was the start of it. The following weekend, the confident schmoozer came to town and escorted the colleen to his new property for a look-see, prior to their Sunday drive. They lunched beneath the poplar trees in Bright and then decided to investigate the mountains and the towns nearby. Both felt comfortable with the casual intimacy of their renewed relationship and neither seemed embarrassed or threatened. There was no doubt, however, as to who pushed the buttons.

"Look, Matthew, a souvenir shop. We should get some souvenirs for our people back home. After all, they would have no idea what the Australian bush is like. Do you agree?"

If the driver agreed, he didn't readily acquiesce because it looked bloody cold on the other side of the car window. He felt snug as a rug in his car with her ladyship's personal magnetism radiating further warmth. The committed tourist finally enticed him out of the car, albeit begrudgingly. If he possessed more charm, he would have opened the door for her, but chivalry was a British thing, so he wouldn't have been interested in that.

"I don't know why they call it Mt. Beauty," came the glum prognostication. "The place is nothing but gum trees and wet ground. You're not wearing your best shoes, are you?"

"Don't worry about me. Just keep a civil tongue when you meet the natives. They don't like to be told their part of the world is anything less than perfect. It is quite cold. Have you noticed that?"

The native turned out to be Greek and not a very friendly one at that. It hadn't been a good day for business and his limited array of souvenirs were covered in dust. He had propped up the shortfall of Aussie knick-knacks with items relating to Hellenic culture, and the couple marvelled at his display of snow globes. It rarely snows on the city of Athens, the Parthenon or the Acropolis so, in this instance, imagination was the winner.

Peter Papadopoulos eyed-off the new arrivals with interest. He always attempted to guess the wallet depth of his prospective customers, and, normally, he didn't have great expectations when he came across anyone under twenty-five years of age. Unbeknown to these prospective customers, his relationship with even younger people was more precarious.

"Are you looking for something in particular?" the shopkeeper asked, trying to be personable. He would only become grumpy if the punters left the store without purchasing anything. The lilting brogue emanating from the female visitor was completely unanticipated and, surely, he must have been disappointed. Two weeks earlier, he had sold his last snow globe of cavorting leprechauns.

"Yes, something indicative of Australian culture," said the long-legged lass with the fresh face. The discreet aroma of her scent wafted across the counter and enveloped the now-attentive salesman. Beguiled and befuddled, he totally ignored the interjection of her consort.

"A warm scarf would be good; or a fur hat. Do you sell hot-water bottles?"

The piece of polished wood with a koala bear sitting on it was a bestseller and the shrewd salesman naturally steered her in that direction, providing a commentary as he went.

"We carve a likeness of our native animals instead of stuffing them, which we feel provides a more iconic depiction of our friends from the forest. The kangaroo and emu are also popular with tourists and are hand-sculptured by our indigenous people."

Of course, the wildlife weren't stuffed because the aborigines ate them, which was too much information. Pat settled on a mildly attractive wombat depiction, which looked like a rabbit with a gold tooth, but would appeal to her nephew in Belfast. Matthew wasn't in a shopping mood but he did feel a token purchase might appease his lady friend. Surprisingly, considering the climatic conditions at the time, he bought a summer garment—a T-shirt proclaiming the wearer to be mean and green. The lad from Ireland would certainly take pride in that message.

Would Pat's initial flirtation with her countryman be enough to sustain her? As she distanced herself from her religious advisors, the young girl discovered exciting new avenues of personal exploration. In a one-on-one consultation with her parish priest, provocatively called confession, she confirmed lust to be her choice as the most attractive of the seven deadly sins. Unfortunately, he couldn't provide constructive advice, as he was fighting similar demons, which would lead to discovery and dishonour in later years.

Matt's physical attributes set her heart a-racing, but caution was promoted by the witness for the prosecution, otherwise identified as her best friend. She failed to detect a riveting personality, and thought the chap to be a little irritable at times. As for that temper—who could anticipate when it would flare-up?

When you live in a regional town for a period and realise that options are limited, many of these issues lose their significance. If bachelor landowners are involved, competition can be fierce, even if some of the opposition are whores, sluts or fast-food waitresses. The chief librarian would never say this but she would think it.

The wedding took place in the spring with the reception held at Paddy McGinty's pub in Main Street. The couple chose sunny Queensland for their honeymoon, and Matt was able to introduce his new bride to Mick Shine, his old punting pal, who had just announced his betrothal to a lovely Italian girl. Sadly, she turned out to be gay, and eventually returned home to Florence.

The months following their honeymoon proved to be a hard slog. Planting vines is no easy task, with the hours long and uncompromising. Matthew usually returned to the house in a surly mood and, if his evening meal was not on the table, he would assume the role of Dr. Jekyll's friend Mr. Hyde.

This intimidating side of marriage had not been anticipated by Pat, nor the realisation that she would initially be the sole breadwinner. Nevertheless, she was grateful to be able to continue working in town, as the alternative seemed unappealing—labouring in the field with her husband. His calculated projections were also unappealing: 2.5 years before they could reduce their debt; 3.7 years before they could afford a child; and 7.1 years before they might return to the Emerald Isle on a holiday.

The dejected woman silently sifted through her own options: 10 months and divorce; 1.6 years and murder; 2 years and suicide. Oh the shame of the long game! He saw a light at the end of the tunnel, but his wife only saw a big hole. During this period, the ogre worked tirelessly in order to impress his bank manager, who continually extended his line of credit.

The good times eventually came. The harvest yielded quality fruit at a time when Australians were well and truly increasing their intake of vino. Profits were reinvested to establish new vineyards but the real owner loomed large—the bank. At least the hard-working, hard-drinking grower could service his loans.

Not much changed for the ever-suffering wife during those better days. She dressed more stylishly and the food on the table became more edible, but her husband's questionable charm failed to improve with the times. His problems with alcohol reached new levels and his personal habits defied description. He often belched when entertaining guests. An ever-increasing flirtation with the ponies was also an ominous sign, but, in the meantime, expansion plans continued with the introduction of crushing and bottling equipment. MOG Wines prepared to debut at the Wahgunyah Wine Show.

"This is a nice drop you're producing," commented his recently-appointed agent. "I think I can place it with some discount retailers, who are looking for quality at a reasonable price. Can you guarantee quantity to match demand?"

"Does Rose Kennedy own a black dress?" asked the excited winegrower. "If I run out of premium product, I can bottle a blend. Most of the competition are wog wines. They won't be able to compete with MOG Wines."

In truth, the latter-named company didn't produce a blend but they would if need be. A mysterious person with a moustache would purchase some skins down the road and rebirth and rebrand them. Such innovation has been replicated and maintained to this day by the most reputable of companies.

Someone also looking for new avenues of expansion was Bing McKeon, the influential horsetrader with vested interests across the northern region. Already well-known for his equine activities, the entrepreneur was now grappling with grapes and had purchased a vineyard from Blake and Al Black in Milawa. It is hard to know what his wife thought of this, his latest hair-brained idea, but could it have anything to do with the fact that his arch-enemy, Peter Papadopoulos, recently re-emerged down south as the proprietor of a brewery?

The lairds and ladies in Scotland mostly consumed fortified liquor, so the new vigneron was on a learning curve in much the same way as Matthew O'Gorman. Not hamstrung by the same financial restraints as the aforementioned gentleman, he spent big money on his marketing campaign. His labels bore the brand Clementine Creek, in deference to his son's pet rabbit. Joe McKeon was now an important cog in his father's corporate wheel of fortune.

It wasn't long before the well-heeled socialites of Melbourne started serving Clementine Creek varieties at their dinner parties. Downstairs, the servants sedately sipped MOG Wines and, around the corner, the suburban hotel couldn't sell enough of Peter Pap's beer. The three European immigrants had made their mark, were independently wealthy, and should have been content with life in their new country.

Matt O'Gorman, wealthy but heavily in debt, fell at the first hurdle, ill-prepared for the blight that decimated his vineyards and others in the region. He was also feeling remorse and rage on the back of Patricia's departure. Yes, she had left him and found digs in Wangaratta, in order to continue working for a community that loved and cherished her. In terms of his projections, it should have been family time, but the love was no longer there. The scoundrel was unpredictable, unruly and under the influence far too often. He definitely struggled with anger issues and who knew where that would lead?

One year of blight can be disastrous, let alone two. This is when the banks stepped-in and Matthew became desperate and illogical. He blamed McKeon for his parlous situation and believed Bing should have tried to support him instead of buying him out.

The man from the north arrived unannounced on his premises some months earlier and attempted to negotiate a sale. Matt would have none of it, even when the Scotsman returned later with an amended proposal. In the end, O'Gorman realised he had no other option. By then, the ingrate had reduced his offer significantly, after obtaining details of the Irishman's outstanding debts.

"You're a bastard, McKeon. We winegrowers should stick together but you've stabbed me in the back and taken my house, my land and my company. I'll never forget this. You'd better watch your back."

Oh dear! Corporate wrangling can be so difficult, can't it? Especially when one of the participants is a closet psychopath. This was not obvious at the time, but subsequent events would confirm Matthew O'Gorman to be a very dangerous person. He was mean and green and most people avoided eye contact if he had been drinking.

With the transfer of ownership papers finalised, the dispossessed winegrower had to find alternative accommodation, but he didn't fancy living in the same city as his estranged partner. He decided on Bright as his home base, and rented a small cottage on the outskirts of town, not far from the road that led to the Gretna Green Stud Farm. He found work at a nearby construction site, and regularly joined his crew for after-work drinks at a local hotel. What a jerk he turned out to be. His companions always departed after the first round had been completed, at which time the publican moved all breakable items to a position of safety below the bar. The police were often called to deal with the pugnacious Paddy, and he spent at least one night in custody every month.

Was his mind blown? Did he harbour thoughts of revenge? Had the almighty dealer on high dealt him a cruel hand? All of that and some. Certainly, some of his bitterness he directed at his estranged wife but most of his bile was earmarked for the darling of the landed gentry: the thoroughbred breeder and real estate speculator, the sanctimonious Scot. A bad bastard for sure.

Some people thought O'Gorman was as mad as a ditch, and who'd argue the fact when they looked back on the night of the fire—the big fire.

"Mattie, I think you've had enough for tonight," whispered the sympathetic barman from Galway. "Some people in the hotel are good friends of the laird. Your obscene tirade against the man might enflame tension and the boss wouldn't like that. You might get barred."

"What people? Where are they?" shouted the inebriated sod on the shaky stool. Trouble was brewing and only the barman's artful guile prevented a barney in the bistro.

"Over in the corner of the dining room: with four members of Jimmy Sharman's Boxing Troupe. They're here for the rodeo, this weekend. Big blokes aren't they?"

One can only presume O'Gorman's confused mind courted discretion, as he grunted an obscenity and stumbled out of the bar into the street. His walk home resembled a stagger rather than a deliberate stride. His destination was not his house but the shed outback, where he managed to find an almost-full can of kerosene. Gathering together some rags, he wrapped them around a discarded axe handle and generously poured the fuel over same. After checking the whereabouts of his cigarette lighter, he set-off on the long walk to Bing McKeon's showpiece property.

It is uncanny how animals can anticipate danger. The mares in the outside paddocks of the farm realised immediately that the man with the flaming torch was not a friend and never would be. They retreated to the back of their enclosure and stirred in a most nervous manner. Too far from the manor-house for anyone to hear their frantic whinnies, they looked-on helplessly as the angry flames took hold of the recently painted white wooden fencing, regarded as the best in the northwest.

Perhaps if there had been recent rain, the grass surrounds may not have ignited as they did, but, after a hot, dry summer, the countryside was littered with brushwood and other inflammable material. The fire perimeter expanded and the flames scurried-off in all directions. The firebug was lucky to escape with his life, as he scampered for the road that would take him home. In the morning, he would wake to the news that rampant bushfires threatened Bright and the mountain towns. Bing McKeon wasn't the only bad bastard in the neighbourhood.

CHAPTER 11

Norm Jones escorted his boss around the paddocks of his property about once a month. He would point out his racing stock and comment on the various stages of their preparation. Peter Pap would always ask probing questions and he knew what he wanted.

"I need the good colt ready for the Caulfield Guineas, Norm," he said, as he gave his star performer the once-over. The two year olds acquitted themselves well in their debut year and one outstanding individual remained undefeated.

"Zorba was too good for them over sprinting distances and I reckon he can get a mile. What do you think? Am I being too optimistic?"

"Not at all. We've both seen his pedigree and it's pretty stout. We go to Caulfield this year and maybe the Cox Plate next year. Is that a plan or what?"

The Cox Plate, the best weight-for-age race in the land, provides the winner with the chance to embark on a stellar stud career, and the owners of prospective runners start to salivate more than twelve months before the event. Peter Pap knew his galloper would need to be an exceptional racehorse to even vie for the prize but he remained confident that his champion was worthy. He enjoyed these conversations with his trainer and positive predictions always enflamed his passion. When the garrulous Greek returned to his house for his midday meal, he radiated cordiality and goodwill, even surprising his wife.

"Darling, we should go to town for the weekend. Demis Roussos is performing at Festival Hall. I can get tickets."

Henrietta Papadopoulos hadn't confided to her husband that she thought the twenty-three stone, kaftan-wearing sex-symbol, had a voice like an Egyptian eunuch (he was born in Egypt), but she would never turn-down an offer to visit her home town, the magnificent metropolis of gardens and good times, sedately situated on the banks of the Yarra River.

The couple had purchased a rather ostentatious townhouse in Toorak, which the good lady lavishly decorated, and it offered succour and shelter during their city visits. He came to town for all things thoroughbred and board-meetings. Her busy social life involved the ladies who lunch—a sphere of influence in any democracy.

On the Monday after the concert, Peter Pap met with his fellow directors at brewery headquarters to discuss expansion. The manager of acquisitions appeared to be nervous, prior to his presentation.

"I'm afraid the deal fell through with that vineyard in Wahgunyah. At the last moment they got an offer from elsewhere and we were left in the lurch."

The takeover tycoon cherished a mantra he frequently espoused—beer with buddies, wine with dinner and any port in a storm. He had become interested in the sticky wines market and that vineyard in Wahgunyah was the most prolific producer of the most suitable grapes. The information he had just been given did nothing to improve his affability. Make way for Mr. Grumpy.

"You're not going to tell me the purchaser was Bing McKeon, are you?"

"I'm afraid so, sir. He completely outflanked us."

What a shame! The Chairman of the Board, a self-made man, never seemed to enjoy the fruits of his success. Whenever he climbed one mountain, he discovered that his long-standing enemy had been there before him. This latest episode was particularly galling and irritably repetitive. The manipulative mogul also wanted to make a move on MOG Wines but McKeon outflanked him on that one, too. He still held the advantage with his thoroughbreds. The Scotsman's neddies were not in the same class as his. At least that's what he thought.

It was rare that the top man missed his monthly lunch at the staff canteen. This token appearance with his workers gave him the opportunity to be more personable with his people, and not be side-tracked by the propaganda of selected executives. When his production line employees were given the liberty to speak freely, he could learn more about satisfaction levels and act accordingly.

On this occasion, Peter Pap would break bread with one of his lesser-known employees, whose off-the-grid activities couldn't be conducted under the auspices of good corporate governance. The fellow had been a grain merchant who sold his business to Papadopoulos for good money, and then accepted a retainer to be his eyes and ears in northern Victoria. Part of his responsibility required him to keep a watch on Peter's daughter, currently being educated at a fancy boarding school in his district. Sam Tromans ordered lobster for his main course, because he would not be picking up the tab.

"What's happening up north? Has my dear friend recovered from his misfortune? I believe his stud farm was destroyed by the fires, but I spill no tears for that Scottish bastard. Would you like some Champagne with your lobster? It really makes the difference."

Tromans nodded enthusiastically and hoped the waiter would deliver the bubbles before he provided his intelligence. He didn't expect his spiel to be well-received.

"The damage didn't prove to be as destructive as first thought. Some of the buildings survived and most of the stock were rounded-up. The manager of the place extinguished much of the fire by himself but, surprisingly, he wasn't keen to take the credit and avoided the subsequent publicity. He's a guy who keeps a low profile."

As Luke Andrews was a shy guy, his reticence would be understandable. He would not know of a fat cat down south cursing his courage and bravery. This fat cat believed that the animals involved in the tragedy would be scarred for life and be useless as racehorses. On this basis, he called for another bottle of Champagne.

Sam the Man didn't get intoxicated easily but because of the generosity of his employer, he was well on the way. They say loose lips sink ships and, because of his now relaxed state, he strayed into the realm of opinion instead of keeping to the facts. His torpedo slammed into the bow of believability and, because of his prejudices, Peter Pap was ready to believe the worst.

"I reckon your friend from Mt. Beauty is going to be the next big thing in racing circles. His spread by the mountains was saved from the fires and this is where they claim his best horses are kept. I wouldn't be surprised if he's a player in next year's Melbourne Cup, and they say he's entering a few colts in the Derby. You've got the favourite, haven't you?"

The former grain merchant had no evidence to support his claims but he figured he needed to supplement a skinny report with some icing on the cake. Otherwise, it might be thought he was not pulling his weight. This last prognostication brought an abrupt end to the luncheon, and an instruction from on high.

"Get back up there and find me some hard news. If there are great expectations coming out of Haggis Mountain, I want to know about it. Do I make myself clear?"

"Yes, sir," said the minion, as he skulled the remnants of his bubbly and burped ungraciously.

On returning to his townhouse, the now brooding businessman was greeted with an unwelcome diversion—an afternoon tea party put on by his wife for her associates, where gossip is always the order of the day. He politely accepted a cup of coffee and an apricot finger from one of the lovely ladies and, after providing his opinion on a number of social and political issues, slipped away for his afternoon nap. He awakened in time for dinner, only to discover it had been delivered in a box by a young lad on a bicycle.

The prospect of Henrietta cooking in her Givenchy gear was slim, so she opted for pizza in the parlour, served with an appropriate glass of vino. Banana cake, left over from the tea party, completed the feast and, to soften the mood, the woman put a Nana Mouskouri record on the turntable. Intimate moments were rare in this household.

The weeks following his discussion with his trainer were filled with anticipation, as the eager racegoer mentally prepared himself for the launch of his three-year-old's spring campaign. By the time Zorba the Geek stepped out at the tight Moonee Valley circuit, he was eighty-percent fit but towelled them by three lengths. His owner couldn't wait to contact his man in northern parts.

"ST, I want you to make sure this gets a good spread in the *Cowpoke Chronicle* or whatever the rag is called, and make sure they print my name. If the editor isn't cooperative, remind him who you work for."

His employee was amused. He felt all this to be unnecessary, as he was sure the man in the mountains would be very much aware of the deeds of the Hellenic horse. Nevertheless, it would be folly to deflate the man's passion.

"Sure thing. Do I cancel our advertising if he doesn't come through? Or do I make him an offer he can't refuse?"

"You're a funny guy, Tromans, but you'll be an out-of-work guy if you can't accomplish this simple task. Do you savvy?"

When Sam rang back two days later, the demanding dictator possibly thought he was going to confirm his brief had been successfully discharged. The news he received set him back quite a bit. In fact, his face paled significantly and his heart started pumping aggressively.

"I'm sorry to tell you this, but your daughter has gone missing."

The reply, curt and questioning, came back like a rocket.

"Whaddya mean, she's gone missing?"

The apprehensive retainer, conscious that his employer possessed quite a temper, wanted to somehow convey his disturbing revelation without reflecting on his own shortcomings, not that he could have done much in this instance. This was not a time to gild the lily.

"Mother Superior called me to say that her charge went off to pony club as usual but didn't return for the evening meal."

The teachers at the elite convent where Lydia was confined didn't give the girls much freedom and restricted their free time to on-campus activities. However, this student had shown remarkable potential as a show rider and received permission to attend pony club once a week. She rode her bicycle to Geoffrey's paddock, and then trotted the animal the short distance to the equestrian centre.

Under pressure and sweating profusely at the end of the phone line, Sam divulged the facts as he knew them. "They found her bike and a hair ribbon in the carpark of the equine establishment."

Because of the Tony Orlando hit song, many young girls had taken to wearing yellow ribbons, but Sister Serena, the sports mistress, confirmed the hairpiece to be Lydia's. Someone found the girl's horse trotting down a dirt road some distance from the facility, with no sign of the rider. Foul play was suspected. Her father immediately became proactive.

"My wife and I will be at the school at around 5 p.m. today. Make sure there is a member of the constabulary in attendance. Also, tell that prissy frocked-up Reverend Mother that if I find negligence on her part, I'll have her guts for garters."

Based on past disagreements with parents, other members of the clergy, and beefy truck drivers who sometimes discharged their provisions at the wrong door, this fifty-something nun projected a fearsome reputation. She would be more than capable of standing-up to the Byzantine bully, should he choose to be critical of her duty of care.

Behind her gruff exterior, this woman was beside herself with grief. Should a felonious culprit be apprehended, he or she should hope that they don't spend time alone in a cell with this bride of Christ. When Peter and Henrietta arrived at the convent, they were escorted to the reception room, to be met by Mother Superior, the head teacher, Sam Tromans and a local copper, Pierre Bowes.

Pierre Bowes was basking in the afterglow of his most recent success, the apprehension and arrest of the infamous Snowdrop Kid. The Kid had terrorised rural backyards for seven months, stealing intimate items of female apparel from clothes lines, and many of the ladies were afraid to wash their smalls. The offender was eventually caught in the act by the sergeant, who immediately became an instant celebrity. He had never been involved in a kidnapping before but knew enough to follow procedure.

"My men scoured the crime scene and talked to potential witnesses, but we can't be sure about anything. If this is a kidnap, Mr. Papadopoulos, the instigator will be in touch and I need to bring in specialists in this field. I contacted our Ballarat substation and they will have someone waiting for you when you return home."

What else could anyone do? The nuns put on tea and scones and the conference dragged-on for two hours. Peter Pap asked questions and so did the policeman, who made the observation that publicity relating to his racetrack achievements may have sparked interest in the multi-millionaire's personal wealth. Lydia's riding credentials were also well known, if not her pedigree.

The two detectives who presented at the Dowling Forest homestead were armed with recording equipment, and took-up residence in the guest rooms. The parents were briefed as to what might be said should a ransom call eventuate, as they expected it would.

The phone trilled loudly at 9 a.m., the next day. The voice was muffled but demonstratively demanding.

"I've got your daughter, fat boy. If you be wantin' to see her again, it'll cost you a million big ones. Put the cash together and stay by the phone. I'll get back to you with further instructions."

Oh for the voice recognition technology of today! In this instance, a handkerchief over the mouth was sufficient to disguise any voice, but, on replay, the detectives produced their theories.

"It sounds like Hank the Yank, said the junior officer, referring to well-known felon Harry Martin. Harry boasted a long list of misdemeanour crimes on his sheet, and he was always the first port of call if they couldn't blame the transgression on anyone else.

"I don't know," replied his female companion. "Is there some kind of accent in there? Scottish...or maybe Irish?"

At the mention of a Scot, the fatigued father grumbled and groaned but then began to think objectively. The Paddies enjoyed a reputation for cocking things up, so this seemed a more desirable situation.

Acting Inspector Angela Pride should have been fast-tracked for promotion because she was so far ahead of the game; her male counterparts wallowed in her wake. However, endorsement from the hierarchy on the top floor didn't appear to be arriving any time soon. Thus the "acting" tag.

The voice, in fact, was Irish and belonged to one-time winegrower and sometime firebug Matthew O'Gorman. Due to persistent rumours concerning certain bushfires, Matt the malevolent decided to leave Bright and found refuge in a bush environment west of Wangaratta, some distance from his estranged wife's rented house. The cottage he leased was run down and hardly liveable but he managed, barely. Another income stream would help a lot and kidnapping seemed the way to go. Big reward for not much effort!

The regional newspaper, *The Wangaratta Chronicle*, provided an extensive sports page, which included hunt club results. The Irishman recognised the name of the winner of the under 19 dressage event and presumed her to be the daughter of well-known thoroughbred personality Peter Papadopoulos. Much of O'Gorman's recent income had been courtesy of the flying colt Zorba the Geek, so he knew what manner of funds might have been generated over the past twelve months.

Over a number of weeks, the rogue staked out the equestrian centre from his perch up a leafy gum tree. With binoculars, he recognised the Greek girl and followed her movements, which were as regular as clockwork. The timing of the snatch and getaway proved impeccable and was achieved without any interference. His luck deserted him when it came to voicing his demands. That handkerchief over the mouth disguise didn't nullify his accent very effectively.

"We'll roll out our inventory of Gaelic law-breakers, Mr. P.," said Angie Pride. "In the meantime, can you get together that kind of money?"

"You think I should pay it?" queried Peter Pap, the penny pincher. His daughter's life was on the line but he obviously wouldn't have put such a high price on her head. He stared at the policewoman, who put his mind at rest.

"Don't worry. We'll get your money back. We usually mark the notes or attach a tracking device to the bag. From my experience, kidnappers are not the sharpest knives in the drawer."

The blunt knife rang back later in the day.

"I want used $100 banknotes packed in a Woolworth's green bag. Lay five packets of Arnott's Shortbread on the brim of the bag and, if the guards mark the notes or attach a tracker, the girl dies. Got that, fat boy?"

"Er, ah, er, ah," stammered the poor soul, absolutely speechless at the thought of losing his money. Losing his daughter wouldn't be a good result, either. How would he explain that to his wife? The kidnapper didn't wait for a response but proceeded with his instructions, realising the call would be recorded and that the pigs would do everything in their power to play it their way. Not on your Nelly!

The drop would take place at a deserted farmhouse, in the old milking shed. O'Gorman nominated a small town policeman from a nearby rural community to be custodian of the money. His instruction to the constabulary was definitive.

"I know Senior Constable O'Regan, so don't be bothered planting one of your bright boys in his place. He drives his car and the rest of you wallopers stay behind the front gate. I want you all gone by sundown, and don't leave any of your lads in the bushes. If I don't pick-up the money, there'll be blood on the moon. It all starts tomorrow at 5.30 p.m. Be there or be square."

"Wow! How do we figure this one?"

This came from the police commander, who would be brought up from the city to take charge of the operation, and hopefully apprehend the odious person who instigated this foul act. His special ops people were ready and committed but how would he deploy them? The perp had thrown them a curve ball for sure.

A map of the region was produced and the deserted farmhouse identified. Surely, the scoundrel gave himself no chance. The property, situated in a small valley, sat at the end of a private drive, emanating from a T intersection, where Anthony McCurry would be directing operations. There would be a sniper in the bushes with night vision glasses and a sight line into the window of the milking shed, so the ransom money would be visible at all times. Did the kidnapper really believe this experienced unit would leave the scene at sundown?

"I think he's as sharp as a sack of wet mice," said the sniper, assiduously polishing his telescopic lens in anticipation of an easy kill.

"Yeah, maybe, but I don't know," said his leader. "What's with the Arnott's biscuits and Sergeant Plod from Hicksville?"

"We've checked him out," replied his colleague, overconfident but, nevertheless, competent. "He might be a Paddy from Pork Chop Hill but he's kosher. There's not a blemish on his record."

Matt O'Gorman also made preparations for the big day. He purchased some provisions to feed the girl (he was not a monster), and, at the same time, collected a Woollies green bag. He would then have to steal a car but that could wait until the next day.

Taking the girl proved to be easy, as she was alone in the carpark when she dismounted from her faithful friend. The wretch pounced, placing the chloroform rag over her mouth, before bundling her into his car and driving away. Her temporary quarters would be the old smokehouse at the back of his cottage. When one of her yellow ribbons became dislodged from one of her plaits, O'Gorman tied the piece of yellow silk around a branch of the old oak tree at the end of his drive. He was a big Tony Orlando fan.

When Lydia regained consciousness, she found herself chained to an old iron bed, and could hear traffic noises that indicated that her prison was near a highway. He didn't speak when he fed her, and she couldn't see his face because of the balaclava he wore. The imaginative girl assumed

IRA, and wondered if the nuns were in on it. After all, her behaviour during the last term could not be classified as exemplary.

When Senior Constable O'Regan left the Tooleybuc nick, he closed the lock-up because he was the only law enforcement representative in town. Crime had taken a holiday in this part of the world, with not one criminal prosecution in three years. He still cashed his pay check, but few people outside of town knew what he looked like. That suited him, as it did Matthew O'Gorman. The reason for his appointment as the bagman remained a mystery and the lie perpetuated by the man on the phone didn't help clear the air. Certainly, he was a liar because there was no way the kidnapper knew the constable in question, but he knew of him and his physical characteristics. They could have been family.

The road from Tooleybuc to the meeting place, where the police team assembled, was narrow. Five miles into his journey, the lawman discovered a traveller in distress, with his engine bonnet up and his bum sticking out. He couldn't drive around the car, even if he wanted to.

"Can I help you?" asked the kindred spirit, not realising the response would come wrapped in a brogue he recognised. He guessed Kerry, Killarney or somewhere down south where they didn't know the difference between a carburettor and a carbuncle. When he bent down to look under the bonnet, Matt O'Gorman hit him with a hunk of granite. Goodnight and goodbye!

The villain dragged the dead body into the bushes and removed the uniform, which fitted him perfectly, although not so the shoes. He hid his own car in a tree-lined siding and then drove-off in O'Regan's police van. The Woolworths bag, full of old rags, was securely stuffed under the passenger seat.

The head of special ops eyed the new arrival with interest, noting that he was taller and younger than he had expected. His ruddy complexion more or less indicated European heritage and his accent confirmed it. Only the unkempt mop of ginger hair on the fellow's head provided any cause for doubt. Surely, every country town boasted a barber shop?

Unfortunately, time was on the wing. The courier arrived at the assembly point only minutes before the appointed time, introduced himself and enquired as to what was required of him. He didn't question why he had been chosen and displayed no signs of nervousness. Just a country copper doing his bit for Queen and country. The operations supremo did note that the newcomer appeared to be limping a bit, but this thought was interrupted by the crackle of the two-way radio: his man in the hills.

"I've got a line of sight and I can see some shelving through the window. Make sure the bag is left in front of the window."

"Got that O'Regan?" asked Anthony McCurry. "Just park in the middle of the yard, then open the shed door and you'll find shelving inside the entrance. Leave the bag and retreat quickly. No perimeter search; no heroics! Just place the money as instructed and get back here."

McCurry gently lowered the package onto the passenger seat of the driver's cabin and arranged the bikkies on top of the money. He ignored the frown he saw appear on O'Regan's face.

The careful cop was supposed to be a cautious man, so O'Gorman drove his vehicle slowly along the drive, knowing that many eyes would be watching him from all angles. The driver didn't know where the watching posts were but it didn't matter. As soon as the van entered the crucial bend, protected on all sides by trees, he braked and switched bags. One million dollars in cash now rested under the seat, and the switch had taken all of twenty seconds. He then continued his journey at his original speed.

McCurry followed the path of the van with high powered binoculars, continually uttering obscenities under his breath. The guy was going so slow, you would think a ticking bomb would detonate if he hit a bump. Eventually, the bag was delivered as requested. When the car returned, the cooperative driver only had one question for his superior.

"Would you be tellin' me what the shortbreads are for? They didn't half make me hungry."

"Probably for sustenance. The perp may also get hungry. He might need something to keep him going through the night."

"Have you thought about the possibility it might be a she?"

McCurry had no intention of engaging in profiling with this underling, so it was time to send him on his way. With a wry smile he thanked the man for his contribution and bid him farewell. It was left to the determined special ops supremo and his unit of trained commandoes to prepare the trap. Sharpshooters were hidden in the undergrowth with night goggles, and everyone was linked with two-way radios. The mystery man might already be in the vicinity, or he could arrive on foot in the darkness, or on a trail bike. By morning there would be no-one at the intersection, but many eyes would be watching.

It would be a long morning.

After the delivery had been made, Matt O'Gorman retraced his route on the Tooleybuc road and collected his clothes from the place where he dumped O'Regan's body. He redressed him in his uniform with a little too much haste, putting the man's shoes on the wrong feet.

Driving through town unrecognised presented no problems and he headed for Seymour Station, only a few miles away. Actually, it was now kilometres as Australia had gone digital a few years earlier. He parked by the pedestrian overpass and then crossed the railway line to catch the rattler to Wangaratta. Here, there was an anxious moment. A local man, exiting the pub, thought he saw his friend Liam O'Regan. When the chap didn't respond, he let it go.

The limited express from the city arrived on time, almost full, and the man with squillions in a supermarket bag shared a compartment with five other passengers. After a long day, hunger pains are not unexpected, so why not open his food parcel? He hadn't left all the goodies for the pigs.

"Thank you, kind sir," said the little old lady on the receiving end of O'Gorman's generosity. Biscuits for his fellow passengers! "What a nice chap."

What a dumb idiot! The man on the run was leaving behind a trail that could and would be followed. Nobody loses a million bucks and doesn't try to get it back. By the same token, his pursuers were already on the back foot. How would they feel when they realized they had been duped?

"We've been duped!" cried Anthony McCurry in dismay.

The commander of Russell Street's most elite unit didn't sleep during the night and was still at his post when morning broke. His people reported the bag to be still in place, and no-one reported any furtive activity. Elsewhere, there were developments but sometimes it takes a while for information to trickle through to the people who need to know.

The stolen car had been listed as missing but nobody questioned the absence of the Tooleybuc police van. Mrs. O'Regan became agitated when her husband didn't appear for breakfast, and was inconsolable when advised that a hitchhiker had found his body. Lydia the lost then turned up at a city truck depot.

Hurting the girl had never been part of the plan. O'Gorman couldn't care less about his countryman. After all, he came from Ulster. The problem was to release her into the community without giving any clues that might lead the investigators to his isolated cottage. He assumed the searchers would start from the wrong place, which is a typical problem for search and rescue missions in Ireland.

The twenty-four-hour service station on the main highway, just past Wangaratta, was a popular stopover for many of the long-haul truck drivers. They scheduled their dinner break there, before continuing-on to Melbourne. The parking bay was large and not very well lit, and somebody with a comatose girl under his arm could slink around at will. This particular sneak used chloroform with all the skills of a practiced anaesthetist. He was sure the teenager would be away with the angels for at least forty minutes. On awaking, she would find herself in another place. How good was that?

Not many millionaires could untie the strapping on a rig and then re-tie same to its original secure state. He lifted the unconscious girl onto the cargo bed of one of the semi-trailers and pulled the flap tight, expecting his tie to pass muster. Most truckies performed a walk-around before they resumed their journey.

When the grisly details emerged, regarding Constable O'Regan's demise, "Mad Dog" McCurry was frothing at the mouth.

"That bloody limp! He was wearing the copper's shoes."

His next call on the walkie-talkie alerted the sleepy sentry nearest to the milking shed. "Billy, I want you to break cover and check the package. Tell me if the money is still in the bag."

The reply hit him like an arrow to the heart, although the news was not unexpected.

"There's nothing but old rags in the bag. Does this mean we've been conned?"

The hard man with the sharp mind was not about to disclose his distress and discomfort over the radio, and instructed all his officers to stand down. There was one final exchange.

"Chief!"

"Yes, Billy?"

"None of us have had breakfast. Can we eat the biscuits?"

"Mad Dog" McCurry

CHAPTER 12

If it wasn't for the truck driver who found the girl in his rig, the whole episode may have passed without a media circus. However, news of the kidnapping appeared in the dailies and most people throughout the state became aware of the fugitive at large. Bing McKeon read the exclusive report over his morning coffee and admitted to himself that he had learned something new. He was familiar with his adversary's corporate achievements, and the publicity concerning the success of his bloodstock knew no bounds. However, Peter Pap as the father of a teenage daughter... that was a revelation.

He should have asked his son Joe, fast establishing a reputation as a skilled horse conditioner. His accomplishments in the show ring were also making people sit up and take notice, and even his mother was now onside. It was probably inevitable the youngster would meet Lydia, as they competed against each other frequently. Any dark-haired beauty with an agile body and a playful personality was likely to come under scrutiny from a lad whose hormones were in freefall.

On one occasion, she asked him to adjust the ribbon on one of her plaits. Many of the girls wore a ponytail but if you can project a point of difference, the judges are sometimes impressed. As it turned out, the plaited performer scored well in the dressage and won the point-to-point event. In recognition of Joe's contribution, she gave him a hug, willingly accepted and reciprocated as the foundation for further bodily contact at a later date. If they had known such a friendship was incubating, Peter Pap and Bing McKeon would have been outraged.

The former gentlemen, already mildly outraged, chose to engage in a heated discussion with his feisty daughter regarding the continuance of her education at her elite college in the country. The kidnapping had made him very nervous.

"Why can't you go to school in Ballarat, like most people who live in the area?"

"It was Mum's idea," replied the girl, adept in the art of attributable blame.

"Of course it was," conceded her father, disillusioned but not beaten. "But she didn't know about that crazy nun, did she? Is it true Mother Superior has bought herself a rifle?"

"It's a shotgun," replied little Miss Know-all, and it belongs to Sister Mary Joseph. The student loved winning a point over her dad, no matter how pedantic the victory.

Her frustrated father would never win the argument, so he made arrangements that gave him some measure of satisfaction. Sam would escort his daughter to pony club and watch over her until she returned to the convent. The minder would also improve his own security capability by purchasing a firearm.

Some weeks later, Lydia and Joe won prizes at the same gymkhana and they compared their awards near the unsaddling paddock. What else could they do but kiss? A long, lingering, intimate kiss that belied their inexperience and lack of technique. Sitting in his car, Tromans slowly placed his hand on the shotgun on his passenger seat. Could there be a wedding in the spring?

Although Sam's distant memories of first love may have blurred his thinking regarding the reality of this situation, he admitted to himself that he couldn't see Mother Superior as Matron of Honour at the nuptials, and the father of the bride would be even less pleased. With these thoughts in mind, he decided to investigate the credentials of this randy Romeo. The kid appeared personable enough, but one had to be particularly vigilant where virtue and virginity were concerned. So, the observer picked-up something he had never bothered to read before—the program of events. There on page three he saw the name of contestant number five, Joseph McKeon. His name also appeared on page six and eight... Joseph bloody McKeon.

Immediately, the muscles in Sam's chest tightened, making it difficult to breathe, and his anxiety levels rose alarmingly. He was sick in the stomach, sweating all over and delirious. He imagined a wedding scene with all the guests carrying weapons aimed at him.

These episodes often pass and the man in the car slowly reclaimed his sanity, although the gravity of the situation remained ever-present. What would he tell his boss? Did his watching brief include intrusive spying? Obviously, if the Lothario looked suspicious, he needed to be alert, but reporting bad news to his boss was fraught with danger. He correctly believed the directive to shoot the messenger had its origins in Greece. If women are looking for love, why can't they get themselves a pooch?

In the car on the way back to the convent, Sam tried some subtle interrogation. He didn't know whether the girl was aware of the feud between the two tycoons. Or if, in fact, she even knew of Bing McKeon.

"I noticed you getting a bit friendly with the opposition, today. Did you manage to obtain any intelligence that might help you defeat them next week?"

Lydia, aware that she was always under observation by her bodyguard, grinned profusely at the absurdity of his question. If he wanted information, why didn't he just come out and ask it directly?

"Joe and I are in love, which is nobody's business but ours, so I trust you will give me the option of telling my folks before you do. He's a lovely guy and I'm sure they will appreciate the fact that I am now a grown woman, and able to make my own decisions."

Oh yeah, thought her intrepid escort. *Let's hope he's not married. From childhood to adultery in one easy leap would be too much for Peter Pap to cope with.*

"It's not over 'till it's over."

Detective Inspector Angela Pride lived by parables, advertising slogans and motivational messages. The latter one, inscribed on a wooden block in gold lettering, sat snugly on the corner of her desk, next to her phone. The Chief Commissioner rarely called on the hotline but on this occasion he wanted to see her urgently.

"I don't have to tell you, we've been severely embarrassed by this kidnapping. Sure, we got the girl back, but we lost one of our own and the public derision will be unpalatable if we are taken down by an Irishman. It was a Paddywhacker who did this, right?

The policewoman smiled thinly and realised she would be obliged to consider her position if she couldn't get a result. The knives were already out for any female in the force who harboured elevated ambitions. She decided to project confidence and hope for the best.

"We think so, although it is strange that he would kill a fellow Paddy. Of course, Senior Constable O'Regan came from Ulster and they don't like the people down south."

"The bloody IRA!" shouted the man behind the desk. Lindsay Dove didn't lose his cool very often, but he knew of a cartel in town, mining for operating funds to send home to help bankroll their terror campaign. A number of recent bank robberies had been traced back to Irish insurgents. The minnow from the fourth floor didn't see it this way, but she was happy to humour her lord and master.

"My meeting with the young girl is tomorrow and I'm confident we can expand our knowledge base. I will keep you informed weekly, if that's alright with you, sir?"

"Make that daily, Inspector. Remember, we've got our eye on you and something positive for us means something positive for you. Capiche!"

The lady took her leave, wondering if the police chief watched too many mafia movies. Her one-on-one with Lydia Papadopoulos took place at the family home in Dowling Forest and although the lass presented as forthright and honest, Angie didn't learn much.

"I previously told your people about the highway nearby, where I heard the sound of traffic. He fed me baked beans, canned stew and meatloaf; just like the chef from the convent. Did you interview the nuns? I wouldn't put it past them."

Inspector Pride's education did not evolve out of a cloistered environment, so she found it difficult to believe the Sisters of Charity would stoop to kidnapping as a discipline measure. She tried to divert the conversation in the direction of the pony club.

"What about your equestrian friends? Did any of them dislike you or become jealous of your achievements? This is often a motive for revenge."

"I don't believe so," said the girl, trying to be as objective as possible. "Being younger than most of them, I competed in a different grade. The success I experienced washed over the whole club and that was good for everyone. We all hang our ribbons in the clubhouse."

"Talking of ribbons, one of your yellow hairpieces was found in the carpark. Do you know what he did with the one he removed from your plait?"

"Not really, unless there were old oak trees in the area."

Driving back to Melbourne, the thoughtful policewoman reviewed her conversation with the victim and perceived her to be bright and intelligent with an acerbic wit. She hadn't seemed to appreciate the extreme danger associated with her imprisonment. After all, the kidnapper had killed viciously and she was lucky to be alive.

The first break came with the discovery of the stolen car outside Seymour Station. The forensic boys moved in and so did the dog squad. Rupert the Rottweiler determined that the perp had caught a northbound train, and was rewarded with the remains of Ms. Pride's quarter-pounder from McDonald's.

With a million bucks in his Woolies bag, O'Gorman could have hired a helicopter, but he probably wanted to keep a low profile. Angela wondered whether he ditched the bag, the smart thing to do, but they were dealing with an Irishman, so anything was possible. Victoria Rail came to the party by releasing details of all tickets purchased for that particular train—four travellers departed from Platform 2 to Benalla, Wangaratta, Wodonga and Albury.

A few of the commuters on the train from the city were regulars and happy to be interviewed. One of them remembered a man with a green bag, who gave out biscuits to his fellow passengers. She thought he disembarked at Wangaratta.

Because of Anthony McCurry's personal relationship with the cop killer, he provided a description which reproduced brilliantly on the *Wanted* posters, pasted all over the targeted town with double bills at pubs and betting shops. The police set up a mobile information unit outside the library and Inspector Pride sat erect and businesslike behind a card table on the footpath, not knowing it would only be a matter of time before Pat O'Gorman emerged from the reading room on her lunch break. Being Friday, it would be salad and beetroot sandwiches, followed by a walk in the gardens.

Patricia strode confidently through the portals of the historic building and down the steps, heading for the park but only getting as far as the caravan. Her jaw dropped and so did her thermos flask. There is nothing worse than seeing a picture of your estranged husband before you have eaten. The alert detective observed the reaction and immediately leapt to her feet, providing the woman with a shoulder to lean on. She guided her carefully to the spare seat at the table.

"You obviously know this man. Is he a close friend?"

"He's my husband, replied the ashen-faced librarian. "What does it mean 'Helping police with their enquiries'? I'm not familiar with that expression."

The inspector, picking up on the girl's accent, understood and accepted her ignorance but didn't feel inclined to make it easy for her.

"It means that when we catch the murdering bastard, we're going to beat the shit out of him and send him to the gallows."

"He murdered someone? I can't believe it."

"And kidnapping; also a Federal offence. Your husband is a dangerous man. Are you expecting him home for dinner?"

It became obvious to Patricia that this probing interrogation lacked substance. They were unaware of the present circumstances regarding her marriage and his whereabouts. She said as much.

"We've been separated for some time and I can't understand why you are looking for him here. I believe he moved to Bright. Did you say kidnapping? Surely not the convent girl? I read about it in the papers."

"That's the one, Mrs. O'Gorman, and your hubby is the prime suspect. Should I regard you as a hostile witness or are you prepared to help us with our investigation?"

"What do you want to know?" asked the poor woman. The salad and beetroot sandwiches were opened and shared and Pat provided background to her relationship with the former owner of MOG Wines. When she returned home that evening, she poured herself a stiff whisky.

For Angela Pride, her day would not be over that soon. The lead came from the local plods late in the afternoon. A regular patron from a pub on the outskirts of the town remembered the guy whose face figured prominently on one of the widely distributed posters. He thought he leased old Wilson's shack on Drover's Way, but old Wilson was senile and probably couldn't provide any details. It took Angie fifteen minutes to get to her destination but, once there, she didn't stop. She didn't need to. The silly sod had tied the girl's yellow ribbon around an old oak tree near the front drive.

Half a mile further down the road (more of a track), an elevated rise presented itself behind a clump of trees, which provided concealment. The excited detective immediately called-in the elite team. They arrived by helicopter, under cover of darkness, and Commander McCurry spread his boys around the dwelling and waited...and waited.

Apart from eight beating hearts and the frustrating mating calls of the resident cicadas, not another sound could be heard from the vicinity of the property. With no lights showing from within, the obvious conclusion was that nobody was home. Then, right on the dot of 7 p.m., music started wafting through a half-open window—"The Anniversary Waltz." Tony McCurry immediately recognised the melody, and recalled playing the tune on the piano when the postman delivered his divorce papers.

It only required a quick finger snap from the chief for the forward scout to creep towards the shack and investigate the open window. You couldn't blame him for what he did next. No-one can resist a window only partially closed. You need to raise it a fraction, don't you?

The shotgun blast took the poor fellow out and that started World War III. The team unleashed a barrage of gunfire that George Patton would have been proud of. The frontline lads let loose with their AK 47 automatic weapons, some tossed tear gas grenades, and one fired-up philistine hit the bazooka button. The ramshackle cabin started disintegrating before their eyes, and one shocked observer felt she needed to say something.

"I hoped we might be able to take him alive. Do you think you could cease fire for a bit?"

For the first time, the moderate from Melbourne understood why they called McCurry "Mad Dog." His eyes had narrowed and he barked his orders aggressively.

"Stand down, everyone. Approach with caution. Cover all entrances."

Did they find the remains of Kilkenny's most embarrassing export? No, they did not. They found a booby trap shotgun tied to an old chair and pointed at the window. They also found a clock radio set for 7 p.m. Who was going to explain the damage to Mr. Wilson?

It is always poignant to look back at what might have been, and this was particularly relevant in Angela's case. Had she continued up the hill in her car, instead of stopping to order the hit, she would have come across Matthew O'Gorman sitting by the side of the road, looking back at his residence with binoculars. The appearance of a car on Drover's Way didn't seem to worry him, as he placed his glasses on the grass verge and diverted his attention to the piece of grilled whiting lying defiantly over his double serve of chips. He wanted to finish his dinner and read the latest news from the wrapping. When you're on the run, you don't often have time to catch up with all the breaking stories.

CHAPTER 13

The library in the homestead at Dowling Forest was old wood and musty nostalgia. Shelving dominated two walls of the room, being home to books of all description: historical novels; classic literature; romantic potboilers and boy's own adventures. Many of the volumes were leather-bound and well-worn, some of them first editions. Peter Pap had read none of them, as they came with the house. Nevertheless, he designated this to be his favourite room and the place where he held court, seated behind his grand mahogany Chippendale desk. At various stages, the wife, daughter, foreman and house staff appeared before the fearsome presence, to be coerced, cautioned, congratulated or condemned.

The conversation with Lydia in relation to her future was deemed to be an open discussion with opinions from both parties to be considered and evaluated. Should the truth be known, Peter's attitude regarding the girl's destiny had not changed since the day of her birth. As his only legitimate heir, he still saw her as the future chair of his business empire. However, to get her to see it his way, he would have to recommend a different path, because this lady would always do the opposite of what her parents wanted. Her father pretended not to be offended by this attitude, a common trend among the rebellious youth of that era.

"Now that you're done with Lacryma Christ, it's time to think about a university degree. I know your mother would love to see you in medicine, but I think you should make up your own mind. There are many noble professions, such as teaching, the law and animal science. I'm sure Geoffrey would be thrilled for you if you went down that path."

The animal in question, grazing contentedly in a paddock near the open window of the library, might well have been summoned to confirm his stance, if his protector had given him that chance. Her quick and definitive response shut off all avenues of debate.

"I don't intend to go to uni, Dad. I want to win gold at the Olympic Games."

You can always rely on the younger generation to surprise you and Mr. P's reaction came out all splutter and stutter.

"B...b...but, but you can't swim. How can you collect a gold medal?"

Until they introduced thoroughbred racing as an Olympic sport, this man's interest in international sporting competitions would be minimal. Like many people, he assumed Australia only won swimming trophies. It would be left to Lydia to educate him.

"We boast a proud record in equestrian disciplines, and I can name our medal winners if you would like. This is my goal, but, unfortunately, it can be an expensive exercise and I will have to find another mount. Geoffrey is getting too old and, quite frankly, I don't believe he would like Los Angeles."

Although still bewildered by the brazen preposterousness of this proposal, the shrewd businessman saw an opportunity for negotiation. He lit-up a cigarette, looked his daughter in the eye, and then strolled over to one of the bookshelves, where he selected a hardback at random. He opened it but read nothing. Slamming it shut, he proceeded to roll-out his proposal.

"I'll tell you what I'll do. If you take on a paying job at one of my vineyards, and commit to a part time business management course in Ballarat, I'll sponsor your equestrian activities and even let you have one of my retired thoroughbreds to groom for LA."

"Really, Pa? That's fantastic. Are we talking about Zorba the Geek?"

The girl's father couldn't help but be impressed by her impudence. This kid pushed the parameters and that pleased him.

"You should be so lucky. Get the hell out of here. I think you mother needs some assistance with her shopping."

The possibility of Lydia making the LA Olympic team seemed remote, but the renewal in Seoul might not be a bridge too far. A lot would depend on the horsepower her father would gift her. Joe McKeon would be in her corner but unlikely to join her on either team, as his other duties limited his availability on the eventing circuit. Bing had increased the size of his stable, and burdened his son with the job of conditioning the horses at Aberdeen.

Does abstention make one hornier? It sure does. The now independent young lady looked for her guy at week-end events and sometimes Joseph would turn-up, all primed and passionate. They often slipped away to one of the local motels to endorse their affection for each other, thus taking the relationship to a whole new level.

The convent cutie had never bothered to probe into Joe's home life details, although she knew he looked after his father's stock, and spent time at one of his wineries. The lad knew everything about the child-beater, due to the fact that he had lived through the whole episode. With the completion of Lydia's schooling, Sam Tromans was relieved of his responsibility and didn't disclose the intimate knowledge he possessed. This was a guy who continually lived on the edge.

Lydia Iris Zoe Papadopoulos also failed to inform her father that, as a grown woman, she was entitled to have an affair with the knave of hearts from northern parts. The lady possibly harboured concerns relating to her father's blood pressure. Little did she know that an introduction to the McKeon son and heir would probably kill him. To be brutally honest, if the darling daughter learned of those antics at Mt. Beauty, everybody's world would come crashing down. Joe didn't want to deceive his parents, but this feud impacted on his relationship. He would eventually 'fess up to his beloved, with certain details held back. Being co-conspirators gave them a degree of collusion that was exciting, but it was also tiring having to avoid the old folks all the time.

There came a period when the committed couple didn't see each other for quite a while. While Joseph was representing his father at regional and provincial racetracks, his sweetheart was coming to terms with her new steed, the recently retired Colossus of Rhodes. This supposed superstar performed ingloriously in his eight starts and proved to be a total failure, which devastated the owner. His mood didn't improve when he learned his daughter had renamed him Souvlaki.

It takes time to nurture a partnership that works but, once you get it right, there is no end to where it might take you: e.g. Laurel & Hardy;

Abbott & Costello; Batman & Robin; salt & pepper. Souvlaki coped with the transition from racetrack to show ring quite well. The obstacles gave him no problems, having seen them before. Most trainers put their charges over the jumps when they want to get their mind back on the job. Lydia didn't rush her new pal and he responded by adapting to the challenge in his own time. Well-conformed animals impressed the judges, and both horse and rider were expected to be well groomed. This colt ticked all the boxes.

The busy equestrienne also commenced her business course, registering as Liz Pap. The teacher might get vocal cramp if he had to cope with the length of her extended surname. Then there was her day job. PP presented the lass with a compact car for her nineteenth birthday, which she drove to the Great Western Winery four days a week. The father/daughter pact was working a treat.

With all that going on, daddy was surprised but delighted when she offered to represent his interests at the forthcoming race meeting at Benalla. His colt came up second favourite in race three, but his daughter was more interested in a starter in the last event. Owner's representative, J. McKeon, would be in attendance, and would arrive early to greet the hornbag.

After preconditioning, the Aberdeen horses transferred to the stables of legendry trainer Marcellus Thomas at Seymour, who would bring them to peak fitness and map out their programs. On arrival at Benalla, the fellow slipped into the Members Dining Room for a sandwich, only to find the owner's representative holding hands under the table with his girl. He pretended not to notice them in case it was a covert assignation. Joe didn't see his trainer because he was intent on giving the girl the benefit of his punting experience.

"Gee, honey, if your father thinks your horse will win you should have something on it. Do you want me to place a small wager for you?"

The girl gave him twenty dollars, before proceeding to the mounting yard, where she would listen to Norm Jones briefing the jockey. The kid looked all of sixteen but sounded as cocky as a one-eyed parrot.

"Don't worry, Mr. Jones. I'll ride her one out and one back and then run away from them when it matters. I reckon this one is better than the others."

The hoop wasn't the only one brimming with confidence. Joseph was just about to proffer his redback to the bookmaker when a bloke stepped in front of him and bet five thousand large on Thunderball. Completely flabbergasted, Joe momentarily lost concentration, and also a good price, as the odds tumbled. What he didn't fail to notice was the chap's Irish accent.

Because of the nature of his current situation, Matthew O'Gorman had changed his appearance and his new disguise was one for the ages: a bushy moustache and blond hair. Unfortunately, the hair on his lip and head didn't match. Peroxide is such a gamble, isn't it?

Congratulate the man on the run him for not going on a spending spree with his ill-gotten gains. The kidnapper asked for unmarked bills, but who relies on the fuzz to be straight? Money laundering was the way to go and the racetrack is where this takes place. In this instance, there were a few dirty jocks in the laundry. They conspired to keep Thunderball three wide for the journey, and he went down by a short half-head. It was the bookies who acquired Peter Pap's ransom money.

His daughter's purse was also considerably lighter.

"You did your dough, kiddo. Sorry about that. I saw some looney put five grand on the bloody thing. He must have been hot to trot."

Lydia grinned, because she guessed the money might have been put on by a commission agent working for her father. The Irishman, prior to his investment, saw the girl from a distance and considered the spirited female to be his lucky charm. In this instance, luck was not a fortune.

Come into money and there is always the joy of sharing it with your nearest and dearest. The good woman may get a fur coat, and wouldn't your best friend love a Harley-Davidson conveyance? It was sad that Matt O'Gorman didn't have any friends, so his generosity could not be tested. He was happy enough to keep it all for himself and frequently played with the bank notes, now stored in a less obvious carry-all. The bored fugitive needed a daily regime to while away the hours in the isolated boarding house he had discovered in the shadow of the Strathbogie Ranges. He rarely ventured outside but occasionally took a walk in the moonlight.

The man was intent on keeping a low profile until he could make a dash for the border.

In all the scheming that preceded the snatch, the Irishman had not hatched an escape plan, because he felt confident he would not be exposed. He hoped to continue living in old Wilson's place until the heat died down, and then move interstate, where he could spend his money. He now found himself on top of the wanted list, with a picture provided by his dear wife. Neither was he impressed with other personal matters she leaked to the press. The fact that he farted in bed was too much information.

With the onset of the Autumn Carnival, the money-laundering punter was tempted to attend some of the key meetings, but, on reflection, he accepted that the danger of identification would be greater at these venues. His increased dependence on the ponies was probably born from necessity, but general boredom may have contributed to his zealous participation. He studied the form every day and took particular notice of the starters owned by Peter Papadopoulos. He also noted the McKeon entries and conjured up ways in which he could nobble them.

One of these occasions presented itself at a minor meeting at Kilmore. Marcellus Thomas produced an improving stayer over a sprinting trip, as a conditioning run. Nobody anticipated a winning performance from the colt, but the former firebug decided to interfere with the 15/1 outsider anyway. When the strapper left the stall for a toilet stop, the Irishman suddenly appeared, clutching a handful of chopped carrot, mixed with a strong laxative. Horses don't care who delivers their supper, so the mixture went down a treat.

The beast produced three smelly dumps on the way to the barrier and, when the gates crashed open, was considerably lighter and keen to run. He duly saluted by two lengths and totally confused the punters and the doper.

There were few things this son of Erin could do right, but still the Victoria Police could not capture him. It had been a number of weeks since the trail went cold and Inspector Angela might not be the pride of the force for much longer. Those daily updates with the commissioner didn't go well because she was clueless, and he was on Valium.

"For Christ's sake; are you telling me you have nothing? This is the fifth day in a row you've come up with zilch and I'm being besieged by the media and the minister. They think we're the Keystone Cops."

"Yes, Chief, but the fact is he's laying low and not spending any of the marked bills we stashed in the bag. We know his passport specs, so I can't see how he can leave the country. What we need is patience. Would you like me to speak to the media?"

The man behind the desk glared at his subordinate, who was possibly being mischievous and, certainly, sarcastic.

"No, I would not, acting Inspector Pride," said the furious overlord, stressing the word "acting." "For now, continue with whatever leads you have, but if we don't see any progress by next week, there will be a new broom in the closet."

While waiting for the elevator to whisk her down to her own level, the chastised copper couldn't help but think about her boss's parting words. She was about to break bread with a probationary sergeant from her division, having major closet problems himself. Being gay, his prospect of promotion in this homophobic organisation was slim but things might be better for him at a regional station, where serious crime officers were in short supply.

"Rom, I want to transfer you to Wangaratta," said the forthright detective, immediately hitting him with her knockout punch. He didn't seem fazed and simply asked for an explanation of this out-of-the-blue declaration.

"For a start, it will get you away from this toxic situation at Russell Street. It's bad enough being a woman in uniform but you are really pushing the parameters. Secondly, I need a man on the spot. The prime suspect's wife has been denigrating him in the media, so he might come after her, which would give us a chance to catch the bastard. Would you like another glass of Chardonnay?"

Section heads rarely invited their juniors to a slap-up lunch, and Rom Remus appreciated the ambiance of the elegant restaurant. Most of those in the squad room were beer drinkers who downed their pots at the sleaziest pubs. Officially, the young man could not be classified as a shirt-lifter but this didn't stop him getting a hard time from those around him. Homosexuality had only recently been decriminalised but reform would be a long time coming for the police in this state. Wangaratta might not be such a bad move. The place was well-served with entertainment options and restaurants and his partner, a waiter, would find employment easily.

"Another glass would be fine. Will I get a pay rise with this transfer? Wang is some distance from town and certain readjustments would need to be made."

Angie laughed at his boldness. She also anticipated the response from the chief financial officer and put him out of his misery quickly.

"Good try, Sergeant. Accommodation and cost of living are far cheaper in the sticks, so you would need to get promoted to get a raise in salary. Of course, that is always a possibility if you do well."

What he said next surprised her.

"I was actually thinking of resigning and moving to Canada. This change might be an alternative. Can I let you know tomorrow after I talk things over with Marty?"

Angela had never met Marty, his partner. Evidently he made a very good chicken cacciatore.

CHAPTER 14

New Year's Eve is not only a time to remember old acquaintances but a night of hope and anticipation. In early 1982, Australia, decimated by drought, and on the back of an energy boom that went bust, cried out for innovative salvation. The dinosaurs of historical precedence were replaced by brash young entrepreneurs, who trashed the technology and traditions of the past and forged new empires.

Bing McKeon and Peter Papadopoulos were not of this ilk. They had made their mark through good fortune and ruthless tenacity. If they looked back at the old year and considered their achievements, they may have concentrated on the progression of their feud. As far as they were concerned, this was the only game in town and they just had to come out on top. Like surly children, they were determined to win at all costs.

This particular year commenced like most of the others—a cricket test started in Sydney and a yacht race finished in Hobart. The first wine show in Adelaide saw a win by Bing's Clementine Creek Reserve Malbec, and Mr. Pap won in Canberra with a Rine River Riesling. Rine River, the moat around his Great Western fermenting shed (door sales on weekends), had been named by the Poppledofs. Only the most ardent observer would have noticed an entry from MOG Wines had snared the major prize in the category of "Best Blend under $5."

On the racetrack, the McKeon stable improved its record in leaps and bounds and all credit to Marcellus Thomas, the wily trainer who knew exactly where and when to place his team, be they stars or progressive horses. Although the feuding fathers often attended the same meetings, they had yet to exchange pleasantries and it is doubtful they ever would.

The Scot, still smarting over his colt's defeat in the Derby, was keen to turn the tables in one of the classic races, perhaps later in the year.

Meanwhile, Zorba the Geek continued on his winning way, running away from them on his reappearance, and bookmakers marked the star performer down as the favourite for the Australian Cup, held in March. Questions still remained regarding the sprinter's staying credentials. Surely the colt couldn't run a journey with such a pedigree, although history teaches us that champions often outperform their breeding expectations. Norm Jones also nominated the gritty Foregone Conclusion. It was a measure of the owner's confidence that he now regarded his horseflesh as unbeatable.

One often needs a big carrot to entice country people to travel and the Royal Melbourne Show was and still is one such enticement. Folks come to town with their animals and their ambition, plus their home-grown produce; everything from pickles to pork pies. The racing carnivals were another magnet for the regionals, as quite a few of the participants came from way down yonder. The social program supporting the equine activities taxed many of the men, but their partners harboured no such inhibitions. Henrietta Papadopoulos led the way with planned functions diarised for most of the week. Much to the chagrin of husband Peter, their townhouse would always be available should any cause for unplanned celebrations arise.

The big autumn social event is always the Moomba Ball, held at the Exhibition Building, one of the world's few remaining heritage-listed pavilions. Boasting a spectacular domed roof, this 1879-built structure hosted the opening of the first Commonwealth Parliament in 1901, and there would be many pollies in attendance for this jolly celebration. Moomba, an aboriginal word meaning *let's get together and have fun*, draws big crowds, who are happy to explore all the entertainment options. The lord mayor sponsors a march through the city streets, with a king and queen atop the royal float. For the first ten years, the queen was actually female.

Peter Pap would be at the ball under sufferance, because of considerable pressure from wife and daughter, but the nomad from the north proffered an apology. Helen, by preferring to stay home, provided an excuse he sorely wanted. Observers might have been underwhelmed by Joe's urging.

"Come on, Dad. Why not come? There will be other old farts at the function and I'm sure you'll find something to talk about. The Exhibition Building is only ten minutes from our digs."

The urger was being duplicitous, secretly hoping his stubborn father would travel the anticipated path and beg-off the ballroom boogie. As far as Joseph was concerned, Cinderella would be at the ball, and avoiding one father would be difficult enough. Lydia, now aware of the feud, agreed that a continuation of their relationship in a clandestine manner might be the best way to go.

"No, son. Away and enjoy yourself. I'll be studying the form for tomorrow, but available to celebrate should one of our neddies win."

McKeon would not field a starter in the prestigious event, but the form lines were clear. Zorba, having recently failed miserably over a trip, was scratched, leaving Foregone Conclusion to represent the greedy Greek. Lawman, owned by Chief Commissioner Lindsay Dove, seemed the obvious favourite, but illegal SP bookmakers across the state would bet against that one.

When Joseph entered the Great Hall, his jaw almost hit the floor. How would he ever find his true love in such a crowd? There were thousands of people dancing, drinking, talking and singing along with the band. The noise level was beyond belief. Refreshment bars had been erected against the side walls, and supplemented with contemporary seating areas. Bold hussies brazenly sat on knees, and already a whiff of naughtiness permeated the air.

The young man couldn't recall seeing so many beautiful women in the same room before, and didn't mind taking time to track down his girl. He finally found her, back to the wall and almost surrounded by red-neck pubescents, drowning in their ill-fitting formal attire. Lydia's shimmering jet black tresses and willowy figure would mesmerise anyone, and the revealing sheath dress she was wearing could possibly have precipitated a medical emergency for those with heart monitors. Joe could only focus on the semi-circle of admirers, none of whom made any effort to suppress their drooling.

"Hello, sweetheart. Who are your friends? The Hellenic Hockey Team?"

The new arrival was being disingenuous. There are eleven players in a hockey team and this group only numbered eight, but she knew all of their names. The offer of an introduction to her father proved enough to disburse the youngsters. In fact, a couple of the lads literally bolted at the mention of his name.

Joseph could see PP in the distance, involved in a deep discussion with a person whose physical dimensions implied that he was probably a favourite brewery client. Young McKeon took Lydia by the elbow and steered her in the opposite direction. After a ten-minute wait, drinks were obtained, as were seats, and the youngsters sat demurely, sipping carefully on their Alabama Slammers. The conversation would revolve around their continued subterfuge at the track on the morrow. Lydia the loquacious had ideas.

"Pa never goes out back to the stable area. If I can avoid Norm Jones, we might be able to catch-up there. We can easily mingle with the other observers."

"My God, how come my lady knows so much about racing, all of a sudden? Will you be wearing a big hat?"

"Of course! Why? Do you think I've got a big head?"

"Not really, but something less obvious would be good."

"Oh," responded the rather crestfallen fashionista. Lydia's questionable sense of style had come from her mother, but her sly planning was borne as a result of forever trying to outwit the nuns in the convent.

This whole furtive exercise might have seemed inconsequential in the extreme but important for those mired in duplicity. By the same token, Joe understood the depth of feeling between the two adversaries and their decision to maintain secrecy was sound. If peace were to break out between the two hard-heads, the wives would be the ones to promote same. In the meantime, the lady with the latest information encouraged Joe to bet on Foregone Conclusion before the odds plummeted. "It's all over bar the shouting," she said.

Her ladyship wore an elegant green felt chapeau of modest dimension, and the lovers met as planned, near the stall of one of the fancied runners. Lawman, to be ridden in the big race by premier jock Roy Higgins, eyed-off the girl and her companion, but there was little time for the lady to channel her most malicious thoughts.

The race proved to be a competitive contest, but, when the field turned for home, Higgins was caught napping and beaten three-quarters of a length by an honest performer called Kip. Foregone Conclusion finished with the also-rans.

The atmosphere within the confines of the black Daimler DS420 limousine, returning to Dowling Forest, was anything but cheerful and even the darling daughter couldn't lift spirits. Her father had been fined five hundred dollars for abusing a jockey in the unsaddling enclosure, and mummy embarrassed herself when confronted by a fellow socialite, wearing an identical outfit. Could you believe it?

"We didn't win, but we didn't lose," chirped the pacifier, paraphrasing a local politician, trying to explain his election loss. "Sack the jock, and mum will know better next time. Never wear *prêt-à-porter* in the Members."

"I feel so small," gushed the disillusioned dilettante, now being lectured in fashion by her daughter. Perhaps her hen-pecked husband might provide aid with soothing words and understanding compassion? No such luck. PP put the day behind him and lived for the next challenge, whenever that might be. These weeks of wonder appear on the calendar only rarely, and soon it would be back to the grindstone for all concerned.

The potential business manager and show-jumper extraordinaire had seen her indentures transferred to a local club. New friendships were established and even Souvlaki befriended new pals, adapting well to this different regime, which included less whipping and more grooming. Who doesn't like to be pampered 24/7?

Great Western conjures up images of cowboys with carbines, tombstones and tumbleweed, gamblers and good-time girls—also, a gunfight at a half-decent corral. This town in North-West Victoria is none of that. Most people don't bother to stop unless they have grapes on their mind, but will gaze in awe as they travel by many hectares of land under vine. Lydia enjoyed working for new manager Klaus Heiglespitter, a former employee of the Poppledofs, who embraced his new protégé with enthusiasm. Quite frankly, he embraced everybody after an afternoon tippling in the tasting room.

Commuting to and from the vineyard was time-consuming for this busy lass and sometimes she went straight from the winery to business college, ready to impress with determined concentration and diligence.

Her understanding of commercial theory surprised many, and she received plaudits for her essay on corporate takeovers in a modern era—a commendation that particularly pleased daddy. Not so pleased was the occupant of the desk near the door in the back row. A perennial late arrival, Jack Glover would sneak into the room and claim the back-row seat, which annoyed the lecturer no end. The confident fellow firmly believed he should have won the composition prize, not that one would criticise the winner, the very beautiful Liz Pap.

One day he decided there was no point admiring her from afar and made the momentous decision to arrive early. Prior to the lecture on horizontal mergers, he laid claim to the seat behind the stunning student. The aroma of her fragrant perfume washed by him like a tsunami of seductive sirens. Would this be his Ulysses moment?

If the attractive student had turned around, she would have discovered an extremely handsome guy breathing heavily near her neck. He was good-looking alright, and well-dressed—quite a fashion plate. In Mr. Glover's world, one never wore a jacket without a pocket handkerchief. Shoes should be handmade and shirts monogrammed (with the 007 brand in his case). The bulge in his pants was the latest digital calculator, calibrated to perfection and ready for any mathematical problem that might arise. He always carried a comb because of recalcitrant hair-strands needing constant repositioning. That unpredictable part down the side of his head was as straight as a ruler in Rwanda. Styled licks need to be kept in place with a generous application of Brylcreem, and he must have been a shareholder. There was no argument. The fellow was a cool dude.

The man also displayed a playful personality. During a lecture, he attached a number of spring-back paper clips to Liz's locks. She found them when trying to wash her hair. A week later, the prankster lowered a glow-worm onto her scalp, which generated giggles from the rest of the class. When the minute monster crawled around to the top of her eye, she screamed and the creepy crawly fell to the floor. He attacked it with his shoe in the same manner in which he had seen James Bond dispose of a Tarantula.

The next night, he and she dined at Chez Bertie, at her expense.

"Thank you for saving me from the beast."

One could only guess what her other young man might have thought of this gesture and, in fact, the whole episode. After all, if there were to be any *knight in shining armour* moments, Joe should be the one arriving on the white charger. At that time, the young man was attending a meeting of the CFA volunteers in Mt. Beauty, with no seductive sirens in attendance. Just a determined bunch of men! No longer would anyone take fire prevention for granted.

"We offer a very good house wine that would complement your scallops, sir," said the supercilious servant of subservience, who had tagged the young man as a fraud. *They spend all their money on their appearance and then struggle through to the next payday.* Although the waiter recognised Lydia (her father owned the place), he presumed the lad would be paying. She snapped him out of his presumptuous train of thought.

"For God sakes, man. We're not real estate agents. Get us one of my father's wines—a late-picked Spätlese would be good."

As the hired help obligingly disappeared into a black hole at the rear of the restaurant, Jack Glover stared across the table and marvelled at the assertiveness of his new friend. This may not be the easy conquest first envisaged.

The young woman smiled, melted his heart, and continued the conversation.

"Don't mind Antoine. He's so far up himself he doesn't know who he is anymore. Real name Tony Lopez from Yarraville. He acquired his skills at a catering firm servicing Pentridge Prison."

"How do you know all this?" demanded the fascinated listener. They had covered the first half of her life and heritage over pre-dinner drinks, and a reappraisal of his usual misogynistic opinions was on the cards.

"Most comes from the supper table at home. My dad has so many contacts, and horrible Henrietta, that's my mum, is a society gossip. I hear everything."

The attentive dinner guest disposed of his first glass of vino quite quickly, due to the fact that his table companion was doing all the talking. The gun-shy Antoine had deserted them, so he poured a refill, which gave the gal the opportunity to reverse the polite interrogation.

"You have told me little about yourself. I know you report to a German boss, which is a coincidence, because so do I. He loves grapes, but he also gropes the girls. We're always vigilant."

"Ha, ha, ha!" laughed Jack, another potential groper. "My guvnor is not that way inclined. Too serious and a workaholic. They sent him out from Munich to lift car sales and that's a difficult task in these times."

"You're a car dealer?"

"Yep, the BMW franchise downtown, and we call them luxury vehicles. I can see you in a sweet little three series, and I can offer you a good deal."

Get out of here, she thought. *I'm paying for dinner and he's trying to flog me a new car.* There was some degree of respect for his efforts but not much.

"I'm alright, Jack. Perfectly happy with my little princess. She's not a gas guzzler, and understands all my little foibles."

"You do know," went on the overbearing salesman, "that BMC no longer produce the Princess series and resale value will plummet. As for spare parts!"

"Can we talk about something else?" said Lydia, now getting rather bored with the direction in which the conversation was heading.

So, they discussed other things and other people and the hours passed rapidly. The bill went on the family account, and the odd couple prepared to part in the carpark, where the showroom scoundrel got to inspect the Austin Princess.

"This is very you—Aegean Blue duco, white leather upholstery. And what about that Nana Mouskouri doll on the dashboard? However, if you would like a ride in a real car, think about chow next Saturday on me."

You have to love a guy with confidence. Well, actually, you don't, and this flower of Athens was not yet ready for plucking, if that is the right expression. She unlocked the car door, saw him trying to intrude into her space, and decided to discourage further advances.

"Let's settle for coffee after next week's lesson. I'll need to reflect on this evening and consider my options."

She gave him a quick peck on the cheek, slipped behind the wheel and drove off. The Nana doll had a shocked expression on her face—possibly a production flaw.

Jack in the box seat, thought the would-be seducer, in no way deterred by her rejection. Women often played hard-to-get, and he figured after coffee would produce the same result as after dinner, and be cheaper. He whistled a happy tune as he walked to his luxury vehicle, overwhelmed with lewd thoughts.

Over the next few days, Lydia reflected on her date with the bulldog from the Bavarian Motor Works and psychoanalysed herself with some trepidation. Was her acceptance of his invitation borne out of boredom or desire? Did she violate the special trust between committed lovers of the separated kind, and what would their respective horses think of such a betrayal? With the forthcoming coffee rendezvous coming up, Lydia Iris Papadopoulos pondered over the possible outcome. She understood these types of men had one thing on their mind. A careful girl would need to nominate a well-lit café for their late-night dalliance and, certainly, wear two pairs of knickers.

When Joseph McKeon attended CFA meetings, his mother always kept his supper warm in the oven. One never knew how long these talkfests lasted. The business of the day didn't always take that long, but with other matters to discuss, such as town gossip and recent scandals, an early night is a rarity. The fire chief insisted that there should always be an adequate amount of cold liquid in the station, so a slab of beer resided in the refrigerator at all times.

Joseph's mother always anticipated his drinking opportunities, and shepherd's pie was the ultimate soak. She hoped to sober him up before young Edwin started asking pertinent questions that might lead him down the path of experimentation. On this occasion, the silent person in the room was the Scottish laird. Puffing on his pipe, a habit inherited from Ron Stokes, he flipped through some horse-breeding manuals, not expecting the first son to be in a talkative mood.

"What's going on, Dad? You have been extremely quiet since that call from the city. Bad news?"

"Not at all. Just Andrew's report on Gurner's Lane. He wants to set him for the big one."

"Bloody hell!" gasped the surprised youth. "You mean the Melbourne Cup?"

"Aye, I do. We've got the St. Leger coming up at Flemington and, if he can put in a bonnie run there, ye cannae go past the first Tuesday in November as a target race. Ye had better get yourself a top hat for the Committee Room."

Bing became involved with this animal because of his gregarious nature. He had befriended a small band of William Street professionals, who frequented the club where he stayed on his city trips. They had been sweet-talked into the purchase by rough and ready trainer Geoff Murphy, who bought the yearling in New Zealand. Andrew, the syndicate manager, couldn't speak highly enough of Murphy's ability, which was corroborated by the man, himself.

Owners sometimes employ multiple trainers for their steeds and Peter Papadopoulos had gone down that path, his Derby winner having been prepared by a legend of the turf in Sydney. Most of his other horses were conditioned by Norm Jones. It was not unusual for Norm to be confused with singer Tom Jones, so Peter Pap provided some of the foals with musical names like Thunderball. Sadly, this colt was a rig (possessed a particular birth defect) and was gelded before his time. It happens occasionally.

At Aberdeen, it was unusual to see the wrinklies last to bed but, on this occasion, Bing and Helen sat alone in front of the fireplace, sipping hot chocolate. The man of the manor enjoyed the occasional bush sounds that seeped through the half-open window and the silence in the room relaxed him. On the other hand, his wife, a student of observation, craved conversation and possessed the generosity to share her opinions around.

"Top hats and committee rooms! My, my, how the wheel has turned."

"What are ye going on aboot, woman? Dae ye no understand the concept of traditional Spring Carnival dress requirements?"

"Yes I do, darling, but I also recall the rage of your youth. Don't you remember Lord Rugby, Earl Grey and that dissolute aristocracy? You've become one of them."

"Bollocks," was the response from the resolute racegoer, who would claim the traditions of many years circumvented all attempts to classify the human participants. "There is nae any class distinction. We just love oor sport."

"I see," said the woman whose opinions regularly differed from those of her husband. "And the Members Bar? You won't let us in. What kind of disparity is that?"

In heading in this direction, the crafty woman had subtly changed the focus of her argument to that of female emancipation, a hot topic right across the nation. The big man produced an answer totally endorsed by the *Male Chauvinist Pig Association.*

"It has naught tae do with gender. The lasses are allowed in if they're members. It just happens there are very few lady members."

The journey to their bedroom would become long and laborious for the now irritable aristocrat, and he yearned for the instant cloak of darkness that would obliterate the memories of recent conversations. He envied his son and his youthful snoring, which wafted out through his open bedroom door. The lad had only managed to remove one shoe before collapsing on the feather doona. The joys of alcohol as a sleeping draught!

We just love our sport.

Some distance away in Ballarat, the days also became long and laborious as the goddess of Athena contemplated her forthcoming coffee stop with Jack. She nominated the Duck Inn, another one of her father's franchise restaurants, as their meeting place, and he started rabbiting-on, even before the door closed. Their tutor, who had discharged them ten minutes late, was copping a serve.

"Why does that nutty professor always quote Bill Gates whenever anyone needs motivating? Did you need motivation to come here tonight, sugar lips?"

"Well, er, ahhhh," stuttered his shell-shocked companion, with no opportunity of reply.

"Of course you didn't, did you? You're here because I'm the man; charming, stimulating, terribly handsome and extremely sexy. Isn't that right?"

Having regained her composure, Lydia put on her best Liz face and proceeded to bring him down a peg. She had to admit that Jack's self-assurance was one of the reasons she found him to be mildly irresistible, but his ego did spiral out of control on occasions.

"Have you been taking personality pills since last week? You're on something for sure."

The waitress interrupted their exchange and Lydia greeted her with a benign smile.

"I'll have a short black and a glass of port, thank you Dorothy."

Mr. Glover grunted his order, waited for the girl to leave, and then continued his outburst.

"You know the hired help. What is this; a shakedown? I thought we came here because you liked water birds."

Lydia gave him her most dismissive reaction as she unfurled her napkin, which was strange, because she hadn't ordered anything to eat.

"My father owns the place, and it is one of the few cafes open late. I also want someone to pick you out in a line-up if I'm never seen again, so I hope your intentions are honourable."

In the spirit of honesty, the car salesmen admitted that his intentions were anything but honourable, and enquired if he could have it away with her as soon as possible. She said no but allowed him to buy her an iced doughnut to go. This kind of encouragement kept one in the game. As she drove off, he wondered how many restaurants her father owned.

CHAPTER 15

Martin McGrath always produced good references, but the manager of the Duck Inn, Wangaratta (branches also at Ballarat, Bendigo and Barnawartha) made it difficult for him.

"I know you've been employed at Fanny's for two years, but this is a middle-range bistro that caters for simple folk who like comfort food. You'd do better at our upmarket sister restaurant Chez Bertie (branches also at Ballarat, Brighton and Baxter) in Main Street."

"I've been there," replied the out-of-sorts waiter, still coming to terms with the recent upheaval of his living arrangements. His favourite man, Sergeant Rom Remus of the Victoria Police, continued to wax lyrical about the delights of rural life, but, so far, he had seen little to get excited about, and now this trumped-up toe-rag kept telling him he was overqualified to wait on tables.

"They're not hiring at the moment but, as you are part of the same organisation, surely I could be transferred if a vacancy arose?" The vitriol that dripped from this last sentence remained unnoticed by the smarmy manager, whose own honey-infused words belied the fact that he was a five-star jerk.

"Yes, that is a possibility I suppose. You do realise that tipping is a rarity at our modest venue, and wages are paid at casual rates. You would never become a millionaire working here."

Given the available vacancy, some might be confused by this negative approach by the hirer. Nevertheless, he appointed the applicant and asked him to report for work on the following evening. At their rented apartment, that night, Marty poured scorn on his partner's posting and feigned suicide with Rom's gun. The policeman tried to downgrade his grievance with the promise of an unsavoury alternative.

"It's either this or Canada. Did you know the Mounties eat maple syrup with their cereal?"

Rom's own first day on the new job appeared less stressful. The fact that he was gay had been transmitted via unofficial channels and accepted without too much concern. They needed the manpower and a recruit arriving from Russell Street didn't happen every day. The capture of Victoria's most wanted was a priority for the station and the word was out that this very person might be in the vicinity. Rom Remus would be the go-to man if a confrontation should take place.

Pat Malone stood out as a person her husband might pursue for refuge or revenge, but resources were not available to give her twenty-four-hour protection. An elderly gentleman from the RSL's security division was stationed in the foyer of the library to deter the murderous madman, should he choose to strike during working hours. These old soldiers, deployed at the turnstiles of many community events, were not even armed. At least someone provided Patricia with a can of mace pepper spray (her library associate).

Matthew O'Gorman's malicious thoughts concerning his ex-wife certainly evoked the possibility of physical payback, and these were the issues he contemplated as he sat alone at his chrome smoked glass kitchen table. Although they were still officially married, he knew she had shed his surname and this didn't sit well with him. The lady's comments in the media also disappointed him and, to his mind, sullied his reputation. He didn't appreciate the fact that kidnappers and killers don't have much of a reputation to protect.

Returning to Wangaratta, where people might recognise him, would be risky but this man danced with danger. South Australia, his desired destination, gave-off casual vibes and rumours persisted that law enforcement officers in that state were as sharp as marble.

He would need to alter his image (that bushy moustache would have to go) and spend some of that kidnap money on elegant clothes. An upmarket motor also seemed appropriate, perhaps purchased in an out-of-the-way town, and Flemington on St. Leger Stakes day cried out as one last chance to launder his money. Having considered all this, there wasn't much else to resolve, apart from his desire to liquidate his wife before he left for greener pastures.

A St. Leger win would be a big deal for Bing McKeon. He had made his mark and many people knew who he was, but he didn't have the same public image as Peter Pap and his super stable of stars. Being the owner of a Derby winner also gave PP a lot of respect, which he craved. The upcoming contest only ranked as a Group 2 classification, but rated as one of the few staying races to count as a guide to the Melbourne Cup. Another one, the Caulfield Cup, held later in the year, would determine the public elect.

Bing received an offer from Andrew and the other syndicate members to come to town a few days in advance for some pre-race carousing at the Australian Club but, because of his wife's recent scolding, he begged-off the gathering of silver spoons. Instead he took Helen to dinner in Bright.

Not far away in Wangaratta, Matthew O'Gorman meditated over his dessert at the Duck Inn, prior to launching his felonious attack on the woman he promised to have and to hold. Admittedly, that *'til death do us part* clause gave him a bit of an out, and his intention of finally putting an end to the relationship would be enforced once he consumed his wine trifle.

Marty McGrath had taken the order, served up his meal and asked permission from the king of the kitchen to leave early, as there were no other customers to serve. Considering the boss departed for a similar reason, Chef Eugene acquiesced. Forever grateful, the gifted *garçon* rushed home to find his partner snoozing in front of the television, and gave him a dig in the ribs.

"You're not going to believe this but that Irish bastard you're after—I reckon I've just served him a stale dessert and some after-dinner mints. He ordered mayo with everything."

The desire to support your partner without question is inherent in every loving relationship, but the confirmation came with the reference to County Mayo. Checking his ammunition clip, Rom led the way to the patrol car in the garage, and turned over the souped-up engine. Then he tried to determine a destination.

"Will he still be at the restaurant?"

"No way," answered the deputised dandy, wondering what to do with the shotgun now nestling precariously on his lap. "He was about to pay the bill when I left."

"Shit, he's after his wife," growled the driver, slamming the car into gear and burning rubber. The local goons usually fined the local hoons for this kind of erratic driving, but Rom could apologise to the neighbours the following day. When there is a damsel in distress, all members of the precinct try that little bit harder and, in this instance, Pat Malone was on her own and unaware of the lurking danger.

Every member of the local nick had memorised Ms. Malone's address, should a crisis arise. Her telephone number was written on the notice board beside the front counter but no-one could raise the duty sergeant, trying to placate a drunk in one of the cells.

Masticating Matthew, relaxed and stress-free over dinner, reflected on the ease of the operation, so far. He downloaded instructions for making a lavatory bomb from the Internet and the only hiccup related to the differing specifications for a hang-pull, compared to a flush button. He guessed his wife would be in the contemporary corner and this was confirmed when he broke into her house to prepare the device. His only other task was to prepay a home delivery from the Curry in a Hurry take-out restaurant. Their motorcycle transport, en-route to the supplied address, had to move to the side of the road to let a patrol unit speed past.

Every available police vehicle headed for the Malone residence. The duty officer, once aware of the circumstances, managed to ring the lady and warn her of the imminent arrival of the cavalry. Naturally, she would have to spruce herself up to receive them and headed for the bathroom. Mad Matt, sitting in his car with binoculars, couldn't wipe the grin off his face.

The temporary repairs didn't require a toilet stop or perhaps there was no time, as the door buzzer heralded Rom Remus and his gun-toting side-kick. Redoubtable Rom told it like it was.

"You're in grave danger, Ms. Malone. Your husband is in the area and we believe he is seeking vengeance.

Does he really fart in bed?"

Pat didn't have time to answer that question, as they had been joined by a motorcyclist, dressed in leather and carrying a pouch containing a steamy concoction. He was a long way from his country of birth.

"I am thinking you ordered the chicken vindaloo, fried rice, pickle and poppadums. Number 7 Celestial Court?"

The lady of the house looked at him with undisguised contempt and then at the other two people standing on her doorstep. Marty stepped forward and, on the basis of his experience with chicken, provided his professional opinion.

"I wouldn't touch it, Miss. You never know where these chickens have been. That's why they vindaloo them. Did you order the takeaway?"

"No I did not," replied the perplexed resident. "What is going on here?"

Suspecting foul play, Sergeant Remus confiscated the delivery and placed the courier in temporary custody. Some distance from this doorstep confusion, the villain who had initiated the prank laughed uncontrollable and far too loudly. One of the motorcycle cops looked around to see a van pulling out from the curb and a fleeting glimpse of the driver. Seeing the same, Rom barked out his orders.

"Officer, record that number plate and chase after the van. I think that's our perp."

As the boys in blue scrambled, Rom led the now frightened librarian away from her house, and promised her protection in the cells, if she didn't mind the drunk. He classified the property as a crime scene, even though no crime had been committed, and his men roped-off the area. The Indian patsy, in an effort to vindicate his suspect food, ate the meal himself and proclaimed to one and all that he was still alive. Ten minutes later he went to the loo.

Matt the malicious heard the blast as he reversed his car out of a neighbour's drive, where he had been hiding until it was safe to move on. He then manipulated his way through a number of darkened streets until he found the highway. Expecting to be hunted north and south, the shrewd Irishman decided on a westerly route towards Castlemaine and Ballarat, towns big enough to offer asylum to a madman. The fellow carried all his possessions with him, including his ill-gotten gains, neatly packed in a suitcase in the trunk. He was well aware he needed to launder some of that money before he reached the border.

Truckies are well-served for road-stops in this country, and sleepovers are common on most arterial links. The man in the van found himself between two eighteen wheelers and felt secure. They didn't even know he was wedged between them. The throaty engine noise that awakened the fugitive at 5 a.m. served as an alarm clock and off he went, looking for a highway café serving breakfast. Matthew figured it was far too soon for the highway patrol to get a fix on him. All the same, could it be time to change his appearance and acquire some new wheels?

At Messer and Opie, Ballarat, the doors always opened promptly at 9 a.m., in the manner of a confident and efficient organisation. With a reputation for personal service, they were ready to take as much time as needed to please their clients. It takes quite a while to be fitted for a bespoke garment and, if accessories are involved, that can also take time. The first customer of the day headed for the tailor with a tape measure draped around his shoulders, which screamed-out authenticity. The man may not have been working on commission; otherwise it would be hard to explain the lack of excitement when the newcomer indicated he wanted two suits, a sports jacket, five shirts, some underwear and ties. He did get excited, however, while measuring the customer's inner leg.

The tailored clothes would be available for pick-up the next day. How efficient was that? Before he exited the store, O'Gorman asked directions to the BMW dealership. Here, the welcome mat had been dusted and greased.

"Good morning, sir, and a very smart choice, if you don't mind me saying so."

Matthew didn't mind what the spiv in the shiny suit said, because whatever he decided would be a smart choice. He responded as if he hadn't heard the ingratiating toad.

"It's a grand motor car. Not many clicks on the clock, I see. Would you be tellin' me that a little old lady only drove it to church on Sunday?"

"Not exactly," replied Jack Glover. "One of our clientele traded-up to more horsepower. This car is a diamond, believe me."

Matthew O'Gorman couldn't help but smile. When one rogue is up against another, who do you believe? He pushed his bullshit barrow a bit further.

"I'm after decidin' between a Merc and a Beamer. It's a difficult choice, to be sure."

Now it was salesman Glover's turn to smile.

"But you've come here first, I'll wager. That must mean something," said the smooth-talking sycophant, wondering how long this would take. He had a luncheon date with the alluring Liz Pap, which he was much looking forward to.

"An alphabetical decision," remarked the cool client.

"Would you be doin' a trade-in, now? A lotta people would be after a van like mine."

In the end, Mr. Super Smooth took the Ford Transit off his hands and sold him a six-cylinder 520 for a ham sandwich (a moderate profit), only possible because the purchaser paid cash.

It proved to be a long lunch with the dark-eyed delectable and the urban Lothario considered his prospects to be moving in an agreeable direction. When he returned to the dealership, he found the police waiting for him.

"My name is Angela Pride, Mr. Glover. We believe you have sold a vehicle to a wanted felon. The van you have accepted as a trade-in is on our radar. The aforementioned owner is a person of interest."

"You mean he's a crim," offered the salesman, not wanting to mince words. Being taken down by a Paddy is a humiliating experience, and the spiv in the shiny suit felt it acutely.

"I'm afraid so," replied the detective, aware of the shame involved with loss of face. It was almost as bad as loss of commission.

"Was anything said that might give us a guide to his whereabouts?" continued the policewoman, not expecting any kind of positive answer from a guy who probably listened to himself more than others.

"Sure, he's going to the races at Flemington on Saturday."

"He told you that?" queried Angela, incredulously.

"Well, not in so many words. I complimented him on money wisely spent, and he said he would win it back at Flemington. Of course, this doesn't necessarily mean he's going there, with TAB outlets all over town."

"Nevertheless, it's a lead, isn't it? Do you think I could ask you to do something for us? We need somebody who can identify the fellow, who maybe a master of disguise."

So it came to pass that Glover the lover found himself togged up in his Sunday best and strutting with the socialites at the track on St. Leger day. Beside him, Pride of the Force set her walkie-talkie to a wavelength connecting her to Commander McCurry and Marty McGrath, two other sequestered souls who had seen the kidnapper in the flesh. One patrolled the bookmakers' ring and the other was upstairs in the Members Bar, enjoying the unencumbered view of the lawn and surrounds. There was another person on-course who would recognise the kidnapper but Bing McKeon, preoccupied with his starter in the big race, begged-off the invitation. He was also trying to find his son, who had slipped away for another of his clandestine meetings with Lydia. It was pretty much old home week.

The man they were looking for was there alright, with money stashed in every pocket of his new jacket. He was ready to start laundering his cash but decided to avoid the bookmakers. If he won, they would likely pay him with his own notes, so he invested through the tote and placed his winnings in the attractive manbag, acquired on the advice of a radio guru, who was renowned for forecasting coming style trends.

Matt collected on the first and Dancing Deborah looked good in the second, with Paraparap and Tynia the only dangers. However, he was spotted at one of the totalisator windows, and everyone was alerted, including the two uniform lads who had tracked-down his BMW in the carpark.

Some people have a sixth sense. They know when people are looking at them, even when their fly is not undone. O'Gorman's immediate reaction was to depart the room under the grandstand by the nearest door, the exit racegoers used to access the mounting yard. From a balcony on an upstairs level, Marty McGrath spotted the Irishman on the grass, walking away from the action. By now, the waiter was enjoying the intrigue. He passed-on his information to the others and the chase commenced—not a frantic pursuit, just fast walking with plenty of ducking and weaving involved.

In-between Matt's car and his current position was the Birdcage: no birds but a lot of horses being prepared for their upcoming test of skill and stamina. Two rows of open stalls ran the length of an adult egg and spoon race, with a green verge separating the punters from the horses and their handlers. A couple of large oak trees gave shade for the onlookers and limited weather protection for the two park benches in situ for my lady, if she wished to take a load off. On one of these seats, Lydia and Joe sat entwined, gazing lovingly into each other's eyes. Jack Glover and Angela Pride skipped into the Birdcage, some sixty seconds behind the fleet-footed runner, heading for the carpark entrance at the other end of the stable complex. He gained valuable breathing space when the pursuers stopped in their tracks to renew old acquaintances.

"Oh my God, Inspector Pride," blurted out the puzzled girl.

"Liz," said Jack

"Oh shit," responded Lydia.

Joe McKeon looked from one to another in complete confusion. He was saved from an explanation by a call from trainer Geoff Murphy. Their horse often played up and an extra pair of hands was needed.

The policewoman couldn't stay, as she had been joined by Tony McCurry and they continued the chase, but not before instructing the car salesman to remain with the young woman and explain the manhunt. This was something he very much wanted to do. Lydia suggested the Champagne Bar.

If O'Gorman thought he was home free he was mistaken. Two uniformed policeman hovered around his car, one of them with a walkie-talkie up against his ear. Turning towards the course proper, Matthew figured the grass to be greener on the other side. Wrong! Southside of the green divide was a housing estate for horses, consisting of multiple structures, each containing accommodation for twenty odd animals, and kindly rented out to various trainers by the racing club.

The reactive runaway chose the midway mark of the Straight Six course to make his crossing, but he was unaware the next event was about to start, as he scurried across the track. Once the starting stalls activated, it would take around a minute for the sprinters to complete their journey, so most of them would be going faster than a speeding bullet—well, at least thirty-five kilometres an hour.

The Straight Six at Flemington often attracts a full field and that can mean two dozen starters ready to run for the roses. Fortunately for the man in the middle, the field usually splits into two divisions, each group needing a running rail to guide them. O'Gorman couldn't have moved if he wanted to. His legs were not responding and the hurtling hooves on hard ground gave off a thunderous roar as the belligerent beasts, breathing heavily, hurtled past him on both sides.

By the time he made it to the far railing, the fellow had regained his composure and, looking back, could not see anyone following him. Perhaps they were waiting for the announcement of correct weight. During the pursuit, they had passed many bookmakers; more than enough time for a bet?

Desperation would kick-in when he realized all the exits were behind him with police units moving into place to block the escape routes. The noise of an approaching helicopter was an ominous sound, and it would be only a matter of time before they brought in the dog squad. Where to hide?

Saturday in the stables is always quiet, with a skeleton staff doing as little as possible. They congregate in the equipment room and absorb all the action on TV. A sleek-footed smarty could always slip by and take refuge in one of the boxes, and a docile animal might appreciate the company. Or not. Matt also realised that privacy could not be guaranteed as stable staff constantly changed the straw in the boxes. It has long been a bone of contention that our equine friends have a rather lax attitude to personal waste disposal. They just raise their tail and crap anywhere at any time, including their bedding. The offending material plus straw is swept away and stored in a large community shed, to be collected at intervals by the night man. It is not a place one likes to walk past, much less enter. The perfect hiding spot!

By the time the furtive figure of the hunted emerged from the palace of poo, night had fallen. Eight races had been run and won and, in one respect, the canny punter was considerably richer. Dancing Deborah streeted them to win by four lengths, and that winning ticket in his pocket would be worth plenty. In another respect, he would have to consider the fact that the law had impounded his car with most of the kidnapping money in the trunk; together with the clothing and haberdashery he purchased from Messer and Opie. How he yearned for some clean clothes.

The day had been brighter for the William Street Syndicate, with Gurner's Lane winning the major event. However, Joe was not in a celebratory mood because of the situation between his sweetheart and that peacock from the provincials. He couldn't track her down, possibly because she partook of too much Champagne and saw out the day comatose in the ladies loo.

Fun days like this happen far too rarely and the accomplished competitors and their jockeys move on to another state to compete in their signature events. They would all be back and ready to go for the Spring Carnival. Bing McKeon and Peter Papadopoulos would both be key players, and, above all other considerations, they had to beat each other. People with power and money needed an incentive like this to keep them going.

Lydia needed two days to leave her hangover behind, at which time she thought she had better get going. The LA Olympic Games beckoned and potential performers would have to impress the selection committee in various trials over a number of months. Souvlaki showed promise but he was not rapt in the dressage caper. The jumps and cross-country proved to be no problem because he liked to stretch his long limbs, but forget all that prissy stuff. Some of those horses looked like they had a broom up their arse.

These equine problems gave her ladyship little time to think about her romantic dilemma. Now back on the circuit, she would see more of Joe but forever worried that her secondary suitor would turn-up at a tournament in a late-model Beamer. However, it was the family feud situation that really bothered her. She had seen the movie *West Side Story* and knew how these things often ended. In fact, her last theatrical production at Lacryma Christi had been *Romeo & Juliet* and there were similarities, if you ignore the fact that the convent Romeo was a girl.

Although Joe's appearances for the Mt. Beauty team were to become infrequent, the consistent presence was Margaret Dow and her mount Jungles. They would prove to be the biggest threat to Lydia's lofty ambition. The youngster had the bloom of youth on her side, but Mrs. Dow still looked good in a tight pair of riding breeches. Awkward moments materialised when the scheduling put the two competitors in sequential order for any tournament because Souvlaki and Jungles didn't like each other. When the latter animal savaged Souvlaki in his meaty bits, Miss Pap cried foul.

"Margaret, keep that brute away from my mount. You have no right to encroach on my space."

"I'm trying, but they're not friends. You should protect your leg. He's a biter."

Here the famous Papadopoulos temper came to the fore and, for those who could remember, the creek bed incident was a perfect example. Lydia raised her riding crop and whacked Jungles hard on the rump. The gelding reared and lashed out, scattering all the other competitors in all directions. From that moment, Los Angeles became an unattainable dream, but there was a bright side. If the Greek goddess acquired her business degree, Daddy would spring for a holiday in Hawaii.

CHAPTER 16

At Aberdeen homestead, the residents celebrated the acquisition of a degree. Young Edwin, after acquiring a solid grounding in the family business from his brother, had been shuttled-off to Marcus Oldham College, where he studied equine management. Established in the early sixties, this institute of pastoral perfection imitated a model set in place by Harvard—combining theory with practical experience. Ed's mother didn't need to know any of this. As far as she was concerned, someone in the family possessed professional skills. What a relief!

The graduate and his sibling readily accepted the responsibility of their birthright. In Ed's case this meant complete financial control of the family's racing and breeding interests, operating out of the office in Mt. Beauty. His brother retained the hands-on role and the patriarch took a back seat.

"You're getting on a bit, Dad," said Joe, fortified by alcohol and empowered with confidence. "Why don't you potter around with those wineries of yours and leave all the crap work to Ed and me?"

"Joseph, I wish you wouldn't speak to your father like that," reprimanded his mother, momentarily releasing her grip on her knitting needles. "Bing is more than happy to let you both run the show and he appreciates the time he will now have to do other things. However, you must never believe you will be able to do this without the firm hand of experience to guide you."

"The same firm hand that clipped ye laddies behind the lugs when ya stuffed-up. Do ye no ken?"

The laird hadn't meant to be an addendum to his wife's prognostications. He was still coming to terms with the fact that she virtually retired him on the spot. It was not the way he planned on going, but, on reflection, if they did stuff-up, he could step in and set things right. He loved his racing stock, but the vineyards were becoming more interesting by the day. Winning wine trophies delighted him as much as track victories.

One of the revelations of the previous year was the increased profitability of MOG Wines. The innovative manager, having introduced a new variety, expanded the demographics of the brand. Miniatures were quarter-size bottles, mixed with various fruit additives such as blackberry, strawberry and peppermint. The kids went for them like bees to a honeypot, buying not only a honey version but a sports selection, which smelled like John Newcombe's armpit. Ad executives with few scruples marketed the product as the healthy alternative.

Needless to say, word of mouth is the best marketing tool and, for those youngsters not reliant on hard drugs, this alcoholic spurt proved to be quite a substitute. The Scotsman realised his small vineyard couldn't keep up supply and he started looking for another business to purchase. Peter Pap had Victoria covered, so the man from the mountains looked to South Australia, famous for cultivated regions such as Coonawarra, Clare, the Barossa Valley and McLaren Vale. He could attend the Morphettville gallops, sound out a few prospects, negotiate over dinner, and be home by the next day. Bing never lacked confidence.

Life in Adelaide changed Matthew O'Gorman, again sporting red hair to complement his regrown moustache. He moved around town with impunity as the biggest police presence was on point duty and crime was where you found it. His choice to live in the hills at Basket Range demonstrated his preference for living in isolated areas, away from the long arm of the law. He led a simple life, attending the track on Saturday and Wednesday, and dabbling in a bit of housebreaking on Fridays, when many families ate out, and Sunday, while people attended church.

When the original owner of the best blended tipple under $5 saw his successor at the racetrack, he couldn't believe it. It was him alright—all la-di-da and spruced-up, coming from the Committee Room in the company of the doyen of horse trainers, Colin Hayes. The fact that the visitor came to town on MOG business gave credence to the concept of coincidence, but the surly punter with the marvellous mo didn't know that. He blamed Bing McKeon for ruining his life, and revenge came easily to a bitter man. A rich and contented criminal might have let it go, but this offender lost his wife, his money and his new car. He really loved that car.

Given this apparent friendship between the Scottish bastard and the trainer, the seething sulk elected not to bet on any of the Hayes horses. You've got to love a man of principle, especially considering the odds. The Lindsay Park animals won seven of the eight races. In a grumpy mood, the low-life followed the Victorian visitor around. He saw him leave the course and return to his hotel. Then he tailed the chap to an up-market restaurant and spied on him as he dined with friends. Given his state of mind, the plotting parasite might have done something with the *Bombe Alaska* but he chose not to strike until the next day. Adelaide is renowned as the city of churches, and you don't have to be a hardened pilgrim to respond to the beckoning of the bells on Sunday morning. Would there be an extra degree of satisfaction if he could kill him with God as his witness?

Matt had his prey down as a Presbyterian and, at 10.15 a.m., the Irishman was conspicuous in the courtyard of their kirk in Archer Street, just north of the city. The churchgoers gathered inside, except for Mr. McKeon, who was conspicuous by his absence.

At that time, the gentleman in question was on his way to inspect the winery he was ready to purchase. Should the property and facilities please him, he would sign the papers and declare the estate to be the new home of MOG Miniatures. This is exactly what happened. After meeting the staff and sampling some of the current product, he voiced his approval, signed the document and asked his driver to take him directly to the airport. On the way, he passed the stud farm belonging to his new friend Colin Hayes. The astute horseman lived in a thirty-eight-room sandstone and marble mansion on two thousand acres. The new neighbour made a note to send his mate a case of Miniatures—a wee drop to cement the relationship.

O'Gorman brooded silently in one of the back pews of the chapel, listening to a sermon on the sanctity of marriage. He understood these parishioners to be good people and regretted poisoning the altar wine. How was he to know that the target of his wrath wouldn't show? Perhaps he hadn't thought out the implications of collateral damage because when the bodies started dropping, he did the decent thing, rushing into the sacristy and dialling the emergency number, thus saving at least twenty-five lucky souls. The other fifty odd victims couldn't have chosen a better place to die.

At the airport, the Melbourne-bound vineyard mogul purchased jubes and chocolate frogs for his wife, a tradition based on the little woman's repeated requests. The confectionary franchise stocked a comprehensive choice of chewable items, which sold well on the back of perennial departure delays.

Helen, at that very moment, was involved in a religious service near their home—the blessing of St. Barnaby's Wayside Chapel, a small prayer hall at the base of Mt. Bogong, dedicated to those who had perished trying to reach the peak in adverse conditions. Richie Papworth funded the facility with good grace and a snide comment.

"There would have been no need for a memorial if those who perished had procured the right equipment at Papworth's Ski Hire."

The post-blessing activities took place at the shire hall and the Country Women's Association put on tea and scones. The celebrations expanded with the announcement that Margaret Dow had made the short list for the equestrian team for the LA Olympics. Everyone was pumped. The event would not take place for two years but the teams needed to be pruned and then fine-tuned before then. Edwin McKeon seemed very impressed.

"Wow, does this mean you might meet Farrah Fawcett and Charlie's Angels?"

"Probably not," replied Margaret, amused at the young man's choice of role models, unaware her husband shared the same role model plus Cindy Crawford and Elle MacPherson.

After a long day travelling, Bing made it home to the bosom of his family, just in time to catch the evening news, reporting on the horrible events he had left behind.

"Did you not see anything?" asked Helen, shocked at the enormity of the mass food poisoning. Fake news is where you find it.

"Nay, lass. It had naught to do with me, but it does nae surprise. You should see the kind of food they eat over there. Someone offered me a "pie floater," a meat pie dunked in a bowl of pea soup—shite. On the plane they served cold tongue. One auld biddy refused to accept anything that came from the mouth of an animal. They gave her eggs and she was thrilled."

His wife liked him to be in a talkative mood. A holiday from that aggressive Scottish bombast always proved good news for everyone, and what better time to bring up difficult issues?

"Darling, are you aware Joe has a girl-friend and wants to get married?"

The silence proved deafening and lasted for some time. Helen wondered if he heard her and tried an encore.

"Ed got it from Marg Dow, who knows the girl from gymkhana circles. I've not met her. What about you?"

The big fella had dropped the ball. A romantic liaison in the family without his knowledge and approval was ludicrous and highly suspicious. Eventually, the man found his voice, heralding the re-emergence of that Scottish bombast.

"It's no that cow from Shepparton, is it? I thought she was just his fancy girl."

Helen had little time for the new-age colloquialisms that menfolk seemed to delight in and narrowed her eyes in disgust, prior to dismissing his ill-informed conjecture.

"He escorted the mayor's daughter to her debutante ball, a one-off. I don't believe he has seen her since. I thought you might have discussed your son's social life with him man-to-man. Or haven't you the time?"

If this wasn't a personal jibe at his slack parental responsibilities, what was? Some people possess the knack of making you feel guilty in the nicest possible way and the peeved parent certainly felt rebuked. The lady of the manor might have also called herself out for being blind-sighted. After all, a woman without knowledge is a woman wasted.

After some discussion, it was agreed there should be some measure of sensitivity regarding the situation, sensitivity not being Bing's strongpoint. The best means of getting the goss would be through Edwin, but the second son took the Fifth Amendment.

"Gee, Mum, why pick on me? Joe will kill me if he finds out I spilt the beans. I've never met the girl. I told you my source and you and she are mates. Oh hell, is that the time?"

The lad was out the door and heading for his office before his mother could draw breath. How frustrating. She stared at the phone for a long time before committing to ring her former vice-principal. In the end, she decided to dial M for Margaret.

"I know we caught-up at the dedication yesterday, but there is something I need to talk to you about. Would you like to meet for a cuppa in town, perhaps this afternoon?"

Did the former subordinate understand what this would be all about? Possibly! She and Joseph were the only locals to have met Lydia, and to understand the ramifications of her parentage, but it would only be a matter of time before rumour raged, and the clansman reached for his claymore.

Some might consider the two equestriennes to be rivals because of constant competition, but Margaret didn't have a mean bone in her body. She was practical and knew Joe sought closure, neither being aware of the suitor from Ballarat, who might appear over the horizon in his high-powered BMW. The whole scenario had the makings of some penny dreadful pulp fiction.

"I'm so sorry, Marg. I forgot to congratulate you on your Olympic selection. What a wonderful achievement," said Helen, wanting to sound magnanimous and sincere. The brow-beating would commence with the serving of the rum balls.

"I want to talk to you about Joe. I appreciate the fact that he hasn't been able to spend much time on the circuit lately, but information has reached me that he's in love and keen to get married. Bing and I are shocked he hasn't sought to confide in us, his parents. Naturally, we're disappointed."

"Yes, I understand," said the now nervous Olympic contender, choosing that moment to order another pot of tea. "There's a reason you've been uninformed."

The mistress of Aberdeen didn't bother saluting two departing customers, as her table companion did. She could see her friend was trying to delay the inevitable and probed once more.

"You said there's a reason. I would like to hear it."

"OK, here goes. Your son has kept his romance secret because the girl's name is Lydia Papadopoulos."

Call for the smelling salts. It was a tense time in the tea house. The customers looked concerned. The owner brought water. The waitress suggested an ambulance. Mrs. McKeon was hyperventilating and her face was a whiter shade of pale; or was that the song playing in the background?

Some doubted the poor woman would get through it but she did, with help from her young friend, who provided first-aid advice.

"Breathe slowly, sip the water, and think of Richard Gere."

If Richard had been there, he might have suggested a slap across the face, but nobody possessed the nerve. They could only listen to Helen's feeble cries of anguish.

"You can't be serious. Oh my God, of course you're serious. Oh my God!"

You don't expect an articulate schoolmarm to be hog-tied by doubt and despair do you? One would have thought those entreaties to God to be a thing of the past, with no longer any nuns to intercede on her behalf. Once the big man heard about these covert lovers, there would be hell to pay in heaven. Cupid, in particular, would be under the gun.

Margaret retired to the bathroom to refresh her make-up, while her friend aged ten years. As the youthful teacher looked into the mirror, she pondered on her flawless complexion, and wondered how long it would take for her children to accelerate her physical decline. Chris had been talking-up the prospect of family, and his fiscal plotting indicated that a child would be an acceptable blessing, as long as he or she arrived after the end of the financial year. As Margaret snapped her handbag shut, she could only grin at her husband's devotion to the predictable. But, she was not here to daydream about her own circumstances. Her friend was in need of enlightenment and she would tell her tale.

This day was a long time coming, and the girl in the middle knew that her silence over the journey would be seen as a betrayal by her former boss. Why does one have to get involved in family matters; especially other people's family? Joe might be relieved that the situation was now out in the open, but he would not thank his riding partner for being the one who cleared the air. The poor lass felt damned from all sides.

Nevertheless, Margaret was prepared to tell all and it wasn't a short story. The other patrons had all departed, and the staff were resetting the tables for the next day's trade. Quite slowly, mind you. They had tuned-in to the conversation and didn't want to miss out on a word.

The story, in all its glory, didn't diminish the foreboding in Helen's soul. With no desire to return home, she forestalled that inevitability by picking around her last treat sluggishly. Her worried confidant ordered more tea and asked the obvious question.

"What are you going to do or, to be more precise, what will Bing do?"

Her blank look revealed nothing. That's what blank looks are for. In truth, Helen didn't know what her husband would do but expected destruction of some kind, and a coronary wasn't out of the question. She knew she would have to handle this delicately.

"I'm going to need to handle this delicately. Joe might need a place to doss down for a few days. Can you and Chris put him up? There will be too much testosterone under our roof tonight."

The horse lady consented, Helen paid the bill, and Our Lady of Sorrows looked down on them both with suitable empathy. These romantic dramas took-up so much of her time, but her brief was to give love a chance. What else could she do?

Tea for Two

CHAPTER 17

Because of her flamboyance at Flemington, Lydia ended-up back in the library with her father in denunciation mode.

"Young lady, your performance at the races was disgraceful and unacceptable. Your mother and I were severely embarrassed to bring you home in such a state."

"Yes, Pa," replied the contrite daughter. "The hangover proved a lesson for me and I will imbibe more carefully next time. I'm sorry I embarrassed you both."

Peter Pap had been warned about the dangerous years of teenage rebellion but thought he had worked his way through all that. The next agenda item was the matter of the blue BMW that kept appearing outside her quarters. This observation brought an aggressive response from her ladyship, who took the opportunity to remind her father that she was now a grown woman, independent and liberated.

But still intractable, unpredictable and feisty, grumbled the retort from deep within his inner self.

In the kitchen, Mrs. P could hear the raised voices and hit the dinner gong thirty minutes early. Henrietta's home-made hommus would calm the stormy seas and her moussaka would placate the combatants. The telephone call from Norm Jones gave the girl some respite but the mood didn't improve.

"Bloody hell! Zorba the Geek has broken down!" cried the distraught tycoon.

The fellow owned other prospects and the loss of potential prize money would be a drop in the ocean for him but, having tasted success, the expectation is that your luck will be ongoing. Some experts promote a theory that only good horses break down because they try harder and overextend with their fragile limbs. Another theory is that God likes to dabble with the distress and despair of his delinquent disciples, a notion also actively promulgated by the Mormons.

The moussaka remained on the fellow's plate as he rushed out of the house, boarded the farm runabout and headed for the grassy enclosure, where his trainer was in consultation with the vet—a rather bulky figure with an appetite for delivering bad news before breakfast, lunch or dinner.

"Sorry, but he's done a tendon. Three months in the paddock and then we'll look at him again. Shocking luck with all those Group races coming up. Are those chickpeas I can smell?"

The man was obviously late for his supper and PP let him go, begrudgingly grateful for his opinion. The bandaged animal seemed oblivious to the concerns of the humans and casually nibbled on the green grass. Norm Jones was ready to get on with business.

"We need to look at our alternatives for the Spring Carnival. I didn't want to bring on Thunderball so soon but I reckon he's the best three-year-old we've got. The Guineas could be the go. Of course, Brewery Boy is on target for The Cup."

"Let's do it," said Peter, not wanting his cupboard to be bare at a time when his arch enemy could be well represented by a number of live hopes.

"Lydia missed out on Olympic selection, I've missed out here, and Hen's flowers didn't rate at the Begonia Festival. We seem to be doing everything wrong at the moment."

The Ballarat Begonia Festival, the biggest flower show in the country, provides opportunities in many categories. The city celebrates every Labour Day weekend with a parade through the main street, and sponsors multiple activities in the Botanical Gardens. The most recent headliner, the inimitable Mr. Whiskers and his dog Smiggy, are crowd favourites.

Mrs. Papadopoulos wasn't a headliner but an enthusiastic competitor. Unfortunately, that blue BMW backed into Henrietta's floral patch and destroyed her best blooms. A more observant parent might have investigated the case of the luxury vehicle a little earlier. At least, Mrs. P might have discovered Jack Glover snipping her roses every time he stopped-by to pick up her daughter. What went on in the back seat of the car was anybody's guess.

Lydia had an answer on tap. Her friend always picked her up for class when her auto was being repaired. She didn't mention that the service continued during the term break. Then again, she failed to mention many things, including the existence of her equestrian lover, who had recently proposed.

In America, there is an obvious agony aunt for these kinds of situations. Dear Abby has been dishing out advice since the fifties and Dorothy Dix personified the readership of the *Australian Women's Weekly*. *Cleo* also provided counsel for teens, if they could get past the male centrefolds.

Peter Pap's reluctance to initially investigate the car salesman was a mystery. The nature and cost of the vehicle would indicate an older man might be behind the wheel, and every father bristles with that kind of situation. In this instance, the premise was wrong, but the alternative no less terrifying. If there was an upside, it was that at least the chap wasn't a politician, or in advertising.

When PP tried to enter the city showroom, they relieved him of his shotgun but didn't call the police. Everyone is a prospective customer. Jack Glover saw the irate father coming and exited by the back door, thus avoiding an awkward confrontation. On reflection, he realised his days reversing over Henrietta's honeysuckle were over. There would be a meeting with Liz on neutral ground, and he would explain his marital status. His wife, on completion of a sabbatical in Swaziland, was now homeward bound.

During the Cold War, spies employed disguises quite effectively. On one such occasion, an agent, masquerading as a sportsman, was challenged at an event in Gdańsk.

"Are you a pole-vaulter?"

"Yes," replied the surprised infiltrator. "But, how did you know my name was Walter?"

Matthew O'Gorman's disguises were rubbish—ill-fitting wigs and cheap hair dyes, and he never wore gloves. His fingerprints appeared everywhere, and those identity changes (always Irish people) also failed to impress. The forensics folks in Adelaide didn't contribute to the subterfuge that labelled the mass killing in Archer Street as food poisoning. They knew the Presbyterians served-up fresh tucker, even at their shelters for the poor. The perp loomed large as a dangerous man and his ability to get his hands on lethal material was worrying. Little did they know his housebreaking expertise contributed to this ability?

To upgrade the manhunt, the authorities pulled a sizeable number of officers off point duty, and Madman MOG realised they would soon start to appear in the hills. Reluctantly, he moved back to Melbourne and accepted a position as a security guard for an organisation that made feminine products: vacuum cleaners, washing machines and white goods of every description. Some of these units cost plenty, so he needed to protect the company from people like himself.

He managed his reappearance at the track with surprising stealth and awareness. Initially, the punter avoided the city courses and travelled to provincial meetings, where public attendance and a police presence were minimal. Naturally, he followed the form lines of the McKeon and Papadopoulos stables and noted that the laird's son always attended, when their horses ran. At the time, this yard claimed a number of victories with a neddy called Aberdeen Angus, named after Princess Alexandra's husband, a patron of the Scottish Wildlife Trust.

While the gendarmes regarded the fugitive as psychotic, maniacal Matt didn't agree. Certainly, he could be brutal, but you expect that from a fiendish feral, don't you? Sometimes, the man could actually evaluate his decision-making before he rushed into impossible situations, and it was this kind of thinking that relieved the pressure on the old man and transferred it to his offspring. O'Gorman reckoned he could hurt his adversary more by killing his heir apparent. Such an act would give him a great deal of satisfaction, magnified by the Scotsman's grief. Every moment would be a memory.

The scoundrel also contemplated visiting his former partner again and wondered if she still lived in Wangaratta. The beastly bomber, disappointed with the outcome of his last foray into fireworks, felt sorry for the Indian victim. Evidently the chap's widow had discontinued deliveries from the restaurant, and upgraded their toilet facilities. If she had done that earlier, her husband might still be alive today.

161

The night-time security job gave the Irishman a perfect cover, should he wish to nick a few things in the course of his employment. During his down time, he was able to read the form and other racing journals. Such dedication eventually brought a reward, because he noticed an ad for the annual yearling sales at Newmarket, an event Bing McKeon always attended. With so many Irishmen associated with the horse-breeding industry in Australia, one more participant would go unnoticed, even though his crass disguise would surely be a point of interest.

Should you want to look like a racehorse trainer, you buy yourself some R. M. Williams boots, chinos, a big belt buckle and a wide-brimmed hat. To avoid the expense, the experienced housebreaker broke into an exclusive men's outfitter and kitted himself up. It was the first time in history this retail outlet had ever been burgled. Who, in their right mind, would want to steal that kind of gear? For good measure, he accessorised with a pair of black horn-rimmed specs and a false moustache, to confuse those with access to the identikit posters still in circulation.

The auction space was designed with semi-circle viewing seats, making it simple to detect and follow. However, in the stable precinct, prospective buyers viewed the horseflesh and moved quickly from one box to another, making it easy for a chance meeting.

The first sighting of McKeon confused the persistent predator. The towering Scot was examining the conformation of one of the yearlings, while providing explanations to the young man beside him, who looked like a junior version of the laird, but it was not Joseph. The Irishman hadn't realised the blaggard had fathered a second son. He recognised and accepted the fact that he now enjoyed the luxury of two targets. Only an idiot could stuff-up such a heaven-sent opportunity.

The financial controller of the family equine business decided he should learn all aspects of the industry, including the exercise of budgetary constraint. His father often got carried away with his bidding and, therefore, the young man would accompany his dad to all auctions and be an agent of restraint.

The Melbourne bloodstock people conducted their auction over three days, with morning, afternoon and night sessions. There was not much free time for the country visitors, who had booked into the Victoria Club for the duration. The club did a nice lamb roast during the week, so the two men dined and discussed the first day's activities. Bing had snared two colts with his eye on a filly for the next day.

"Well, lad, yer first yearling sale. Whit dae ya ken?"

"Quite thrilling. I'd say that. But not so good on the blood pressure. I also observed the clock on the wall produced more bids than anyone else. Did you notice that?"

The wise father sighed gracefully, secretly proud his protégé had picked-up on such a small detail. Over the course of the day, the young man hadn't said a lot but he didn't miss much.

"I fear auctions are a bit like that, laddie. They dinnae gie you much time to think and that's part of the plan. Nonetheless, I'm happy w'oor purchases. Great value for money. Let's hope the wee filly in the morn is just as affordable."

The McKeon deputation didn't go to the horse sales the next day. The prospective champion they had their eye on was withdrawn from the catalogue, which is not an uncommon practice. The owners may have changed their mind or the vet changed it for them. Bing used the time to visit some of his wine outlets and Ed went to the movies. When they returned to the club, they heard of the catastrophic events that had taken place that afternoon.

The highlight of the day was expected to be a strapping colt from New South Wales, bred in the purple with looks to match, and the first catalogue item for the evening session. There wasn't a spare seat in the auditorium as the auctioneer mounted his podium and called for bids. The usual suspects came to the fore and dollar figures bounced from one bidder to another like a beach ball at a boring sports event. Gasp followed hush as the figure headed for the magic million, a record purchase. With only a single buyer breaching that meridian-mark, one and all prepared for the auctioneer's final call and the thunderous applause which would undoubtedly follow. It didn't come to that.

As soon as the man with the melodic voice slammed his gavel down, the rostrum in front of him, behind him and all around him exploded, sending slivers of wood panelling all around the facility. Some patrons got it in the neck, others in the eye. One man walking down the side aisle was speared in the belly button. Blood oozed down the seats and splattered on the people sitting on them. The three-person deputation from St. John's Ambulance couldn't cope, and the thoroughbreds became severely traumatised. Those in the pre-parade ring broke away from their handlers and bolted.

Matthew O'Gorman, comfortably seated on the number 57 tram, heading back to the city, saw two horses shoot past the conveyance in Kensington Village at speed. A short while earlier, he had heard the explosion and, knowing the Scot wouldn't pass up the chance to see the prize colt go under the hammer, guessed his evil deed to be finally done. The barbaric beast would have been disappointed to learn that at the moment of the explosion, the Scotsman was signing up another retail outlet for MOG Wines.

Due to the inability of law enforcement to catch the will-o'-the-wisp the first time around, Angela Pride didn't get her promotion, and found herself in charge of a mundane arson investigation. Admittedly, the subsequent discovery of victims upgraded the status of the crime, for which she was well equipped to handle. The modus operandi of this shocking act bore a striking similarity to the lavatory bomb incident. Thankfully, the gunpowder residue the forensic people examined wasn't tainted by extraneous odours.

"What are you thinking?" queried her junior, a man with little experience but a lot of questions. "Are we the right people to be investigating this?"

"Sure we are. There are fatalities, so we're looking at homicide. Do you have a problem with that?"

The young man didn't have any problems. He just liked to make conversation in-between his operational errors.

"Phil, please don't touch the evidence without gloves. And don't stand in the blood. You're contaminating the crime scene."

The pensive detective thought she might be able to connect the explosions, but she couldn't see a motive for this second vile act. Pat Malone didn't fit into this set of circumstances and she didn't see a Greek angle. The big time brewer was a horseplayer but not involved in the proceedings of that week. After a long night, the weary woman must have been happy to get home and kick off her shoes. She opened one of those small wine bottles, so popular with young people, rather liking the raspberry-flavoured low alcohol content. Later, she would question why she kept having so many blood-thirsty dreams.

The future of the Victoria Police force arrived to pick up his boss in the morning and they drove back to Newmarket. A forensics expert, still on site, provided his condensed opinion.

"Devastation and desolation," decreed the dour dynamo from the fine detail department. "The incendiary device blew up instead of out, so the flying debris caused most of the injuries. As you can see, the furniture has been burnt or scorched and the upward blowback of the blast made the roof struts unstable. The ceiling could come down at any time."

The auditorium wasn't an enclosed room and the ventilation gap between the rooftop and the walls provided the people below with some clean air. Those guys who walked behind the animals with their manure scoops did a fine job, but who knew when they might go on strike?

There were seven fatalities in total and thirty non-life-threatening injuries. The bloodstock company lost two of their auctioneers, a female clerk and three floor-walkers. The prize yearling had to be put down and the inside toilet closed for repairs. A memorial wreath was placed in the foyer (unscathed) in memory of the departed, and the auctions continued in the back paddock, where human traffic was boosted by the number of insurance assessors combing the area. Angela absorbed most of this in an instant but only had one question for the man beside her.

"CCTV footage?"

"Yes, ma'am. The bidding action goes out online to quite a few cities and countries and around the premises. There are screens in the foyer, restaurant, stables, pre-parade shed, you name it. We've got a very clear picture of the perp for you."

Could this be Christmas? wondered the enthused detective as she tracked her man into the office to watch the replay. Her little lapdog trotted along beside her. Lo and behold, there he was—the inimitable mad bomber himself. The current disguise resembled Groucho Marx in a cowboy movie, but his distinguishing features were definitely distinguishable, as he sauntered up to the rostrum prior to the start of the evening's activities.

It was common practise for a cleaner to spruce-up the auctioneer's stand before each session and O'Gorman was suitably attired in a cleaner's jacket. As he dusted the dais, he neatly lifted the wooden mallet and replaced it with another. Very smooth, Matthew. The man with the feather duster even managed a smile for the cameras, although he may not have anticipated the possibility of electronic surveillance. On the other hand, the villain might have wanted the widow to know who had done away with her nearest and dearest.

"The detonator was in the gavel," Angela blurted out, after watching the replay.

The forensics guy looked on approvingly. He usually had to rerun the video half-a-dozen times before the retards from Russell Street embraced the obvious.

"You've got it, girl. A bit of ammonium nitrate, some Semtex and diesel oil. It's almost as easy as making a lavatory bomb."

The retard from Russell Street needed some air. She asked her flunky to rush off for some coffee, while she settled down on one of the park benches beside the burnt-out interior. In the background, the voice of a new auctioneer cut through the stillness of a windless morning. Seven hundred thousand dollars for a half-brother to the sister of a Caulfield Cup winner. What a bargain!

There was little more the investigation team could do on site, but they knew where the responsibility lay, and that culprit could not be far away. While waiting for her coffee, Angela instigated an all-state alert and asked her people to provide the media with relevant pictorial content. How hard would it be to find a Paddy with a daggy disguise?

Bing and Ed wheeled-by in the afternoon, on their way back to Aberdeen. After inspecting the rubble that was the remains of the auction ring, they drifted down to the back stables, where the bidding continued unabated. With nothing there for them, they headed home, passing the float carrying their two colts along the way. It was Edwin who experienced a sudden pang of guilt on his father's behalf.

"Dad, you didn't forget to pick-up mum's goodies, did you?"

"Are you daft, son? My life would nae be worth living if I was that forgetful."

When Helen had released the bad news concerning Joe's romance, he had been rude and unreasonable, blaming her for lack of parental surveillance, amongst other things. His blistering denunciation also implicated God, Allah, Krishna, Buddha, Margaret Dow and those bloody equestrians.

It's easy to be contrite after the fact, but, in this case, a superior gift was required and he opted for some imported chocolates and candies, and hoped the local folks at Darrell Lea wouldn't be offended. For years, this popular confectionary outlet fed Melbourne's sweet-toothed community through thick and thin. Their local liquorice was to die for and some people did (the store was situated on a busy intersection). Rumours that the business was owned by a group of greedy dentists didn't influence Bing's buying habits in any way.

The horse float arrived at Aberdeen about forty minutes after the sedan, and Joe led the two colts off the transport, anxious to see what his father had purchased. One boasted a deep girth, strong hindquarters, good bone, and had an intelligent head and eye. The other was a loose walker, lighter in the rear, and possessed a longer rein and more delicate legs. They appeared correct in every way, which is not always a given. The laird had already decided what to do with the yearlings.

"Put them in the lower paddock and they can natter tae the brumbies as they pass by."

Many years had gone by since the Scotsman first laid eyes on the high country brumbies, but they were never far from his mind. The younger generation found it difficult to understand his attachment to these wild creatures, and he often needed to lecture them concerning the foundation on which he had built his empire.

Inside the house, Helen circumnavigated the chocolate box. She had accepted her gift with muted passion, and now untied the bow that would unleash all kinds of pleasurable possibilities. There is a standard operating procedure when contemplating the choice of a sweet delight. For a start, read the condensed bible of contents, which describes each delicacy in detail. The narrative always promises ultimate gratification. The retinal survey comes next. Slowly scan the treats on offer and note their various shapes and sizes. You will be aware that some of the tasty morsels feature soft centres and others don't. If you spend too much time on this, you'll end up a nut case. Your reach then needs to be quick and definitive with no time for hesitation or doubt. Just flick the confectionary into your mouth and close your eyes. The indulgence is complete.

There have been a number of investigations into whether chocolate is an aphrodisiac, but the results aren't conclusive. The person who would always volunteer to be a gourmet guinea pig was in a better mood when the menfolk came in for their meal and full of chatter when they sat down. Bonhomie still reigned because Bing had yet to approach Joe regarding his romantic relationship. Neither had Helen or Margaret Dow. This saga had all the makings of a radio serial, if the ABC ever decided to terminate *Blue Hills*, their long-running soap opera. The lady of the house was a fan and also a movie aficionado, so her first question to Ed didn't involve racehorses.

"So, Edwin, what film did you see? There is so much to choose from in town isn't there?"

Although her better half walked the same streets at the same time, this is a question he refused to ask, and for good reason. Most youths of that age are reticent to review with their parents the likes of *Hollywood Hookers* or something of that ilk. Fortunately, for this conversation, the lad's entertainment choice proved not to be so raunchy.

"I saw a preview of a picture to be released next year, *Risky Business.*"

Joe chose to attack a bit of pesky potato and lowered his eyes as his brother looked hard at him.

"A guy called Tom Cruise starred and spent most of the film in his underpants. Not a bad soundtrack, if you like that kind of thing."

The production, in fact, turned out to be a blueprint for teenagers wanting to arrange a party while their parents were away. The movie has a lot to answer for. Not finding the discussion she hoped, Helen moved on to other subjects and, after what they considered to be a polite eternity, the boys excused themselves, thus avoiding the washing-up—a post-dinner move in which they excelled.

Over coffee and port, the chocolates reappeared and were shared by the senior residents. The elephant in the room didn't get any but it was time to recognise his presence. Helen cast the first stone.

"We have to have it out with Joe. He should know that we know and we need to know how serious the bond is. In either case, it will be a load off his mind. It must have been a terrible secret to carry around for so long."

"Hoo long is soo long?" replied the man still coming to terms with the reality of the situation. Instead of waning, his hatred of Peter Pap had intensified over the years and he couldn't see him as Joe's father-in-law.

"Evidently, since he started eventing, so it is not a flash in the pan. We have to be careful not to go too hard at him. This could fracture our relationship with Joe completely. I don't want you going off like a bull in a china shop."

The small grunt that greeted this cautionary warning was a typical response. Of course, the Scotsman's reaction would be only one part of the equation. Mr. Papadopoulos would also be a dicey proposition in a china shop. The decision was made to conduct a mature discussion with the young man when Edwin was out, given it would be a rocky road one way or another. An additional determination was made to replace the lid on the chocolate box.

CHAPTER 18

The history of the shotgun reveals that this firearm is often a tool of coercion in marital matters, but rarely as a deterrent, as in the case of the car salesman. Lydia, now done with the chancer in the BMW, turned her thoughts to her special beau and his marriage proposal. Should Peter Pap meet Joe, there would be a fair chance a machine gun would come into play. At the least, a tongue-lashing in the library would be on the cards.

The youngsters discussed the possible reaction if and when they divulged their secret, both being oblivious to the fact that the McKeon elders were already informed and taking blood pressure pills. Elopement loomed as a possibility but was a bit old fashioned, according to the convent-educated realist. Joe thought it encouraging that his unofficial fiancé was discussing options, even though there had been no commitment. He presumed that fear of her father precluded all rational thought. Then again, facing Bing wouldn't be a picnic, either.

Lydia was first to grasp the nettle, and took advantage of PP's absence, travelling interstate at the time.

Having discovered that McKeon had purchased a vineyard over the border, the peripatetic proprietor did likewise. Bing opted for the Barossa Valley so he chose McLaren Vale. The vendors didn't want to accept his offer to stay on, so the mover and shaker needed to find a new manager and winemaker. At home, his daughter needed to find her mother in a good mood—the perfect time for a heart to heart with Henrietta.

"Mum, I know you and dad have been worried about my dating choices lately."

"Make that very worried," replied the queen of the quip, looking sternly over her glasses at her rebellious child.

"Well, there's no need to be. I've actually been going with a fella on the circuit and we've been tight for quite some time. I think you'd really like him."

"Is that so?" responded Henrietta in a voice devoid of enthusiasm. "Is he a good driver? Why haven't I met him?"

"Don't worry. He would never reverse over your roses, and you've not been introduced because of his birth defect."

"The poor thing! What is it?"

Here goes, thought the daring daughter, crossing her fingers.

"His name is Joseph McKeon."

In males and females, there is a definite disparity in terms of reaction to shock. Men are aware of their incapacity to withhold vulgar indecencies and, for that reason, double insulate their homes in order that neighbours are protected from audible obscenities. This is all predictable stuff. It is the silent objection that confuses and confounds. Henrietta's mouth was open, but her voice seemed paralysed. Even the birds on the tree near the kitchen window stopped tweeting, in anticipation of some juicy titbit that might be relayed down the line.

"We don't need to talk about it now," said Lydia, pre-empting her mother's response. "However, you can understand why I told you, rather than Pa."

"Yes, I do," came back the retort. "You want me to tell him, don't you?"

"Well, er, ahhhh, if you think that's best. I would leave it up to you to pick the right time and the right place. You're not bad at that type of thing."

That was it with no further details required. Not being part of the feud, Mummy Dearest couldn't have cared less, but her husband would be a different matter. She would need to bring this out in the open in a public place. Otherwise, he might not restrain himself and she could end up in the emergency ward. The most public place in Ballarat was the largest retail outlet in town, and they even welcomed grumps like you know who.

"What am I doing in the homewares section of Myer? We never go shopping together."

"True, darling, but I need access to your wallet. We're going to purchase a going-away gift for cousin Con and his bride."

"Cousin Con, the teacher?"

"That's right, dear. He's acquired a position at the English Language School in Venice. They're going to live by the Elementary Canal."

"It's called the Grand Canal."

"Whatever," murmured the experienced shopper, deftly handling an outrageously priced Spode serving dish.

"I always think English bone china is the perfect gift, don't you?"

"Whatever," parried the bored wallet carrier, spying an espresso facility, and hoping it wasn't a mirage.

"Let's order coffee while they're wrapping the present."

So, they sat, and while PP simmered, she let loose with a truncated version of what was starting to look like a modern day Shakespearean tragedy: Hamlet without the eggs; King Lear without the humour.

His response provided proof as to the marvels of the human body and what it can withstand. Veins are supposed to accommodate blood flow in a way that is inconspicuous and workmanlike. Peter Pap's veins were trying to leave his body and his eyeballs bulged like Marty Feldman doing a Homer Simpson impression. God knows how his blood pressure maintained stability, but it did, and he made it through the first stages of shock with the addition of a little brandy in his coffee. Henrietta always carried a hip flask in her handbag for crisis situations.

From her point of view, the danger period was behind them, and she now had to convince her husband to ignore his usual approach of fire and brimstone, and strategically overcome the problem as an astute businessman should.

"What do you suggest? I understand she'll want to do the opposite of what we demand, so we don't demand. That much I know about young women, but you know more, Hen. I'm sure you have a solution."

Henrietta's solution proved to be a finishing school in Switzerland. Absence doesn't always make the heart grow fonder and time with the sophisticates in Europe might be just the thing to make her forget her mysterious lover. PP didn't dismiss this possibility but thought Lydia would understand their motive and reject the plan. Nevertheless, he thought the separation solution appealed, which gave him the inclination to advance an idea that would be advantageous to them both. He asked his wife not to divulge the fact that he knew of their daughter's significant other.

Lydia entered the library the next day, prepared for the worst. Her father's proposition caught her unawares.

"Sweetheart, I'm in a jam and I think you can help me. I've just purchased vines in South Australia, but the key people aren't staying on. I need someone to oversee operations and appoint a new winemaker."

"Gee, Pa, I wish I could recommend someone but I only know the folks at Great Western. Have you spoken to Klaus? He would be better informed."

"I have and he tells me you would be up to managing a small producer on your own. He thinks it would be useful experience."

"Me?" spluttered the shocked girl. "You want me to manage the place by myself?"

Touched by her modesty, her father smiled benignly at his daughter. Now that she boasted a business degree, what was holding her back? Experience is always the best teacher.

"Yes, I do and I think you'll make a go of it, but finding the right vigneron will be the key to success. Your first task."

He further explained that he didn't want to rush her but the place was presently unoccupied with a confused workforce wondering who would take over. A decision by the next day would be appreciated. He kissed her tenderly on the way out and recommended some reading material on the shelves, if she wanted to bone up on grape varieties.

Matthew O'Gorman decided to relocate back to South Australia, which was difficult to understand. Being wanted in two states, one would think he would head in the other direction. Even more puzzling was the decision to get a real job and he actively pursued this option at a place with a minimum police presence. The ad in the local paper interested him. They wanted a winemaker and he found himself across the desk from an old friend. Lydia Papadopoulos, now a beautiful young woman, came across as being rather businesslike with her interview technique. Given that he had not spoken a word to her during the kidnapping drama, she would not recognise him or his voice.

"I am impressed with your deep knowledge of our industry but I'm perplexed that you possess no written references. Is there a reason for that?"

"Course there is, darlin' girl. D'you think they're goin' to endorse an expert virtuoso for the competition? They'll be wantin' me for themselves, cause I'm a hot shot. You'll be lucky to get me, to be sure."

When you're continually exposed to blarney, you take these kinds of comment for granted, but Lydia's Gaelic experiences were minimal. Sister Bridget at the convent didn't count because she always told the truth. Nonetheless, the young woman considered herself to be an excellent judge of character and liked the cut of his jib, not that anyone would ever let O'Gorman near one of their seafaring vessels.

"I am committed to seeing a few more applicants, so I'll get back to you. The appointment also includes free accommodation at the gatehouse, if that is suitable," said the interviewer warily. She had no idea of his marital status but finally asked the question, which opened the floodgates. Some people don't like to talk about their divorce, but his rant continued incessantly.

Lydia, keen to get him out the door, called time on his outburst but couldn't stop giggling after he'd gone. Such a character would brighten up the place, no argument. A number of items appeared on her to-do list but this appointment was a priority. She would ask around to discover if anyone in the trade might vouch for him.

They talk about the luck of the Irish and, in this instance, it worked. How the brazen BS artist passed the credentials check is anybody's guess, but he landed the job.

Lydia could find no-one with any knowledge of his new pseudonym. Why didn't she ask another Irishman? They are all familiar with Kevin Barry: patriot, martyr and the subject of a popular song. Without casting aspersions, it was fortunate the schemer put his daughter in charge of a small winery, rather than mismanage a large one.

The thing about wineries is that it takes a number of years before you discover your vigneron is crap. Sure, the former owner of MOG Wines could cut it at harvest time, but the skilled practitioner has to marry yeast and bacteria and know about aroma and acids, tannins and taste, fermentation and fruit, as well as problems like cork taint and rotten egg gas.

At this time, the rotten egg employee had yet to read any back issues of *Wine News*—otherwise he might have read the article on his old company's new complex up north and headed in that direction. For now, the smooth talker envisaged an easy ride with his naive female boss. He was used to having women under him so this would be a new experience.

When Peter Pap learned his daughter had recklessly employed a male of single status, who would reside on the property, he hired a live-in cook/housekeeper, who would feed his child, prepare lunches for the staff, and cater for the occasional corporate function. Madelaine the Mouth would also be the information conduit back to her employer in Victoria. She would ring him every Thursday after Lydia departed the house. Most of the telephone traffic came the other way, including Joe's weekly long-distance calls.

"I just called to say I love you. You're not going to a party tonight, are you?"

In fact, every Saturday afternoon, the whole workforce headed off to the old Noarlunga Hotel to enjoy the change of environment and mix with the local community. Mr. Barry was usually the star of the show, eulogising the merits of Guinness and other concoctions. His definitive pronouncements excited the publican, who occasionally slipped him a free pint.

"Vino is grand for dinner parties, but if yer on the lash and lookin' for real craic, ya need the black brew— the tears of angels. And it's good fer yer health."

This health angle was the tack taken by the Guinness advertising agency, and they systematically hoodwinked prospective customers all around the world, ready to imbibe in this elixir of life, no questions asked. The likes of Brendan Behan and James Joyce supported this medical scientology in a big way—the oil that greased their moving parts.

The fellow's co-workers enjoyed the homespun blarney and found the Irishman to be entertaining, as did Ms. Papadopoulos. All the same, when a difference of opinion became critical, neither would give an inch, and there was many an argument between the two hard-heads. The biggest barney concerned the discovery of cork taint when opening some of the product, ready for market. The new arrival could hardly be held accountable for this Shiraz consignment and he said so.

"Don't you be after lecturin' a son of Ireland about cork. It seems to me yer've got a dodgy supplier. Yer should be balling *him* out. I'm advocatin' screw caps but nobody's listening. Yer need to read-up on the future, young lady."

The young lady in question didn't like being talked-down to, so she let loose.

"You may not be responsible for the tainted corks but you should be paying more attention to the production process and less on the tasting process. If you haven't got the bottle for this job, you should consider your position."

With that, he stormed off to his bachelor's retreat, where the hiss of opening beer bottles indicated his afternoon intentions. He would not be a man anyone should go near for quite some time. Although those in the field didn't hear this quarrel, someone in the house did. Madelaine the Mouth, about to serve lunch, abruptly reduced the table setting by one. She wondered what she should tell PP when they connected later in the afternoon.

The next day, with peace restored, production continued unabated. Quite frankly, the man's shortcomings were often overlooked by Lydia and also by Madelaine; therefore, there was little in the way of criticism finding its way back to Ballarat. Because of this, Daddy Dear had no cause to visit on his frequent interstate trips on brewery business. His girl would travel up town and father and daughter would have a quiet lunch somewhere. Sometimes they would be joined by David Walkden, the brewery's marketing man, who provided assistance whenever required.

People often talk of six degrees of separation. Walkden, a regular at the Presbyterian Church in Archer Street, survived the purge precipitated by Matt the Murderous. Not being a hypocrite, he never took communion and had avoided the wine, laced with anti-freeze. His shrewd investment in a topless bar in Rundle Street might be condemned in religious circles, but you can't ignore a nice little earner, can you? Some of these profits ended-up on the collection plate, so where's the harm?

You can't compare Rundle Street to the Reeperbahn or Ramblas, but it did the best it could. Scantily clad sensual women solicited for sex and peddled soft core solutions to those who liked that kind of thing. Why not pay three times above market price for alcohol, if a dolly bird will sit on your lap? To be critical of such an amusing diversion would be un-Australian.

The Paddy never came to town at the same time as Lydia and, even if he did, it is doubtful they would ever run into each other. Returning to the scene of his crime (one of them) was a bold move and he must have been confident in his almost indescribable disguise. Consider a union between Adolf Hitler and Phyllis Diller on a bad hair day. That little red moustache served as the clincher, but it also made him unforgettable, which is not the intention of a disguise.

The girls of a certain gentlemen's club liked it and they liked him. Unlike many of their patrons, he stifled the stench of booze with the aid of a Fisherman's Friend. This little lozenge boasted a long and illustrious history, and even Margaret Thatcher happily admitted to be a consumer. If the anti-English kidnapper had known that, he may not have become a constant user. If Lydia had concentrated a little harder at her police interview, she may have remembered the distinctive menthol bouquet behind the mouthpiece of that black balaclava.

It is probable that Dave entertained the schmoozer in his establishment, but he never let on to her ladyship. He did drop hints that he thought the Irishman should not be trusted. This man about town maintained a businesslike relationship with his boss's daughter and he knew all about the tough competition. The largest producer in her area, Hardy's Wines, correctly claimed to be a family organisation. Their chairman spent most of his time sailing, but the company was well-run and profitable.

Should a plaque of platitudes be awarded to the pioneer winemakers of South Australia, it ought to go to the Germans who pioneered the industry in that state. Names like Kaiser Stuhl, Leo Buring, Hahndorf, Wolf Blass and Rufus Heidenreich just rolled off the tongue and their banal packaging fooled everyone—Cold Duck, Barossa Pearl, Cherri Pearl, Mardi Gras and Tiffany. These sparkling white or rosé refreshments were as legitimate as Leipzig, so Matt O'Gorman and his toothbrush moustache fitted-in nicely.

Lydia contemplated warnings about her new employee from a number of sources but she ignored them, putting it down to idle gossip and jealousy; that is, until the night of the Long wives.

Vicki and Renée Long were married to two brothers, Robert and Lyle, both staunch members of a swanky golf club at Reynella. On the first Saturday of every month, at about 5 p.m., the girls would meet for a cocktail or two at the Noarlunga Pub, while their husbands finished-off the back nine prior to joining them. As often as not, they would then retire to Papparone's for a pepperoni pizza or pumpkin pasta.

There were a number of reasons why the pendulum of predictability was out of kilter that night. No-one expected Robert to hole-in-one on the fourteenth green, which necessitated the implementation of a time-honoured tradition—you shout the bar. Along with this came the blow-by-blow description of how he did it and everybody needed to hear this. Well, at least people who could appreciate the feat.

The girls appeared at the hostelry on time and planted their pert posteriors on two of the cushion chairs in the lounge bar, not far from the room where Kevin Barry and his friends socialised without Lydia (on this occasion). In what must be described as a design triumph, the passage to the men's loo passed through the Ladies Lounge, and it was here that Ireland's own produced his peculiar brand of repartee for the benefit of the two women in the room. The first walk-by consisted of a humorous aside. The second came with a lame joke and an invitation to join his group. Who could refuse such a smooth operator?

Mrs. Long and her friend Mrs. Long drained their Tequila Sunrises as if there was no tomorrow, and their new chum seemed happy to buy them another. At that time, it was not known whether he might have added something to the mix. Eventually, the drinkers thinned out, with their group down to three and no husbands on the horizon. The publican then called last drinks and started to wipe down the bar, as his customers left. He would later report that he remembered the sound of a car departing from the vicinity of the front door, with a hole in the muffler.

The randy rogue convinced his new friends that a ride on the wild side was warranted, and he bundled them into his conveyance and headed for the beach. If there had been a police vehicle patrolling the road, things might have turned out differently, but resources were thin on the ground. Just a short walk to the dunes and beyond, the choppy waves beckoned. The moon was new, the sea was blue and there was only one thing to do.

"C'mon pretty colleens; last one in is a virgin," bellowed the urger, as he started stripping off his clothes. Renée materialised right behind him but Vicki had trouble stepping out of her dress, being very drunk.

The waves were substantial and the undertow dangerous, but they didn't drown. To cut a long story short, both lasses made it back to the dunes where O'Gorman raped them; or was it consensual? Either way, there was brutality involved. He just left them there, stark naked and exposed to the elements. Sleep came easily until sunrise, when reality set-in, as did the hangover. Vicki awoke first and found the words she never expect to utter.

"Oh my goodness! What happened to us? Where are our clothes?"

Her friend, equally flabbergasted, just pointed to the line of garments dotted along the sand. Fortunately, the low tide saved them from extreme embarrassment.

"I think we went skinny dipping and goodness had nothing to do with it."

Most of the clothing was retrieved, although Renée's bra had been seized by a jellyfish, keen to use one of the cups as a retreat, possibly to hatch eggs. The woman shuddered as she evacuated the guest from her underwear.

In the clear light of day, the girls realised their immediate problem; in fact, two problems—Mr. Lyle Long and Mr. Robert Long.

Explanations would be sought, especially with half the town out looking for them. The brothers arrived at the pub late, so the golfers presumed their women had decamped in anger. But why leave without their cars? They couldn't find the publican, at that time driving his barmaid home, and his wife knew nothing because she retired upstairs early in the evening with a migraine.

After checking their homes, the two men alerted the law, and the desk sergeant posted a missing person's bulletin. Oblivious to this turn of events, the two women conspired to deceive.

"Hey, Vicki, let's not start walking home until we get our story straight. How did we get here with our cars still in town? This is the question everyone will be asking."

"OK, we say we were too pissed to drive so we started to walk home and then decided to go for a swim."

Renée thought this story to be half plausible as the beach was less than four kilometres from the drinking establishment. She certainly couldn't think of a more believable tale. Neither wanted to implicate the third person involved in their drunken frolic, but they did agree that he wasn't a gentleman. Should they be pushed for an explanation, they parted company near the public house, a story they hoped the Irish brute would confirm.

A police patrol found the girls a few kilometres along the Seaford road, and they told their story to the senior constable, before their menfolk came to pick them up. The country copper didn't believe their porky, so he hit them with one of his own.

"In cases like this, we are obliged to take a drug test. I hope you don't mind. It will only take a moment."

No objection. Why would there be? The party girls blamed the tequila for their situation, but, as soon as their spouses arrived, they would be blaming them for not turning up on time. Get off the back-foot, ladies. Parry and thrust is the way to go and women do this better than anybody.

Sunday, a day of rest, saw little talking at the respective Long households. On Monday, the lab report came in with a positive result. Both women had Rohypnol, the date rape drug, in their system. For these uniformed boys, anything more potent than marijuana indicated sophisticated criminal activity. Over the previous twelve months, the lads had recovered at least two lost dogs a week, but it was no longer time to rest on their laurels. A phone call, patched through to headquarters in the big city, gave them the back-up they needed.

HQ sent a man down to investigate the availability of party drugs in the area. The initial investigation would determine who might throw a party in that hamlet of hush, normally a pretty quiet place. He teamed-up with one of the locals to re-interview the victims, but the wives stuck to their story and their partners were no help. In fact, valuable time was wasted listening to Robbie relive the moment he had scored a hole-in-one.

This time, the publican made himself available and managed to put the Paddy in the frame. He explained the status of his customer, provided his address, and didn't fail to mention the car with the dicey muffler. Superman from CID, after committing to a vineyard visit, confounded his young companion by taking the long route.

"Hey, Sarge, you're going in the wrong direction. The winery is the other way."

Superman smiled in the way that superior beings do, and quietly explained what they would do.

"Thank you Constable, for pointing that out, but first we're going to canvas the beachside residents to determine whether they heard a car with a faulty exhaust on Saturday night."

The results came in indicating three positives and one maybe. This information would not be released to the suspect until after he had made his statement. City cops—ahead of the game. That's the way the junior lawman saw it and he was impressed.

With no vehicle outside the gatehouse, the canny copper gunned his car up the long drive and came to a stop beside the building advertising door sales: an elongated sandstone structure with a slate roof. The designers had done their best to replicate a small-scale Bockenheim or Bavarian Schloss and two sets of oak barrels sat side-by-side on either side of a large heavy timber door. Above each barrel, window boxes displayed petunias, fuchsias and snapdragons, and privacy was discreetly assured with white lace café curtains adorning each windowpane. The wooden engraved sign above the door hung from two short chains and declared the place to be *Papadop's Distillery*.

The music seeping through the crack in the window pane was strictly Salzburg and one half-expected the von Trapp family to come marching out of the tasting room. Instead, a young lass with jet black hair and dark eyes emerged.

"Good afternoon, gentlemen. Are you here for some vino for the Policeman's Ball?"

This brought a smile to the faces of both coppers. They realised you only got beer or lemonade at these functions.

The senior officer introduced himself and his underling, and asked Lydia if one of her employees owned a noisy car. She immediately glanced at the purple Peugeot parked by the pear tree near the pump room.

"It's my fault. He's been meaning to get it fixed, but we've been so busy. Surely this is not a hanging offence?"

The long pause that interrogators often use is quite theatrical but sometimes effective. The sergeant followed-up with a non-committal answer and a polite question.

"We're here on another matter, Miss. Do you think you could take us to the owner of the car? You're entitled to be privy to our conversation, should you wish."

Lydia entered the barrel room behind the policemen and couldn't help but see the look of horror in her winemaker's eyes when he recognised the uniforms. Here stood a man who had brushed with the law before, and she suspected a vehicle infringement would be the least of his worries.

Then it all came out: the drinking session that involved her staff; the drugged women; the last person to see them before they disappeared. It would have freaked her out even more if there had been talk of rape or abuse, but the good time gals, who now knew they had been doped, maintained their silence.

The man under pressure responded to the interrogation with a determined denial. He said his goodbyes outside the pub and returned home, no detours. Channel 7 programmed a delayed telecast of the All Ireland hurling final at midnight and O'Gorman claimed to be in his easy chair with a Guinness. Surprise, surprise—the lead investigator was a fan with the ability to harpoon his alibi.

"Yes, I watched the game but I thought the Cats were lucky to win. What did you think?"

Hey man! Who saw this coming? The Irishman, entirely confused, struggled to reply.

"Well, er, ahhh, Sergeant...."

"Murphy," replied the cool cop. "I always watch the game with my dad. He comes from Tipperary and was disappointed, as you might expect. Are you a Kilkenny supporter?"

"I am. Black 'n' Amber forever. We'll take the victory, arseways, whatever."

The policeman pretended not to notice the red blush that had broken out over most of his face and invited the fellow down to the station to make a written statement, and have his Peugeot inspected for roadworthiness. Lydia decided to chip-in for her money's worth.

"Make sure you're back by four o'clock, Kevin. We've got a marketing conference and our man is coming down from Adelaide."

From the moment the two cars left the vineyard, strategies were being formulated. Matthew O'Gorman remained confident there were no witnesses to his night of madness, but stressed about the vehicle spot-check, because the car was stolen. He hoped technology had yet to reach the Fleurieu Peninsula.

In the other car, Bruce Murphy trotted-out his instructions.

"He probably won't volunteer his fingerprints, so wipe clean a cup before we offer him a beverage. Go over the car with a fine tooth comb and look for signs of any female presence. Send details of the number-plate to registry and look up the felon's file of people with Hitler moustaches. Whatever we find, we'll let him return for his four o'clock meeting. Does the station have any tracking devices we can attach to that purple horror of his?"

"Fair go, Sarge. We're not MI5. Why don't we hide a member of the dog squad in the boot?"

All in all, the four-man no-woman substation did well. The person helping them with their enquiries took his coffee with the lot, so they had prints on the cup, spoon and milk jug—the only time anyone had ever seen a milk jug in that particular nick. A hair clip was found in the back seat of the car and the registration resonated with the Vehicle Crime Division. When the fingerprints were processed, alarm bells sounded in Victoria and Inspector Angela Pride was notified.

While this was happening, Lydia decided to conduct her own investigation. Madeleine the Mouth found her rummaging about on the coffee table.

"Maddy, where is the TV guide for last week? Have you dumped the garbage yet? I need it."

The seven-day program guide, subsequently found, verified the hurling event televised between Kilkenny and Tipperary. She breathed a sigh of relief and was almost ready to let it go.

"Do you know any Irish friends who could confirm the result of this match, replayed first thing Sunday morning?"

"Can a dog bark?" answered Madeleine, whose expressions were sometimes bewildering to a girl of Greek origins, accustomed to the forceful and direct answers of her father.

"It will only take a few minutes. Where will you be?"

Lydia advised that she would be in the barrel room, but, naturally, didn't indicate that she would be looking for Rohypnol. On the way out, the alert woman noticed her firearm wasn't in its usual place.

"Madeleine, the shotgun is missing. Where is it?"

"Oh, yes," remarked the faithful retainer. "David Walkden arrived early for your powwow and discovered crows attacking the netting near the road. He's a regular Davy Crockett."

Good old Dave, thought the boss lady. *For a consultant, he sure gives us our money's worth.*

She was aware there were a lot of crows in South Australia, but, if there were pharmaceuticals of any description in her cellar, they would be with all the other chemicals, stored behind the last oak cask in the barn. Fortunately, Lydia found everything in order and wondered if she had overreacted. Madelaine's entrance and announcement put an end to that kind of thinking.

"A clear win to Tipp. Not even close. Did you have money on the match?"

Shit, thought Lydia. Her appointee, the liar, may be a felon. She just had to find that damning drug if it was on her property.

Obviously, those prying policemen saw her man as the prime suspect, and she couldn't anticipate his return much before the meeting in forty minutes. With grim determination, she collected the spare keys and drove down to the roadside residence. It was the first time Lydia had been in the cottage since he moved in and the place was a tip. His choice of reading material didn't alleviate her concerns—*Playboy*; *Penthouse*; *Hustler*; *Screw* and *Swank.* He had a blow-up doll in the bedroom and a blow-up picture of Pierce Brosnan in the toilet (taken before he became James Bond).

Lydia found the drug in the bathroom, just before she heard the sound of a reverberating muffler in the drive. *Oh crap!* The feisty woman chose to put on a brave front, not knowing this was where he would be grabbing when he caught up with her. She came out of the bathroom as he came in the front door.

"What the feckin Jesus might you be doin' in my house, you Greek slut," shouted the cantankerous wild man, still smarting from his time with the Fuzz Muppets. He saw provocation in her eyes and that excited him. She chose to challenge him. It had worked before.

"What do you mean your house? This is my house, you overgrown leprechaun, and I won't abide the use of illicit drugs here or anywhere else on my patch. Is that clear Mr. Barry or whatever your name is?"

It was a stellar performance but not good enough. He stepped forward, grabbed her by the shirt and pulled her towards him. With their faces inches apart, Lydia might have seen her own fear reflected in his eyes if her senses had not been diverted. Not by sight; by smell. The distinctive odour coming from his mouth, she now remembered well—menthol. The realisation of her discovery hit her like nothing before—even when they told her the Easter bunny wasn't real.

Ever the gentleman, the enigma from the Emerald Isle spat in her face and then hurled her across the room towards the fireplace. That might have been the end of it if it weren't for six or seven little words. They slipped out before she could plan her strategic withdrawal into a world where everyone loved her.

"Oh my God! You're Matthew O'Gorman."

This momentous uttering changed everything and she knew it. He came at her and she prodded him in the face with a long stick. Only a fool would use a shillelagh as a fire poker. After all, they are made of wood.

It gave her the precious seconds she needed to avoid his advance. She didn't see the front door as an escape opportunity but that open window in the lounge room provided an alternative. She dived through it and shoulder-rolled to her feet. When you're continually falling off your horse, one gets accustomed to the dynamics of bounce. By the time O'Gorman had exited the cottage, she was well on the way up one of the rows of grapes, almost shielded by the white netting which protected the fruit from predators.

He followed and made ground. The poor girl had lost one of her shoes and she discarded the other. She kept falling over in the uneven ground and tore her clothing, as she tried to avoid him by crawling under the vines to a different row. The torn fabric hanging from the plants just gave him a route map. He caught up to the fleeing female within cooee of the main house and overwhelmed her with his superior strength.

Still, it wouldn't be over until the vat lady stopped screaming. She gouged him in the eye, tried to kick him in the unmentionables, and mouthed at least half-a-dozen Hellenic obscenities. His strong hands enveloped her fragile neck, the gritty girl capitulated, and Nirvana must have been moments away. Then the compelling voice cut through the hazy afternoon stillness: the voice of deliverance.

"Stop it!" shouted Dave Walkden, brandishing Lydia's shotgun. Standing on the verge of row ten, he aimed the blunderbuss at Mr. Barry's chest. The brute released his hold on the girl and she scurried away from his clutches. Some people called him Definitive Davey because he always knew what he was going to do. In this case, he strode forward quickly and unloaded one of the barrels at the killer. The pellets scattered but none of them missed the man, who was badly wounded in the shoulder. Blood splattered all over the left side of his face. He didn't go down but he did stagger—quite a bit. The patriotic protestant came closer and then did what he had always wanted to do. He kneecapped a Fenian bastard.

Angela Pride and Tony McCurry came in on the first available flight and visited O'Gorman in hospital. He had survived surgery and was now under police guard, waiting to be repatriated back to their patch to face charges. The South Australian authorities would have to wait in line to implement their indictments.

With the abolition of the death penalty in Victoria, the killjoy from Kilkenny was sentenced to an extended period of servitude at her Majesty's pleasure, thus denying the taxpayers over the border the opportunity to contribute to his board and keep.

Some months into his incarceration, the Homicide Squad learned that the lavatory bomb and altar poisoning were both "Murder of the Month" items on one of Matthew's go-to sites, and his computer access in prison was withdrawn. He turned to literature and an adventurous publisher accepted his handwritten manuscript, which eventually evolved as the bestseller *How to Murder Your Mum and Get Away with It*. Retailers didn't know whether to list it as fact or fiction, but it sold anyway. Pat Malone was mortified and refused to catalogue the book in her library. Could you blame her?

"Oh my God! You're Matthew O'Gorman."

CHAPTER 19

The first indication of Bing McKeon's health problems arose during the memorial corrobboree that celebrated the passing of Bunji Waku. He blacked out.

The elders were not surprised and surmised he was channelling with the dear departed, as they had been close friends. The sprinkling of fire-dust on his forehead brought him around quickly, and it was left to the first son to slow walk his father back to the homestead. Helen did not attend these kinds of functions as she did not approve of men daubing themselves with paint, except for Marcel Marceau.

The old man didn't want anyone to fret over him, but he did take advice, sitting down in his favourite chair and accepting hot chocolate and a muffin. His wife left the men to talk and phoned Dr. Richardson in Bright for an appointment.

Ian Richardson, an old world doctor, usually prescribed Bex and a good lie-down for everything. This omnipresent analgesic was eventually superseded by the likes of Aspro, Vincent's powder, paracetamol etc., but, in an era of few alternatives, this was the remedy that reigned supreme. Of course, every diagnosis came with a health warning.

"Some people seem to think you don't have a heart, but I can confirm that you do and it is beating regularly. Nevertheless, your blood pressure needs to be kept under constant surveillance, so my advice is simple—slow down. Pass your problems to your sons and take a few days off every week. I want to see you again in three months."

They never met again. The physician died the following week and his send-off remains one of the biggest funerals seen in Bright to this day. This unfortunate circumstance meant the master of Aberdeen missed his three-month checkup, as he didn't trust young people. The replacement doctor readily admitted to being fifty-three years of age.

The next time Bing fell over, it was his own fault. With the prospect of an early winter, the evening dews arrived and the terrain became moist and slippery. He fell while stepping over a fallen log and crashed to the ground, scaring the hell out of the creatures lurking in the undergrowth. One doesn't have a lot of sympathy for animals who lurk, and they often scamper in situation like this. In this instance, the fallen fellow found himself in eye contact with a malicious-looking reptile, contemplating its next move. The yellow-bellied tiger snake is nobody's pet, so Bing groped around for a solid stick because he knew what to expect. The serpent lunged and he performed what cricketers call a "sweep to leg," followed up with his renowned pancake flattener. Not bad for a disabled old fart.

McKeon was not totally disabled but his ankle was badly twisted and he found it difficult to regain his feet. In fact, he fell over repeatedly and ended up crawling towards his back door. His wife, returning from town in her estate car, picked him out in her headlights.

"Oh my God! What have you done to yourself? Are you OK?"

How nice to be on the end of a sympathetic enquiry. The curt reply she received in return was not warranted but typical of the Scotsman's bluster.

"Dinna fuss, woman. I just rolled ma ankle. Help me inside afore we freeze ta death."

It was also typical of the man, not to mention the other part of the adventure—the confrontation with the snake in the grass, which would have consequences of its own.

When evaluating his reptilian adversary, Bing missed out on some key points of interest. For a start, the creature's undeveloped body structure is usually an age indicator. Her cute, innocent eyes also indicated that any forward move would be of a playful nature. Yes, he squashed a young female of tender age and little experience, and you had to believe that wherever the youngster might be, big momma would not be far away.

The parent in question discovered her daughter pancaked on the plateau, and, no doubt, quickly decided that reprisals were in order. The vengeful viper looked towards the homestead and started slithering in that direction.

Old McKeon, not a patient patient, followed Helen's instructions to remain still on the lounge sofa while she bandaged his foot. There would be no climbing the stairs, that night, so he accepted that this would be his domain for a few days, with coffee, tea and light meals delivered at appropriate times.

Being a superwoman, the lady of the house completed the first-aid, and then retired to the kitchen to prepare oven-warmed meals for her children. The ritual of turning-down beds was the next job on her agenda, and she also opened the main window in their bedroom. Fresh air freaks tend to do this kind of thing.

Of course, she had no idea a slithering trespasser was half-way up the drain pipe on her way to the upper floor. As Helen closed the door behind her, a tapered head appeared at the window sill, casting an approving glance at the warm interior. Once inside the room, an even cosier destination presented itself, and the banded beast made its way up the legs of the bed and settled in-between the covers. It was convenient that someone had turned-back the quilt.

Given the drama of the day, an early night for everyone seemed desirable. Edwin played music in his room and Joe was not yet home. Helen slipped her husband a sleeping pill with his hot chocolate and then retired to their bedroom.

The lump under the quilt didn't react to the lamp switch being activated, but when the lady sat down on the bed to remove her shoes, the reptile repositioned to strike.

Not quick enough, Tiger Lady. Helen, now on her feet, unzipped her dress and transferred same to a frilly pink hanger in the couple's walk-in wardrobe. Three-quarters of the closet was designated as my space, another non-negotiable caveat, not stipulated in the wedding vows.

Next came the ablutions, and this is when the slippery serpent decided to leave the comfort of the Laura Ashley printed cottons and follow the body warmth, ignoring the sound reverberations set-off by Joe, as he bounded up the stairs in his usual manner. In the bathroom, the defenceless dame would have nothing but a toothbrush as a weapon. Helen caught sight of the approaching stalker in the mirror and screamed. When she turned around to face the intruder, she screamed even louder.

Joe ran into the room and immediately summed-up the situation. He grabbed the snake by the tail, performed a one-and-a-half pivot, and hurled the bloody thing out the window. It is hard to know whether the viper survived the fall. A low-flying hawk saw an opportunity to feed his family for a week and swooped. Inside the bathroom, the traumatised woman had collapsed into her son's arms and was shaking like a Melbourne tram at full throttle. Never again would she be known as a fresh air freak.

Mum's saviour became a hero to his family and all who heard of his brave intervention. In light of Joseph's recently acquired status, Bing agreed to a man-to-man discussion regarding his son's romance with that Papadopoulos harlot, and tried to be reasonable and realistic, as instructed by his wife.

"So, hoo serious is this relationship? Helen tells me it's been nigh on fer a fair time."

In normal circumstances, this interrogation would be a fearful interview but the old man didn't look so fearful, leaning on a crutch. The lad was also energised by his conciliatory tone.

"We're in love, Dad, but there are complications. Geographically, it's impossible and, career wise, we both understand our family responsibilities. All we need is understanding and approval from you and Peter Pap. You don't have to embrace each other."

The last comment recognised reality because these two would never be putting their arms around each other. The female family adviser told Joe as much and indicated that he should work on small victories which might become big ones over time. This was sound advice because it now appeared you didn't need to be a highlander to come down from your high horse.

"Well, son, all I kin say is "let's meet the lassie," and see where that goes. But, if the Greek beats us in the Caulfield Cup, I might no be merciful."

The initial meet and greet opportunity came with the first heavy snowfall of the year. There's no business like snow business for unpredictability. The season can start anytime from June to August and suppliers like Richie Papworth just sat grim-faced, looking at the skies with their fingers crossed.

Lydia's riding club organised a ski weekend at Falls Creek, which gave her the chance to wheel-by Mt. Beauty, at the bottom of the mountain.

Because Daddy had yet to be approached in the same manner as Bing, secrecy and deception still ruled. The girl rang her mother from Great Western and told her they were going elsewhere. Just a small lie. She arranged a marketing meeting in Melbourne on the Friday morning, and then boarded the train to be picked-up by Joe at Wodonga. The family dinner preceded their journey to the peak the following day, to ski with her friends for the rest of the weekend.

The most excited person around the table was Edwin. He gave up his room for the young girl and left a no-snake guarantee on his bureau. Just about everybody in town had heard of Joe's exploits, but it is often the sibling who's first to take the Mickey. Isn't that what brothers are for?

The least nervous person proved to be Lydia, and it is fair to say she charmed Helen and Ed instantly. Bing was particularly circumspect and only jettisoned his cautious demeanour when the brandy pudding arrived, his favourite. The family considered inviting Margaret Dow and her husband but due to their horseback rivalry, they didn't think it was a good idea. Nor did anyone want the conversation centred on equestrian tittle-tattle. Tactical thoroughbred talk would be the way to go if they wanted to melt the heart of the man they said didn't have a heart. It seemed to work.

A few weeks after the veil of secrecy lifted at Aberdeen, a similar breakthrough came to pass in Ballarat, although Peter and Henrietta didn't get to press the flesh with Joe. At that time, Lydia remained unaware her parents knew of the love affair but had started to consider the possibility on the back of her father's strange behaviour.

Papadopoulos was under pressure. The beer baron from Western Australia had moved his brands into Victoria and they were taking market share. The northern brewers were also broadening their horizons. Until then, Victorians would never let a Sydney brew touch their lips. This was interstate rivalry at its best and, of course, that mob didn't even drink from the same size glasses. The upcoming change of season would also be the preamble to the Spring Racing Carnival, a period which isn't always easy on the nerves. Fortunately, Norm Jones provided some encouraging news, which lessened the doom and gloom associated with Zorba's injury.

"The filly we held back, Delilah, has really blossomed and is a realistic chance in the Thousand Guineas."

This was good news but not an immediate priority. Peter Pap had to orchestrate the swap of managers between states in order to bring Lydia back to Great Western. He hadn't lost sight of the reason he banished his daughter in the first place: to separate her from her lover. The new plan to offer her an alternative came completely from left field.

Completely unannounced, Daddy started dropping-by the vineyard with young men in tow, ostensibly for a winery tour. They were usually sons of Greek merchants or confreres of some sort and, as often as not, quite presentable. Most of them were spoiled brats.

One day he turned-up with Richard, a youngish third generation Brit, and a self-made man. He had started a camping/adventure retail outlet in York and now controlled the franchise in all Commonwealth countries. He wasn't backward in coming forward.

"This is the winter of our discount tents, and I'm putting together a team to trek Nepal. You father tells me you are an adventurous spirit. Would you like to join us for the trip? It will be tough but a lot of fun."

In normal circumstances, the fellow might have appealed to the babe with the adventurous spirit, being tall, broad-shouldered and good-looking. His intense blue eyes could be categorised as trustworthy, and the mop of curly brown hair on his head looked as if it might defy the baldness bandit for quite some time. However, being an instrument of her father's guile and duplicity disqualified the chap from consideration. The mischievous miss therefore made it difficult for him.

"It sounds terribly exciting, but I would have to bring my horse, Souvlaki. We go everywhere together."

The man was flummoxed and his reply interrupted by his unexpected stuttering. The explanation that they had already hired two mountain yaks sounded weak. The reality of quarantine and cost would make such a trip impossible for an equine partner, as Lydia knew full well. So did her father, who could only meekly progress the tour.

"Richard, let me show you our cellars. We only use imported oak for our barrels."

In the aftermath of this latest match-making episode, Lydia began to suspect her father might be more informed than she realised. There was only one way to find out. She collected a bottle of the winery's most potent vintage and called on her mother. A few glasses of this brutal beverage and anyone would become a motormouth.

So, the truth came out, and the girl was grateful she had received the news in the kitchen, rather than the library. It would be up to Henrietta to explain to her spouse that she let the cat out of the bag. The remains of the alcohol would sustain her through that particular confrontation.

CHAPTER 20

In Australia, all thoroughbred horses celebrate their birthday on 1 August. It's not a big deal. Gifts are nothing more than a carrot with breakfast, provided by their faithful carer, the strapper who has groomed the beast on a daily basis, ever since the animal entered the stable as a precocious two year-old. Delilah, now three and a real sweetie, gave her handlers no trouble in the yard and always hit the grass running in her workouts. In fact, some of her times proved to be sensational. Her trainer's confidence in her was not misplaced, and he sent reports to Peter Pap on a regular basis, as he did with all his horses. However, this one was dear to his heart and a worthy replacement for Zorba the Geek.

She didn't win her first outing but rattled home to finish fourth over 1200 metres, giving her fans cause for optimism. A Group 1 event over 1600 metres would be targeted, with two hit-outs beforehand, to have her fit and primed for the classic renewal. Jones was beaming when he reported the filly to be in top shape and eating-up—always an excellent sign.

"I can't see her being beaten in the lead-up races. Yesterday topped her off nicely and we might get fair odds at her next start. For some reason, the bookies seem to undervalue a fourth placing."

This was certainly the case through the eyes of a punter named Fingers McIntosh, who maintained a questionable relationship with some bookmakers and certain jockeys. He acquired his nom de plume in the early days, as a pickpocket, before he graduated into burglary, arson and personal injury. The slightly-built fellow was easy to spot in the betting ring, given his liking for colourful clothing. Imagine Frank Sinatra in a Hawaiian shirt. When Fingers decided to support a neddy, it usually won.

He gambled against Delilah at her next start and bribed everyone but the horse. Unfortunately, the jock couldn't restrain the animal and she romped home by three lengths, giving no indication that she was sorry for the financial pain she caused.

Retribution is a rather silly response, isn't it? The deed is done and better to move on and wait for another day. McIntosh didn't feel that way. A reputation, no matter how tawdry, should never be tarnished by the action or lack of action of the little people.

They found Delilah's jockey at the bottom of the trash chute at the Southern Cross Hotel. Fortunately, he had been booked into a second storey room and survived the fall. Nevertheless, two broken legs would keep him away from his chosen profession for quite some time. The discovery at Peter Pap's property, two days later, proved far more disturbing, and the magnate's mood took a turn for the worse.

While doing his rounds, Norm Jones came across a horse carcase lying in Delilah's paddock. It was Delilah, shot in the head and left for the birds. He discovered a live Murray cod flapping away on her prostrate body. Only a Mafia aficionado would understand the significance of this message and Mr. McIntosh did watch a lot of gangster movies. Peter Pap, when he heard the news, went ballistic and spoke to God for the first time in many years.

"Why, why, why Delilah? Why not one of my lessor horses? You've taken Zorba from me and now this. What have I ever done to you?"

Whoa, Pete; hang on there. Don't you remember that creek-bed incident all those years ago? That little girl you hit—her name was Mary. She wasn't the mother of Christ but named in her honour. These things resonate with those above, and there's no statute of limitations in heaven.

Rage can sometimes affect objective thinking, but Peter Papadopoulos, once he calmed down, vowed to identify the killer of his horse, and then react accordingly. Sam Tromans had been rather idle since his child-minding days with Lydia, but loomed large as the perfect man for the task. PP brought him down from the country and set the odd-job fellow up at the Victoria Club, money being no object. His expense account included a budget for bribes.

Men-only clubs: Melbourne is rich with these segregated bastions of male bonding. Get away from the missus and the kids and spend quality time networking with business associates, or just chew the fat in the bar or billiard room. Each of these fraternities attracts a certain demographic and the Victoria Club attracted sportsmen, particularly those in the racing community. The bookmakers met there every Monday for their settling.

This oasis of testosterone was Bing McKeon's home away from home, but he had never met Tromans or Fingers McIntosh, currently under suspension for failure to pay his dues. In the aftermath of the Delilah incident, it was a wonder he didn't receive a life ban. Everyone knew and understood what had transpired because, although jockeys are small, they have big mouths. Because of his generous stipend and living arrangements, Tromans was in no hurry to confirm the name of the culprit to Peter Pap. However, he located the low-life and monitored his movements over a number of days, thus making it easy for those who would deliver the *coup-de-grâce*.

The thugs who accepted this responsibility were two heavies from the milling room at PP's city brewery. They opted for baseball bats and let loose on Fingers when he exited his local pub. They broke his arms and legs and stuffed a fillet of whiting in his mouth, hoping he would now understand what it was like sleeping with the fishes. The poor chap didn't drown because someone saw him floating in the Yarra River and called the emergency number. It is legend that he never placed another bet and, late in life, became a Buddhist. He donated his Hawaiian shirts to the Salvation Army.

When Peter Pap coerced members of his work-force into extra-curricular activities, it was the first time he had crossed the line since that affair in Mt. Beauty. With his moral compass pointing south, he now became a sinister servant of Satan—not that it bothered him. Inspired by his new-found notoriety, he started smoking cigars and cursed regularly. He also joined a gentlemen's club, run by mysterious conman Mal Lovell and his partner Anna Wood, an adventurous gal who always would when others wouldn't. The painted rose now supervised the working girls and her man watered the whisky. PP played cards and encouraged beautiful women to be provocative.

The club didn't advertise for persons of dubious reputation but they materialised out of the Melbourne mist, eager to participate in the pleasurable activities available. Some of these people might be described as racetrack touts. It didn't take Peter Pap long to determine what some of them would do for money, and thus the germ of an idea started to form in his mind. He would nobble Bing McKeon's horse in their forthcoming challenge, which would take place on the opening day of the Caulfield carnival.

The loss of Delilah had seen his prospects diminish in the fillies' event, but his colt Thunderball attracted punters in The Guineas. Geoff Murphy's champion, Grosvenor, deserved to be favourite, but the McKeon entry, Aberdeen Angus, was the obvious danger. Princess Alexandra asked the Governor-General to wager twenty pounds on the beast, not knowing there was a nobbler hovering. However, the instigator of the nobble would see this as a one-off scuttle, as he was confident Brewery Boy would beat McKeon's Gurner's Lane the following week.

It is difficult to interfere with a starter prior to a classic event. Guards are often posted outside the stables, especially at night, and drug testing can be undertaken at any time. Being a brewer, Papadopoulos employed chemists who could concoct a heady mixture, as could his vet, who may or may not be party to any conspiracy.

In the end, PP left it to Bruce Halligan, the tout, to organise the sting and arranged to pay his fee in another country. He would also deny knowing the shady character, as mutually agreed.

This particular fixer would never be a candidate for Mensa, the oldest IQ society in the world, but he could have done better than he did. He bribed the strapper to add two bottles of ouzo to Angus's water bucket, with the result that the colt headed to the barrier in a state of euphoria. He found it difficult to enter his allocated starting gate and, once there, made a pass at the horse in the next stall. The stewards should have picked-up on this, because he had never been involved in a same-sex relationship in the past.

The field jumped as one. Aberdeen Angus held his position for the first 600 metres but, once in the straight, started to wander all over the track, losing valuable ground. The wayward wanderer returned to the enclosure with a hangover and threw-up over the chief steward, who immediately initiated an enquiry. This didn't please Peter Pap, already in a depressed state as Thunderball had been donkey-licked by Grosvenor. He lost money and his self-belief.

With one great race after another, there would be little time for recrimination, as the feuding tycoons had both accepted for the Caulfield

Cup, to be held later that week. Brewery Boy left Gurner's Lane behind in the VRC Derby but the latter horse excelled in the St. Leger Stakes. Neither was fancied behind the exciting three year-old Grosvenor, taking all before him.

Lydia identified this occasion as the ideal time to introduce Joe to her father, but timing would be of the essence. Pre-race he would be nervous and afterwards he would be deliriously happy or grumpy.

She chose his most vulnerable state (nervous) and descended on her parents as they picked at their cheese and greens in the Members Dining Room. Two extra chairs were purloined from another table, and Joe found himself staring into two expressionless eyes, almost concealed behind a whiff of cigar smoke. Henrietta took it upon herself to start the conversation.

"I believe your father also has an interest in the main race. How exciting. Please excuse Peter. He gets a bit tense on these occasions."

"I understand, Mrs. Papadopoulos. My dad is the same, but it's easier when you are long odds. Our trainer also has the favourite, so we're only hoping."

With the small talk over, the youngsters avoided any awkward silence by retreating to the Young Members area. The club always puts on a hospitality marquee for the new generation, in the hope they will become players for life. All the men arrive with folded form guides in their pocket, and the girls parade around in their fashionable hats, sipping sparkling wine, thinking it is Champagne. Some of them would have spent $200 on their outfit, and brought along $5 in their purse to invest on a grey horse, if it winked at them.

With eighteen runners under starter's orders, connections are heavy on the ground and the mounting yard is always congested. Throw in the media and club officials and you know what the Myer sales on Boxing Day are like. It was hard to believe Peter Pap and Bing McKeon stood only a few metres apart but they would not see each other. Both were concentrating on the trainer's final instructions to their respective jockeys, the only dudes showing some degree of tranquillity. They had been through this scenario many times before.

The horses slowly circled the mounting yard, some on their toes while others were thinking about a last minute crap. Every animal appeared to be race-fit and conditioned to the moment. It would be a tough 2400 metres for both horse and jockey and only the fittest and fastest would be still there when the whips were cracking.

The race started at a furious pace. It always does. Those with bad barrier draws tried to position themselves nearer to the rails but only some made it. One heartless hoop saw a fancied runner three wide with no cover and grinned maliciously. He is such a sweet boy in the jockeys' room.

Peter Pap always watches from the owners' enclosure in the grandstand but, because of his natural height, Bing is comfortable at ground level, where he can hear the laboured breathing of the steeds as they stretch out past the winning post the first time. If any of them need to call for hydration, this is when it happens. The Scot only had eyes for Gurner's Lane and kiwi jock Brent Thompson, whose reputation as a big-race rider knew no bounds. Trainer Geoff Murphy didn't know where to look, as he saddled-up three live chances in the field. Tommy Smith sent out four of his best, including Brewery Boy.

There is no doubt the heavy track took its toll on some of the fancied runners, who floundering in the going when Gurner's Lane swept to the front and ran away from them all to win by five lengths. Murphy's other unfancied runner came in second and Brewery Boy finished second last. The TV cameras focused on the excited owners as they escorted the victor back to the winner's stall. Someone reported a fire in the grandstand but it was only the steam escaping from Peter Pap's ears. To be beaten was one thing, but to see his mortal enemy on the victory dais didn't sit well with the grumpy Greek. He reached for his heart pills.

Lydia wisely refused the invitation to celebrate with the successful connections, and thanked her lucky stars that she had initiated introductions before the race. Begging-off a ride home with the folks, she returned to the Young Members marquee, where the lady re-discovered the joys of inebriation.

Matthew O'Gorman saw the race from the recreation room at Pentridge Prison. For some reason, he now bet on his antagonist's horses and twenty cigarettes to one seemed a generous offer from the prison bookie. Ciggies were the currency of custody in Stoney Lonesome and the mad bomber was enjoying such a great run, he might expect to leave the penitentiary much earlier than expected—in a coffin.

The jailhouse punter didn't having a good time of it in the pen. The residents didn't like crimes against young people and his flippant wisecracks would not have endeared him to his fellow prisoners. He was beaten-up a number of times by the inmates and these were not your common or garden criminals. Herb Lavender, in the middle of a twenty-year stretch for killing his wife, tormented the newbies, as did Basil Vine, a creepy stalker with a history of molesting women. Bud Weiser, the American, maimed three people with a broken beer bottle. Each of these rogues had a go at O'Gorman, but none of them could claim responsibility for his death. This was down to a banged-up writer, who should have been incarcerated elsewhere, as he was certifiable.

The screws always like to dispense work orders to prisoners, according to their experience. O'Gorman should have been shunted-off to the prison garden because of his agricultural background. Sure, they didn't maintain a vineyard and the administration didn't know about the still, but this seemed to be an appropriate substitute. No siree! They put him in the library because of his wife's literary experience. Go figure. The author Whip Hooley (not his real name), who might have expected library duties, found himself with the latrine detail. That's probably easier to understand.

Hooley was doing twenty-five years with time off for good behaviour, but he didn't get any time off. He was convicted of murdering a critic, which hardly rates that kind of sentence, but there were after-the-fact considerations. He cut-up the body of the victim and mailed the package to Dr. Hannibal Lecter, care of a Hollywood studio. The judge didn't think this reason enough to send him to the nuthouse.

When O'Gorman told the scribe that the governor had censored his reading material, it was shoot the messenger time, except he didn't shoot the librarian. He stabbed the hapless Irishman with the remains of his dinner. T-bone steaks have since been taken off the menu at all Victorian prisons, because it is relatively simple to sharpen the end of the bone to produce a menacing dagger. The finger grip at the other end is so convenient; it makes one wonder why this weapon is not used more often.

Matthew hovered between life and death for all of seven minutes, time enough to realise the man who stabbed him was in charge of the toilets. He wondered if he knew how to make a lavatory bomb. This was his last thought.

CHAPTER 21

The Spring Racing Carnival is an exciting time for everyone connected with the sport of kings and they salivate when Cup Week arrives. Peter Papadopoulos instructed his brewery people to set-up a corporate tent which would be the envy of all. To this end, they imported a fellow who would show guests how to open a bottle of Champagne with a sword. He called it Sabrage and this would probably be his last performance, as he only had two fingers on his left hand.

The folks at Aberdeen were also excited. Bing and Joe hired their top hats and stuffed shirts and delighted in the fact that Helen would attend, albeit in the Nursery Carpark as a guest of Chris and Margaret Dow. Edwin would be her escort.

The club provides two lawn enclosures outside the entrance gates and members rock-up in their vehicles with fold-up chairs, card tables and chilled booze. The trunk goes up and out comes the pâté, chicken sandwiches, strawberries and cheese platters. Tables can be enhanced with lace cloths and flower arrangements and usually are. The first Champagne cork is popped before noon, and coffee is not required until after the last race.

It is pertinent to mention that the 1982 version of this activity was called a picnic. The Bedouin tents followed and, in later years, marketing moguls micro-managed a mini-Manhattan in the Birdcage area and invited people who, at the very least, were minor celebrities or soap stars. These diabolical once-a-year dabblers would not be seen dead near a horse, but are always available for a TV interview.

The horsey participants get involved long before game-day and the media, conscious that everyone wants to be part of the action, provide essential commentary on an on-going basis. In an effort to maintain the hype, they waxed lyrical about the Sydney wonder horse Kingston Town, having just won his third Cox Plate. He appeared to be a shoo-in for the Melbourne Cup. The jockey, once his seating arrangement was confirmed, couldn't wait to get home and tell his partner.

"Hi, honey, I've got two words for you—Kingston Town."

"Get out of here!" screamed the lady. "I love Jamaica. When are we going?"

OK, so everyone isn't a nailed-to-the-wall supporter, but you can't get away from the fact that a public holiday is convened, and the whole country is in lockdown for just over three minutes on the first Tuesday in November. Not that this is the start and finish of it all. There are two race days to follow and one before, plus the Derby Eve Ball. In a classic act of patriarchal logistics, Bing, Helen, Ed, Joe and Lydia attended the ball, while Henrietta sponsored a soiree at their townhouse. The hostess and her husband introduced their daughter to the assembled guests before Joe arrived and whisked her away to the gala event.

You can't argue with the simplicity of black and white, can you? All the male simpletons wore penguin suits but couldn't compete with the female alternative. The apparition that was Lydia stunned everybody. Her jet black hair cascaded over her shoulders and contrasted with her eye-popping sleeveless floor length ball gown: white satin and lace, embellished with beading and sequins. Consider the collective sigh from jealous women as she entered the ballroom, and salacious drooling from their partners. Helen was thrilled, Bing was stunned, and Joe considered himself to be very lucky. The first glass of bubbly went down a treat for all concerned.

It was no surprise to hear Lydia announced as the Belle of the Ball and called to the stage to receive her sash. Betty Brocade, the renowned couturier, made the judgement and spearheaded the presentation. Unfortunately, the girl never felt the cold silk around her shoulder. The commotion came from stage left and at first the audience thought it to be part of the act. A noisy group of people pranced into view, all sporting horses' heads, while shouting and screaming. They carried derogatory messages on their placards and some scattered firecrackers around the legs of the social committee, in order to confuse.

The reality was that they represented HURT (Humans Unimpressed with Racing and Trotting), an animal liberation protest group bent on harassing the equine community. Their aim, to put an end to horse racing in general and hurdling in particular, would never influence the government, but they did received tacit approval for their ongoing protests, which included street demonstrations, graffiti and picketing events with TV coverage.

Their leader, Emile Lestrange, boasted a background of subversive dissent against authority, church, big business, the military and McDonalds, and he was as litigious as a lawyer who could lip-read. His followers were easily led and Carl James was one of these. He embraced the dirty jobs others rejected.

In this instance, Carl bounced over the boards with a bucket of sheep's blood and threw it over Lydia. It was difficult to correlate the welfare of animals and the sheep with its throat cut, but no-one would deny the theatrical nature of the protest. However, was this the only way they could articulate their crimson comment? What's wrong with red paint?

"You've got blood on your hands, people of racing!" shouted the cheeky youth, as he dropped the bucket and ran for the exit.

The girl's hands were the only body part he missed. She screamed and tried to brush the sticky mess off her white dress. The gore stained her olive skin and matted in her hair. Betty Brocade fainted and the MC remained riveted to the floorboards, unable to do anything. The security people weren't much help either and arrived after the group had bolted. Their blue van departed the carpark at speed but not before someone noted their number plate.

The next morning, Lydia found herself on the front page of all the Melbourne dailies, delivered by Sam Tromans as the family tried to enjoy breakfast. His boss called him as soon as he heard of the atrocity committed against his daughter, and the two men retired to the garden, where Peter Pap explained succinctly what reprisals were required.

"Sam, I'm going to leave this to you. You know who to contact and who to target, but I don't want them killed. I want them to be able to reflect on their actions every day for the rest of their life."

That was it. No more. No less. In one minute, the family fixer had been promoted to hanging judge, a position way above his pay scale. He figured there would be appropriate financial compensation, so he considered his brief and deliberated on how many of the perpetrators he should punish: Carl James, certainly, and Emile Lestrange, for sure. Perhaps he would be lenient with the others, as they would be so scared, they might retire from the protesting business.

Mr. Lestrange was not scared or repentant and hardly grieved for the girl involved in the ballroom fiasco. He knew of her father, although he was not aware of his penchant for punitive justice. The activist regrouped his followers for their Derby Day picket outside Flemington's front gate and the blue van was parked nearby. Without their horse heads, how would anyone recognise them as the people who stormed the stage?

How indeed! That is why at least twenty journalists hovered around the picket line, and Emile rejoiced in the opportunity to espouse his demands and subject them to his usual tirade. He was a little perplexed that the only questions they asked related to Lydia Papadopoulos and her father.

"Tell us, Mr. Lestrange," said one reporter, "did you realise, last night, that you attacked the daughter of the brewery magnate?"

Of course, the man who often manipulated the media wasn't going to fall into the trap of 'fessing-up to the attack. By the same token, he would not deny it.

The press and TV people, still covering the front-gate demonstration, missed the vehicle with the Papadopoulos family aboard. Peter could see the throng through the slit in his window and noticed Sam Tromans in the background, walking around a blue van.

Sam was a thorough investigator with friends in strategic positions, including the media and the police. Already he possessed photographs of the group on stage and on the picket line. He knew the name and address of the owner of the auto (Emile Lestrange) and had identified Carl James, the young guy with the tattoo on his right wrist. Both of these people he photographed from all angles. You never want a hit man to target the innocent by mistake.

Cruelty to animals has always been a hot topic with those outside the racing game. Those inside claim their integrity is without blemish, although in 1966 the brother of two trainers carried a shotgun to the races and threatened to shoot any jockey who whipped his horse. It is believed some bookmakers made similar threats for different reasons. The thing about threats and malicious intent is that sometimes you just pick the wrong person. Would anyone have admonished Al Capone or any of his children?

No-one would ever put Peter Pap in that category but consider the possibility that he thought he was in that league. The two heavies he retained for reprisal work never rejected a job, and Sam Tromans impressed on them that the executive direction was not to inflict fatal injuries. Other than that, he failed to be specific in his instructions, which was bad news for the intended victims.

The bloodbath took place at a rented miner's cottage in Carlton. Carl James, requiring a rest after two days of protest, didn't join his two flatmates at the pub. When they returned home at 11 p.m., they found him floating in a bath full of blood. They observed his crushed fingers but couldn't see where the red stuff was coming from. The paramedics arrived quickly and rushed him off to Emergency Central. As soon as the doctors became aware of the extent of his injuries, they called the police.

The flatmates provided background and details of the HURT protest came to light. At this time, the investigators thought a vet might be their perp because the victim had been gelded.

Emile Lestrange lived with two young women in Kensington. Trish and Penny, the artists who decorated the incisive placards carried by the protesters, were so occupied when the call came through from the hospital advising of the lad's injuries. A devious reporter had established rapport with one of the girls and given her a heads-up, hoping he would get a knees-up in return.

With the man of the house not at home, the frightened females didn't know what to do. The demonstration on Cup Day was supposed to be their biggest yet, but neither of them signed-on for this kind of angst. Making an executive decision, Penny phoned some of the others and told them to pass the word around that the protest had been cancelled. They then packed a few essentials into Trish's car and headed for Sydney. Lestrange arrived home an hour later, to be met by Biffo and Bozo, the hit men. It was the worst day of his life.

You have to respect people who can work within the parameters of their brief and still be creative. The brutes from the brewery repeated the punishment handed-out to the youngster and also cut out Emile's tongue. Other than that, he was fine. They dumped him in a horse trough down the road and retired to an ale house frequented by members of the meat trade. In that way, the blood on their clothes would be inconspicuous.

Sam Tromans subsequently supplied a mission accomplished report to PP, and requested permission to return home to his loved ones. The request was duly granted. Peter Pap was glad he could now concentrate on the races, and hoped Lydia would not suffer any post-traumatic stress from the unfortunate episode.

The morning papers were all gung-ho for Kingston Town at Flemington and even Tommy Smith could not give Peter a leg-up for Brewery Boy. He trained both of them, so he should have known. God forbid that McKeon's galloper should win. That really would be a kick in the guts. The man only owned a minor share but winning the Melbourne Cup meant bragging rights. The Caulfield Cup winner displayed impeccable staying credentials and every starter had a weight advantage over Kingston Town—not the favourite but definitely the people's choice.

PP received his first thrill when Brewery Boy pulled its way to the head of the field at the finishing post the first time and made the running. The King was well placed but Gurner's Lane didn't start well, buried in the ruck out back. Lydia was buried in the ruck at the Champagne Bar and happy to have a foot in both camps. She forgot her promise to go easy on the bubbles and was drinking like a sailor in a salt mine. Thinking of all the possible connotations of the day, a win by her father would be the best option, as he possessed the worst temper. As she looked at the television and recognised Brewery Boy as the horse striding boldly out in front, there was a moment when she thought she may be right. Only a moment!

Bing McKeon fixed his eye on his horse at the tail of the field on the rails: an impossible situation. The roar he heard from the grandstand could only mean one thing—Kingston Town had hit the front. But was it too soon?

Joe thought so, as did Ed. The Flemington straight is a long way home and when you carry 59 kg it is even longer. Nevertheless, the champion continued to fight off all challengers and Tommy Smith was jumping around like a jack rabbit. The jockey looked confident but that's because he didn't have a rear-view mirror. Gurner's Lane made an incredible run from the rear, only going around one horse. With scintillating speed he ate up the ground and descended on the people's choice with fifty metres to go. It was a brave effort by the champ, but the fast lane was on the rails and the hero hoop was scraping the paint, which is a racing expression indicating the fastest way home.

The winning jockey Len Dittman took it all in his stride, and nonchalantly relived the experience with the TV front man. The owners, including Bing McKeon, cavorted around the mounting yard and played pass the parcel with the three-handled gold cup. Joy and happiness proved to be the order of the day, and only Peter Papadopoulos and all the other losers failed to join the celebration. In fact, it was all too much for the defeated tycoon and he collapsed in his corporate tent. Worried associates helped transfer him to the on-course medical facility, where he became reacquainted with his star-turn, the Sabrage swordsman. The chap had chopped-off another finger.

The winner's celebration at the Southern Cross Hotel proved a squeeze, with about five hundred instant friends squashed into the function room. Nevertheless, tradition demanded that this venue be the centre for celebration. This tradition only went back as far as the sixties, when this garish American dream rose from the ashes of the Eastern Market. The light blue mosaic panels of the eleven storey building covered a whole block and stood out from the bluestone marvels already in place, courtesy of convict ancestors. It was kitsch, slightly embarrassing but very popular. The Beatles stayed there, as did Judy Garland, Rock Hudson and John Wayne. Now you could add the McKeon family to the list. Andrew, the syndicate boss, made a speech and they all drank from the Loving Cup. It was Christmas in November.

Lydia missed the party but her place was with her father, bedside at St. Vincent's Hospital. The medics diagnosed a heart attack but they thought he would recover, as long as he slowed down. The doctors decreed no visitors other than family, so the two waiting detectives in the hall retreated to headquarters. There would be another day to question him regarding the savage injuries to the HURT protesters.

The VRC Oaks, run two days after The Cup, is traditionally ladies day, sometimes drawing a crowd of up to 100,000 punters, dressed to the nines. The main event is often overshadowed by the Fashions on the Field contest, which can be brutal but invigorating, nonetheless. Helen McKeon would not be there, due to her lack of ability to see out a week of solid partying. Those with no stamina piled into Chris Dow's vehicle and headed home.

The first few weeks of November are magic in the mountains. The air is crisp and fresh and the spring rains cleanse and purify. As Helen gazed out of the car window on the last leg of their journey, she observed the spread of wildflowers by the side of the road, beautiful and abundant. Certainly, the roses at Flemington were stunning, if not spectacular, but a team of gardeners always conspired to help them bloom on cue.

This vegetation, resplendent in its natural environment, required no cultivation, no artificial fertiliser, and no marauders with secateurs. It was an emotional moment for Helen. With no interrupting bluster from her husband, she meditated on what might be and what might have been. The flowers remained resplendent and resilient until the Bright turn-off, when the huge poplar trees came into their own and dominated the landscape. If there was a wise old owl up there somewhere, he or she would probably recognise Helen's retreat into nostalgia as a sign of reflective reminiscence, not uncommon among the older generation.

The ageing process, now starting to take hold of the senior residents of Aberdeen, was most obvious with Bing. He kept racking-up doctors' visits and his memory lapses became commonplace. Helen's recollections became very much part and parcel of her meditative moments, and she wondered if she should record them for posterity. After all, her husband's pioneering efforts in opening-up the high country were not insignificant. Sure, he had been well-rewarded and his family would benefit from his legacy, but she hoped he would be remembered for more than the Melbourne Cup or worse still, as the owner of MOG Wines.

With these thoughts in mind, Helen positively decided to write her memoirs and committed to sharing her time between her manuscript and the maintenance of her man. Bing's illness would progress, she was sure of that, and he must be made as comfortable as possible in the home that he had built for his family. People with dementia can handle the past quite effectively. It's the previous five minutes you have to worry about. There was still time for the Scottish laird to seek solace in his memories.

The passengers in the limousine heading for Ballarat were also in a reflective mood. Peter Pap had been discharged from hospital on the proviso that he didn't listen to any horse races for the next few days. This was a big ask and both Henrietta and Lydia would stand guard over all listening devices for the duration. Somebody suggested a walk around the paddocks might be good for his blood pressure. The horses had never heard of Bing McKeon.

Lydia had been looking forward to ladies day with her favourite man, as The Cup aftermath had been a little flat, given the situation with her father. Oaks Day always produces an array of beautiful women, all trying to outdo each other with outfits that defied the laws of imagination. The Champagne Bar was the place to be, and you never met a friendlier bunch of biddies. Just ask anyone.

As usual, eight races would be run and won, mostly by a conveyance carrying someone's lucky number or favourite colour. The ladies have other reasons for supporting various contestants and you won't find these strategies in the form guide. Nor are the bookmakers interested in the logic behind female investment. None of them have lost at this meeting for thirty-five years.

Bing was up for the challenge and managed to remain sober and appreciate the equine competition. Not so Joe. In the absence of his beloved, he hooked-up with a charmer named Beth Babcock, and they participated in a lamentable rain dance on the lawn, when the precipitation came, as it often does on Oaks Day. It was a shame to see all those fancy frocks, wet and waterlogged, with their owners slopping around in the mud, carrying their high heels. To make matters worse, the TV people recorded the most shameful antics, which put Joe and the girl in the picture. Lydia saw it all on the television in the library. Thankfully, PP walked the property in ignorance.

Seeing her fiancé enjoying himself in the company of another woman was a reminder that perhaps she might be taking him for granted, or was the Greek goddess just a little jealous? Her thoughts and considerations proved time-consuming and she forgot all about her father. Henrietta raised the alarm. PP hadn't returned from his walk and the light was fading fast.

They collected torches and commandeered the runabout. With no visual evidence of his whereabouts, the women set-off for the perimeter of their holding, which is shielded by rows of trees in certain parts. They found the disorientated landowner in the penultimate paddock by the north track, the field allocated for horses recuperating from injury.

Peter Pap was talking to himself and was incomprehensible. Even the horses had limped-off to the other end of the paddock in bewilderment. The man was rambling-on, and totally confused. He didn't seem to recognise Henrietta and Lydia.

"No way, why, bastard, bastard, Sassenach shit-kicker, Scottish git— lucky, lucky, lucky."

Mother and daughter looked at each other with alarm. PP was losing his marbles, and they guessed the Melbourne Cup result had precipitated his decline. First the heart attack and now this. Lydia tried to placate her father.

"Pa, calm down. It was only a horse race. We'll get over it."

The two women managed to steer Peter through the gate and onto the runabout. Throughout dinner he was uncommunicative and for three days remained morose and sullen, frequently mumbling and muttering. Henrietta rang his secretary at the brewery and urged them to get by without him for a week or so. She saw no need to seek medical advice, and felt encouraged when his demeanour improved over the week.

Peter Papadopoulos then made the announcement that he was going to join the local Lions club, which was a bolt from the blue, but a promising sign. They were nice people who supported good causes, and the interaction would stimulate his mind and help him forget Bing McKeon.

In truth, Peter Pap did join this organisation but didn't attend any meetings. Instead, he presented weekly at the Ballarat Gun Club, a noble organisation of retired servicemen and sport shooters. The proud history of the club could be traced back to the twenties, one of their notable patrons being the enigmatic John Dillinger. At this time, the honorary patron was gun activist, Charlton Heston, and he would be a hard act to follow. Club president, Ben Haire, deliberated long and hard before he approved the Peter Papadopoulos membership application. After all, elderly people who might suffer with Parkinson's disease were not the best people to handle an automatic firearm.

PP started out with an assortment of hand guns, and then graduated to single action rifles, shotguns, automatics, and state-of-the-art weapons with telescopic sights. This type of gun was helpful for a fellow bothered by cataracts, so he purchased his training model.

The gruesome Greek also enjoyed the social benefits associated with membership of this club. They did skeet shooting on Tuesdays and fantasy assassinations on Fridays. Because PP actually had murder on his mind, these Friday evenings were truly inspiring.

Who knew when and where the brewery magnate acquired his hard edge? Certainly, those associations he formed at various gentlemen's clubs around Melbourne may have contributed, and he was quick to seek retribution for his daughter's humiliation. But murder?

One professional not on his payroll was a psychiatrist and this seemed a shame. He wasn't in a fit state to be making bold decisions, which might turn out to be regrettable. There was turmoil and aggravation in his heart which demanded instant satisfaction. Sam Tromans, having recently returned home to the bosom of his family, didn't expect to hear from his employer so soon after the drama of recent weeks.

"Sam, I'm coming your way and I want to borrow your four-wheel drive. You can use my car for a few days until I return from the high country."

Sam Tromans had never denied his boss anything and he wasn't about to start now. Nor had he ever questioned his motivations or impulses. The welcome mat would be waiting for him and it was. PP only stayed long enough for the vehicle changeover, and managed to sneak his rifle into the SUV when Sam wasn't looking. He then set-off on the road to Mt. Beauty, only stopping to refuel and apply his false moustache. The army flak jacket and hood would go on when he reached his destination.

Although it had been many years since Peter Pap had set foot in Mt. Beauty and surrounds, he was familiar with the McKeon property. Who could forget the firebombing incident, and his many visits to the watercourse, now named Bad Man's Creek? He knew where to hide the vehicle, and how to access the tableland in front of the homestead. Timing was of the essence. In the fading twilight, the sniper would seek camouflage in the middle of the plateau among the feeding roos. He knew the distance capabilities of his rifle, and the panoramic expanse of glass frontage of the residence gave him a wide target.

He could see Helen in the kitchen, obviously preparing dinner, and the figure slouched in an easy chair in the lounge could only be the Scottish bastard. He knelt down on one knee and put his eye to the scope. Yes, there he was, with a tartan blanket wrapped around his knees and an open book on his lap. He was dozing. Through the open window came the recognisable sound of young Pavarotti performing his signature aria, Nessun dorma (none shall sleep). Was there ever a more perfect musical piece for a marksman? Peter Pap knew when to expect the climatic finish, and began to trail the lens slowly up the Scotsman's body, past his heaving chest, open mouth, and drooping eyelids. The crosshairs fixed on a spot in the middle of Bing's forehead, as Luciano upped the ante, and the orchestra slipped into overdrive. The fat finger of fate started to slowly squeeze on the trigger when the ground beneath the rifleman started to tremble.

Immediately, the gunman released his grip on his weapon and looked around in surprise. It was a balmy evening and yet there was thunder. The thrashing sound coming from the forest was a puzzle, but all would soon be revealed. When it was, the poor chap just froze. There seemed to be hundreds of them—dappled greys, strawberry roans, bays and chestnuts—all heading in his direction at a furious pace.

If Peter Papadopoulos had eaten all his yogurt that morning, he might have had the strength to make a run for it, but his legs had turned to jelly. He could only think of all the horses he had nurtured and maintained over the years—Delilah, Thunderball, Geoffrey, Souvlaki, and Zorba the Geek. Would they not intercede on his behalf before the pack could run him down, as surely they would? Sorry Pete! That's all in the past. It's Apocalypse Now.

The white leader veered away from him at the last moment but the others were not so fleet-footed. One of them hit him full-on amidships, but he bounced and landed on his feet again. That's when the poor sod was hit from behind and he didn't get up. The rest of the mob didn't bother making any detours, and proceeded to trample all over the rag-doll that

Peter Pap had become. The last animal stood on his head and crushed his cranium, but he was dead before then. The battered and bloodied corpse would lie under a blanket of darkness until the birds of prey arrived in the morning for their breakfast; not that there would be much left after the night stalkers had had their fill. They were certainly around. One could hear owls, howls, and the strident vowels of the kookaburras, high up in the gum trees.

The End

POSTSCRIPT

With artists and authors, death is always a potent marketing tool and the publishers of Matthew O'Gorman's book reprinted the tome, and the paperback walked off the shelves. Pat Malone became a rich woman, and even Lydia purchased a copy for her mother's birthday. *How to Murder Your Mum and Get Away with It* again topped the best seller list for a further fifteen weeks.

Pat Malone finally found happiness with a hotelier in Heathcote. She moved there to become the city's chief librarian and obliterated all memories of Wangaratta and Matthew O'Gorman from her mind. She lost her mind at the grand old age of eighty seven, and lived out her final days in a state of oblivion.

Angela Pride divorced her husband and married Tony McCurry in a simple ceremony at the Police Academy gun range. Jack Glover stood tall as best man and supplied the wedding cars. He was also present for the christening of their first three children. On the last occasion, he brought along wife number four.

Rom Remus became the first gay commissioner in the history of the Victoria Police. Of all his achievements, he is remembered for his improvements to catering services, under the stewardship of his partner Marty McGrath. Their relationship survived through thick and thin, and every year they treasured their vacation, always taken in Canada.

Margaret Dow retired from professional eventing with six Olympic gold medals to her name. Regrettably, she had to melt them down because times were tough. Her hubby Chris was arrested for organising a Ponzi scheme, and her mount Jungles was put down after biting the lord mayor of Bright during a *keys of the city* ceremony in her honour.

Edwin McKeon came from nowhere to be the leader of the next Aberdeen generation. He cut a swathe through the horse sales from Karaka to the Gold Coast and turned pedigrees upside down with regular coups that turned-up champions. In 1989 his horse won the Melbourne Cup and the following year he purchased a chain of liquor stores that would only sell Clementine Creek wines, MOG wines or those from the Papadopoulos vineyards.

For Joe McKeon, there was life after Beth, as Lydia forgave him for his embarrassing rain dance that had soured relations for a short while. They married, as expected, and in so doing, consolidated their two families into the largest conglomerate in the country. Lydia was also forgiven for her sometimes petulant behaviour on the circuit and became the patron for Equestrian Australia. Joe just helped his brother, looked after his mother and, when possible, gazed lovingly into his wife's eyes. They lived happily ever after.

ABOUT THE AUTHOR

Gerry Burke was born in Healesville, Victoria, the home of one of Australia's quirkiest animals, the platypus. He was educated at Xavier College, before taking-on an accountancy course while employed by an international mining company. This was a commitment that lasted for twelve years, partly spent in New Guinea. Dramatically, the author then switched careers and joined an advertising agency in Melbourne, as a copywriter.

Gerry's advertising career took him to Britain, America, Hong Kong, Singapore and a number of Australian cities. He was employed by some of the world's largest ad agencies before branching out and starting his own company on his own terms. GerryCo provided advertising, marketing, film and video production to local and overseas clients.

In parallel with these activities, Gerry maintained an on-going interest in the thoroughbred horse racing industry, as an owner and breeder. Today, he continues this love affair, which has outlasted his dedication and devotion to the world of advertising. With friends, he has raced over twenty thoroughbreds.

The author's humorous stories and commentary were first made available for general consumption in 2009, with the release of his first book, *From Beer to Paternity*. A number of short story collections followed, in which the ubiquitous discount detective Paddy Pest was introduced to the unsuspecting public. *The Hero of Hucklebuck Drive* was the author's first novel in 2015 and *The Europeans* will be his fifth. Six of his books have received international awards in the categories of General Fiction, Humor and Science Fiction.

Gerry is single and lives in Melbourne, Australia.

www.gerryburke.net

CPSIA information can be obtained
at www.ICGtesting.com
Printed in the USA
BVHW081520080719
552848BV00007B/132/P